LORE OF THE LETHARN

BOOK TWO OF THE RAITHLINDRATH SERIES

Robert Ryan

Copyright © 2014 Robert J. Ryan

Cover Design by www.ebooklaunch.com

ISBN-13 978-0-646-92498-4

(print edition)

Trotting Fox Press

Contents

1. Mist and Murk

Lanrik stepped forward cautiously. He made no noise and was nothing more than another shadow in the twilight world of the pine forest. But just as the gloom helped conceal him, it also hid anything dangerous that might lay in wait. And there were dangers. Aranloth had assured him of it, and his instincts told him it was so.

He continued forward. Each slow pace was carefully measured, every movement hushed, and his eyes ceaselessly studied the gloom, searching for anything out of place.

A whisper of movement reached his ears. It came from twenty paces to his right, and he glanced in that direction. He saw the figure of Ruthark. The man's outline was visible, accentuated by the bow he carried. A Raithlin hood obscured his face, but Lanrik could picture his scowl. He was a perfectionist, absorbing everything that Lanrik taught him and hard on himself whenever he made errors.

Lanrik moved on. Twenty paces to his left, hidden by a cluster of shadows beneath tall trees, was another Raithlin.

A long trailer of gray moss hung in Lanrik's way, and he bent low to pass beneath it, careful not to touch it and reveal his presence to anything that lurked ahead.

Some distance behind him Aranloth and Erlissa followed. They had powers to contend with many types of attack, but it was better to avoid problems than put that to the test.

The journey through the forest was slow, but they had avoided its perils so far. Now, they drew near their destination, though not even Aranloth could say what they would find when they reached it.

The screech of a marsh hen ripped through the air, closely followed by a second. Their calls were like a human scream, and Lanrik felt the hair on the back of his neck rise. Though the sound disturbed him, at least it meant that the travelers had drawn near to Lake Alithorin and the ruins they sought, for the birds did not stray far from water.

A vast fog spread from the lake, rolling over the tops of the trees and deepening the forest gloom.

Lanrik stepped cautiously over a long-fallen tree, surveying the other side before committing himself fully to the movement. Orange lichen flowered over the bark's rotting surface, and he smelled the pungent odor of decay.

The Raithlin to his left came into view. Hargil was a cautious man, one of the many reasons that Lanrik had accepted him into the Raithlin. He learned quickly too, finding the scouting skills natural, though his sword-craft was poor and would likely never improve beyond satisfactory. Lanrik shrugged. The skills of the Raithlin were many, and no one excelled at them all.

The trees thinned, and the twilight of the forest gave way to a fog-dimmed sun. Lanrik paused on the threshold of a massive clearing and studied what lay ahead.

There was evidence of an ancient road. It ran straight and true, though the cobbles that had once formed a smooth surface were now broken and rough. Grass, even

4

the occasional pine sapling, grew in the many cracks and widened them. The wild was reclaiming its own.

Long tendrils of mist crept along hollows to the right. Lake Alithorin must be very close now, and on its other side the city of Red Cardoroth. But the lake was massive and the city too far away to offer help should trouble arise.

The mist did not reach the center of the clearing, and there stood the ruins of a Halathrin town. It was small by their standards, little more than a forest settlement. Stone lay in heaped rubble, and some walls leaned at odd angles, nearing collapse. Many buildings were intact, while others were a litter of shattered stone and choking weeds. Everywhere, scorch marks blackened the stonework.

The town had come to a sudden and violent end. Lanrik took a long time to study it, the Raithlin to either side doing the same, but it appeared deserted and there was no sign of danger.

He made a hand gesture, and the two Raithlin joined him. Aranloth and Erlissa moved forward, and the last Raithlin, Arliss, who guarded their backtrail, came up as well.

Aranloth sighed. "Does nothing last?" He whispered the words, and no one replied, for they sensed it was a statement rather than a question.

They were all subdued. Only Arliss appeared unaffected. Lanrik noticed that she stood straight as she always did, giving the impression of being taller than she was. Her face showed determination and the brusque self-assurance that he so much liked about her. It was not false confidence either, for she was the best of the new Raithlin. She ran a hand beneath her hood and through her short blonde hair. It was too dim to see the faint red scar that ran across her left cheek, the result of a knife fight in Cardoroth. She noticed him looking at her, and flashed a smile that lit her eyes.

Lanrik turned to the lòhren. "I can't see anything except old ruins," he said. "That doesn't mean much, though. There are hundreds of places where something could lurk unseen."

Aranloth gripped his staff tightly. "We've been lucky so far. Let's hope that continues, but we must be ready for anything."

They moved forward in a close group. There was no cover, only the occasional tree, making it futile to try to hide their presence any longer. They strode quickly, but quietly, toward the destroyed settlement.

The chirping of countless frogs reached them from the wetlands near the lake. The noise was subdued by the mist and the thick belt of trees that lay between. From somewhere faraway came the howl of a single wolf, lonesome and plaintive.

Arliss glanced at Lanrik. "This place gives me the creeps."

She spoke the words so softly that he barely heard them, but her customary smile never left her face, and despite the fact that her hand rested on the hilt of her sword, he detected no fear.

They drew near the settlement. It was still. Nothing stirred the green weeds or the dried pine needles that lay in thick drifts against walls.

Aranloth raised his staff and pointed. "There is the tower of Narvil. At least, what's left of it. Somewhere inside is the book we seek."

Lanrik looked at the building closely. The stonework was the same red marble as most of Cardoroth, only the Halathrin had constructed it well before the founding of

6

that city. Elugs had destroyed it before then, too. Not elugs from the south, Aranloth had told him before they set out, but from the northern mountains. The forests around Lake Alithorin had become a haunt for evil creatures after that. They crept down from the cold mountains in the wake of the battle, attracted by the lingering sense of sorcery unleashed during its destruction.

The tower was a dark pillar near the middle of the settlement. It stood taller than the other buildings, and its walls were intact. Nevertheless, fire had scorched its lofty parapet, and many of the merlons from its crenellated battlement, which once pierced the high air, lay tumbled and broken on the ground. The door was also gone, and a ragged hole gaped in its stead.

They walked down the pockmarked road. The ruined town surrounded them. Broken walls loomed to either side, covered with slime and the gleam of moisture from regular fogs. Near the town's center, the street opened into a plaza. On its far side, the black hole of the tower stared bleakly at them.

The cobbled surface of the square had endured the passage of time, or the destruction of the town, better than the rest. Its surface was smooth. Stone benches, many still unbroken, lined its perimeter. But it was dark here, even in mid-morning. The tall buildings cast groping shadows, and the sun was little more than a silver glow in the fog-shrouded sky.

A single and massive pine grew in the center. Its girth was perhaps a score of feet. Once, it formed the centerpiece of the square, and a border of carved red marble circled it. But the stone was now chipped and cracked, and the tree dead. Its broken crown lay toppled below. Yet it must have survived the destruction of the city, and grown through the long centuries untended and unseen by those who planted it, for a thick wreckage of fallen branches and leaves still lay beneath it.

Something caught Lanrik's attention, and his senses sharpened. He signaled for silence and the group came to a halt. He saw nothing. Nor could he hear more than the constant chirping of the frogs and the slow drip of water from a nearby roof. Then he saw at the far end of the square a great white wolf. And then another. In moments, a large pack padded into view.

The group backed up against a wall. There was no real cover here, but at least the wolves could not surround them.

Aranloth muttered. "I feared it was so. Ever these beasts are drawn to sorcery and the dark tracts of Alithoras."

Erlissa frowned. "But the sorcery was used long ago. Why are they still here?"

"The scent of elùgai lingers across great spans of time," Aranloth said. "I can sense its taint now. And Shurilgar, the elùgroth who led the attack on the town, was powerful."

Lanrik kept his eyes on the wolves while he listened. He did not care why they were here; he was only interested in whether or not they would attack. Suddenly, they raced over the open square toward him and he knew.

The Raithlin had notched their arrows and Lanrik, drawing the string of his own bow, gave the command to shoot.

A volley of white-fletched shafts streaked through the gloom. The wolves scattered. They scrambled away while metal arrowheads smashed into the cobbles all about them. Some struck the beasts glancing blows, but only Lanrik and Arliss brought down their targets.

The wolves retreated to the far edge of the square. Lanrik guessed they would rally and attack again, and it worried him, for the beasts were many and the archery of the new Raithlin not yet to a high standard.

"It's a standoff," Ruthark said.

Lanrik notched an arrow. "We'll think of something."

Aranloth leaned against his staff, deep in thought, but offered no suggestions.

While they were thinking, Arliss acted. She put down her bow, removed her small pack and took something from it, and then grinned at Lanrik. Her teeth gleamed white in the shadows, the smile lighting her eyes. Lanrik noticed, not for the first time, that even her eyebrows were blonde.

He liked her smile; it was infectious, but it worried him too, for it usually meant that she had a dangerous idea. He started to ask her what she intended, but she was already moving.

Her lithe figure raced toward the center of the square, and her doeskin boots rapped loudly against the cobbled surface. The wolves pricked their ears and watched.

Aranloth straightened. "What's she doing?"

Lanrik did not answer. He had not seen what she retrieved from her pack, but he knew she had a plan, though he could not guess what it was.

Arliss ignored the wolves, but they watched intently and began to whine. A few of them paced forward tentatively, and then the others followed. In moments, the whole pack rushed toward her.

"Shoot!" Lanrik commanded.

Three arrows winged across the court. But the distance was longer this time, and none of the shots were

9

lethal. The wolves hesitated, yelped some more, and then raced once more toward the girl.

Arliss had already reached the pine tree in the square's center. She bent down and fumbled with something, but Lanrik could not see properly. He and the other Raithlin made several more shots, but the frenzied beasts barely slowed.

The wolves neared Arliss. She straightened suddenly, having finished what she was doing, and raced back toward the others. The wolves would catch her first though, and Lanrik ran to meet her, drawing his sword. Suddenly, there was a flicker of light in the dim square, and he understood what she had done.

Fire licked over the debris at the base of the tree, and the old leaves, dry and brittle, caught alight swiftly.

Arliss raced on, but the wolves, which were closing on her quickly, shied as the pile of pine needles erupted in flame and illuminated the square.

The wolves yelped and retreated, moving out of the plaza and into the dim side streets.

Arliss stopped running and sauntered back to the group. Her hood had fallen back, and her blonde hair took on a ruddy cast from the flickering light. Flame raced up the tree, and smoke and sparks billowed high into the fog-filled sky.

Lanrik sheathed his sword.

"Good work," he said.

Arliss gave him a cheeky grin. "That's what you pay me for, isn't it?"

Lanrik could think of no response, and Aranloth wasted no time in moving toward the tower. The group followed, the heat from the burning pine pressing against the bare skin of their faces and hands.

The lòhren strode ahead and spoke without turning.

10

"The tree is dry and it'll burn swiftly. We'd better get what we came for, and then get out as fast as we can."

Lanrik could not agree more. He wondered if the book they sought was worth all this trouble, but it was an opportunity to give the Raithlin some real-life training. Most of all, Erlissa wanted it. She had done so the instant that Aranloth mentioned it by chance, for it contained the rare knowledge of a Halathrin healer, famed throughout Alithoras. His skill was unrivalled, and it was an opportunity that she could not pass by. And the lòhren had agreed, even though he knew there were dangers, because it was also good training for her.

Erlissa was becoming more of a lòhren every day under Aranloth's tutelage. It disturbed Lanrik, for she seemed to have time for nothing else, and her studies consumed her. Still, he had thrown himself into his new role as well since the events of last summer. Their ambitions were driving them apart, and he did not like it.

Aranloth halted before the tower's opening. It gaped before them, a black maw of broken and ragged stonework. The wooden door was long since gone; only a few rotting slivers remained. Thick brass hinges lay on the cobbles, twisted and dented by the force of a battering ram, or Shurilgar's sorcerous power.

The lòhren lifted his oaken staff and a faint light gleamed at its tip. It brightened as he stepped over the rubble and into the dark tower. The others followed him.

When Erlissa crossed the threshold, she paled and swayed. Lanrik reached out and steadied her.

"Is everything all right?"

She shivered all over. "I don't think so. I had a fleeting vision of something bad."

"What's going to happen?"

"I don't know, Lan. None of it made any sense."

They moved ahead, following Aranloth's light. He led them along the stairs that wound up the inside of the tower, and Erlissa spoke no more. Lanrik noticed Arliss frowning, as though she mistrusted Erlissa's lòhren senses. It was no surprise, for the two of them disliked each other.

The undisturbed dust of long years carpeted the stairs, and the air was close and dank. The doors to each level were thrown down, and the rooms inside destroyed. The scattered remnants of ordinary household items lay covered by mold. Timber furniture was splintered and broken, tapestries shredded and windows of rare stained glass shattered. The elugs had long ago destroyed all that was beautiful, and what remained was now only the haunt of vermin.

Lanrik's thighs burned while he followed Aranloth up the long stairs. The tower was tall and many-roomed, but the lòhren seemed to pay little heed to anything. He strode toward the highest room, where he hoped to find the book.

At length, they neared the top of the tower. Lanrik looked out of yet another broken window and saw the town spread out below. The great pine was still alight, but the easily consumed leaves and branches had burned away. Now, only the trunk remained. Fire had caught in several places, but there was less light and smoke than earlier. He could see little of the shadowy streets beyond the square and could not tell if the wolves remained.

"This is it," Aranloth said.

The lòhren stood in the doorway of the room immediately under the open summit of the tower. It had once been a library, but books and toppled shelves lay strewn across the floor. Fire had burned much, and what

12

remained had long since succumbed to moisture and mold.

"It's hard to believe anything could survive this," Erlissa said.

Aranloth sighed. "These books contained the accumulated knowledge of centuries. The survivor told me that the Halathrin kept a record of their history since the exodus that brought them to Alithoras. That alone would be priceless." He paused and looked around bleakly. "Knowledge is hard gained . . . but swiftly lost."

Ruthark nudged the remnant of one of the books with the toe of his boot.

"I guess our trip has been for nothing, then."

Aranloth shrugged. "Perhaps, but the book we seek was special. The others were completed, but the author was still writing this one. He used a small room set aside from the main library. It was cramped, but it offered the peace and quiet that he liked."

Hargil looked around. "I don't see any other room."

"Just as well," Aranloth said. "That's what gives me hope that it wasn't discovered by elugs."

The lòhren picked his way through the debris toward a spider-haunted tapestry on the far wall. They trod carefully after him, for the floor, though made of thick timber planks, was fire-damaged, and rain had often wetted it through the windows.

The wall on the other side of the room formed part of a circle, following the outer perimeter of the tower. The stairwell led up to the crenellated summit behind them. Ahead, Lanrik knew, the wall was either very thick, or the tapestry hid a doorway. The survivor had told Aranloth the latter was the case. Now, they would find out.

The lòhren reached up. He took hold of the shredded tapestry, ready to tear it down, but at his touch it disintegrated and fell to the floor. The earthy scent of mold was strong in the air.

They saw nothing but a dirty wall. The mood of the group sank, yet after a momentary silence Aranloth chuckled. He tapped the wall with the end of his staff. The faint light at its tip flared, and dancing shadows leaped and swayed throughout the room.

Under the angle of new light a slight depression was visible. Aranloth pressed it with the palm of his hand. There was a loud click and a puff of ancient dust. The lòhren then eased his weight against the stone.

Lanrik watched in astonishment as a door opened with only a hint of sound. The small room beyond revealed a glimpse into antiquity and how the Halathrin had lived. It was undamaged by the wrecking hand of the enemy and untouched by the slow-footed centuries, except for a fine layer of gray dust.

An exquisite table, crafted of black walnut, stood gracefully at one end. An intricately carved paperweight, of the same rare timber, rested on it, and beside it was a writing quill and a silver inkwell. The ink was the only thing in the room that revealed the passage of time. It had long since dried, but mold and fungus had grown about it and stained the sides of the vessel.

A chair stood next to the table. It was pulled out as though whoever had last sat on it had left in a hurry, which Lanrik thought might well have been the case. Bright tapestries, only slightly dulled by dust, rich rugs and a glorious stained-glass window completed the room.

Aranloth turned to Erlissa. "Everything is just as the survivor told me. The book should be in the draw. Since

14

retrieving it was your idea, the task of claiming it falls to you."

Erlissa did not answer but walked to the table purposefully.

Lanrik knew better than the others what this meant to her. It was not just that her parents were healers and that she wished to honor them. It was also a measure of her guilt at killing the elùgroths who had attacked Lòrenta. She had done what was needed, and he thought she would do it again if circumstances arose, but this was her way of balancing the scales. By bringing the book to light she would advance the art of healing and redress the hurt she had done. It was the first part of her plan to establish a special section in the Halls of Lore; to create a place of learning where healers from all over Alithoras could gather and exchange their knowledge.

Her hands did not pause on the draw handle. She pulled it out smoothly. There, protected from dust, lay the book she sought. It was a large tome, the leather cover dyed black. Gold lettering in Halathrin script ran across its surface.

Erlissa placed the book on the table and gently turned a few pages. They seemed brittle, but otherwise unharmed by the passing years. Beautiful writing in a sweeping hand covered each one.

She turned to the lòhren and smiled. "We've got it!"

"Yes," he said. "At least we can salvage something from all this destruction. But I cannot help wonder about all the other books. What knowledge, what wisdom, what record of an age that was, has been lost forever?"

Lanrik understood that Aranloth felt such losses keenly, but there were more pressing problems.

15

"We've got the book," he said, "but we still have to get out of here. The wolves will be close by, and the pine tree won't burn forever."

Erlissa placed the book in the small pack that she carried, and they left the room. The travelers began the long walk down the stairs.

Lanrik sent Hargil ahead. It would be his job to ensure the stairwell was clear and that the base of the tower was free from wolves. Leaving the settlement would require a different approach. Stealth had served them well on the way in, but speed would serve them better on the way out. And a preparedness to fight. For he did not think the wolves would leave them alone while they walked the dim paths of the pine forest.

They reached the tower door and found Hargil waiting. For a while, he and Lanrik studied the square from the shadows of the entrance, but in the light of the still burning tree there was no sign of the wolves.

"Let's go," Lanrik said.

He gestured for Hargil and Ruthark to move out to either side, and took the point position himself.

They had only taken a few steps when he called for them to stop.

"I don't see any wolves," Arliss said.

Lanrik did not answer. The shazrahad sword at his side suddenly felt heavy, and he had a sinking feeling in the pit of his stomach. A dozen horsemen trotted from the shadows beneath a building and headed straight for them.

"Back to the tower," Lanrik said.

"Musraka!" Erlissa hissed through clenched teeth.

Somehow, the shazrahad had found them, and Lanrik knew what he wanted. He caught a glance from Aranloth and read the same fear there. *He must not have it.*

16

2. King's Poison

Lanrik gritted his teeth and ran back to the tower. There would be no escape without a fight, and they were badly outnumbered.

One by one the travelers passed into the dark interior again. He held back, allowing the others to go first. The pounding of hooves over cobbles swiftly grew loud behind them, and a strident yell pierced the air. He and Erlissa reached the threshold together, but she looked back on hearing the shout and gasped. Then, doing what he least expected, she pushed him hard to the side.

He lurched but did not fall. There was a muffled thud, a cry of pain, and Erlissa went down to her knees. He could not make sense of it until he saw a knife on the ground beside her.

The blade must have been aimed at his own back, and in saving him she had been hit herself. He picked her up and carried her inside the tower. All the while he feared another knife or an arrow, but there was no further attack.

Hargil and Ruthark blocked the entrance after he stumbled through. They notched arrows to their bows, but the horsemen wheeled to either side of the tower and passed out of view. The only way to shoot at them would be to step out into the square, and that would place the two Raithlin in the open and leave them vulnerable. They remained where they were.

Lanrik laid Erlissa down on the hard flagging of the tower floor, and her dark hair spilled out over the dirty stone.

"*Please* be all right," he muttered.

He was not sure where the knife had struck her. He needed to locate the wound and staunch the bleeding, but he was confused. A number of vivid stains marked the white cloth of her lòhren robes.

She grimaced and then struggled into a sitting position. "No need to fuss," she said.

"Tell me where you've been hit," Lanrik asked.

"It's nothing – just a glancing blow to my arm."

Lanrik let out a sigh of relief. There seemed to be a lot of blood, but hand and arm wounds often bled profusely even when they weren't serious, and because people moved their arms, the blood easily transferred to other parts of their body.

Arliss handed him some cloth, and he rolled up the sleeve of Erlissa's robe, found the wound on the back of her arm, and bandaged it carefully.

When he was done, she stood up. "What do we do now?"

Ruthark looked back from his position at the entrance. "I think I can hear them talking, but they haven't tried anything yet."

"Maybe the wolves will attack them," Hargil said.

Aranloth frowned. "There are too many riders, I think. If we're to get out of here, we'll have to find a way to do it ourselves."

"How did the Azan find us in the first place?" Lanrik asked.

18

"It cannot be a coincidence," Aranloth said thoughtfully. "I sense Ebona's hand in this. She often deals with the enemy."

Lanrik mulled it over. "They couldn't get across Esgallien ford, but they might have swum the river elsewhere. An army couldn't do it undetected, but a small group of riders might manage it, I guess. From there they could have used the cover of night to make their way to Ebona. Assuming they knew where to find her."

"Who knows how long they've been in contact and what information they've passed to each other," Aranloth said. "Or how, for that matter. But to remain undetected in the north of Alithoras, and to find us as well, tells me that they had help. Ebona is their most likely ally. And she has good cause to hate us both."

Lanrik moved to the entrance and considered the situation. The square lay ahead, all open ground that offered nowhere to hide or to avoid arrows. The light from the burning pine, though less than it was, still illuminated it, although the fog that blanketed the sky appeared to be thinning. If they tried to run, the riders would pick them off by bowshot before they reached cover. Even if they made it into the streets, the forest lay beyond them. It was perpetually dark beneath the thick canopy of leaves, and there was little in the way of undergrowth to hinder the horses. They could not outrun a pursuit in those conditions.

A voice unexpectedly rang out and broke the silence of the square.

"Parley!"

"Granted," Lanrik replied immediately. While they were talking it would give him time to think. And he needed it, for there was no obvious way out of this mess.

19

Musraka stepped slowly into view. A scimitar, in a decorated scabbard of hardened leather, hung by his side, but he took care to keep his hands in the open and away from its hilt and his clothing, where the suspicious might be wary of a concealed knife. His scarlet headdress gleamed in the flickering light, and the whites of his eyes and upturned palms shone palely.

The shazrahad came to a stop, and the two men studied each other in silence for some moments. It seemed a distant memory to Lanrik since they had last met in Dead Man Swamp. The days had been good to him since then. He and the others had saved Lòrenta from the elùgroth attack, and the establishment of a new Raithlin order was progressing well. Time had been less kind to Musraka. His beard was unkempt; the headdress wrinkled and travel-stained, and his face was gaunt with hollow cheeks and drooping bags under his eyes. But his voice, when he spoke, remained as deep and rich as Lanrik remembered.

"You know why I have come," the shazrahad said.

"Yes," Lanrik replied.

"I promised that I would pursue you across the earth. I told you that nothing would stop me." He gave a weary sigh. "The road was longer than I expected though, and you have cost me much. But war is war, and I no longer hold the taking of the sword against you. If you give it to me now, I will let you and your companions walk from here freely."

Lanrik did not answer straightaway. He thought Musraka would be as good as his word, and the offer seemed the only opportunity to escape, for he still could not think of any plan. But the consequences were unthinkable.

He wanted to draw the conversation out, but he could not stifle a clear-cut reply.

"No," he said. "I knew nothing of the sword when I took it from your tent. But now I do. I know it's the embodiment of a prophecy about the conquering of Alithoras, and I can't let you have it – even for safe passage. If need be, we'll fight. But know this. Battle is always uncertain, and you might be the first to die."

Musraka laughed. The sound was deep and rolled through the square. It was strange to hear in the ruins of a long-destroyed city and by the leaping light of a burning tree.

"A good attempt to seed doubt into my mind. But what is death to me? I have no honor until I regain the sword. And without honor, my life is worthless. But truly, it will not come to that."

Lanrik doubted if the shazrahad's men felt quite as strongly about it, but he felt a stab of unease at the last words and remained silent.

Musraka folded his arms. "You do not ask why?"

The man's confidence disturbed Lanrik, yet while they spoke there was still hope that he, or one of the others, would think of a way out of their predicament.

"I'm sure you're going to tell me."

"Very well. I aimed the knife at you. But your companion bravely knocked you to the side, and it struck her instead. She will come to regret it, for the poison that filmed the blade is now working through her blood." Musraka paused, allowing his last words to have their full effect, before he continued. "But you can save her. Return the sword to me, and I will give you the cure."

The shazrahad watched him closely. Lanrik gave no sign of the sudden despair that washed over him.

Musraka clapped his hands together. "You do not let me see your defeat. Well done! You are a good opponent, yet we both know that in the end you will agree to my terms. Just as you knew nothing about the sword when you took it, I knew nothing of you. But I have learned since then. I know all about you and Erlissa. I know who you are and how you think. I know that you will yield."

Lanrik had no answer. His thoughts reeled, and he heard movement behind him.

Aranloth stepped into the flickering light of the tower entrance.

"What poison did you use?"

Musraka inclined his head slightly at the lòhren.

"I know all about you too, Aranloth. But wise as you are, do not think that you can find a cure. For both poison and remedy are plants that grow only in my homeland on the southern slopes of the Graèglin Dennath mountains and the dry plains in their shadow. Even there, they are rare."

Aranloth leaned wearily against his staff. "I know where your homeland is. What I asked is the name of the poison."

The shazrahad paused and then shrugged. "It does no harm to answer. You would render it in your tongue as *King's Poison*. But I doubt even you have heard of it. And if you have, the knowledge will avail you nothing."

Aranloth sighed. "I haven't heard of it."

"It is a favorite among my leader's court," Musraka said. "Death is certain without the cure – and that is seldom administered in time, for the poisoning is rarely diagnosed until too late. The onset of its effects are slow. It may take a week to become apparent, making it hard to identify the poisoner. It also gives them a luxury of time to escape if they fear suspicion will eventually fall on them. But however slowly the poison works, it is a swift and agonizing death in the end. I tell you all this freely so that you understand the situation. The girl *will* die, unless Lanrik returns the sword to me."

Aranloth hung his head. "We'll think on your offer."

Musraka did not try to hide his sneer. "Take all the time you need. None of us are going anywhere."

The shazrahad walked toward his men and disappeared from view.

Lanrik and Aranloth went back inside the tower. Erlissa's face was pale, but she spoke before the others had a chance to say anything.

"I feel fine," she said. "There's no proof that Musraka used poison – he could be lying just to get the sword."

Aranloth slowly shook his head. "That's certainly possible, but I don't think it's the case. The Azan are a cruel people, but lying is not their way, least of all a shazrahad."

"Then why don't I feel any different from normal?"

The lòhren looked at her gravely. "The poison is slow-acting, as Musraka says. I *have* heard of it, though there was no need for him to know that. It will take several days before you fall ill."

Lanrik felt a sensation of cold settle deep into his bones. "You're convinced that he's telling the truth?"

"I believe so."

Lanrik drew the shazrahad sword. Its pattern-welded surface gleamed in the flickering light of the pine.

"There's nothing for it then but to give him what he wants."

Erlissa fixed him with an implacable gaze. "That's not going to happen. You know the prophecy – the Azan

23

need the sword to conquer Alithoras. It must never get back into their hands."

"I know the prophecy," Lanrik said. "But I know this too. I'll not keep the sword and lose you." He spoke quietly but with force.

"There are more important things at stake than me," Erlissa said. "The fate of Alithoras might depend on keeping the blade away from them."

"Perhaps. But what's the fate of Alithoras worth to me if you're not safe?" He paused. "Anyway, you're forgetting something. The sword is mine. I took it from Musraka's tent . . . and I can return it."

She looked at him silently, and then placed a hand on his arm.

"I appreciate what you want to do. The sword may be yours, but my life is my own. Think on this – would you want me to live, knowing that in doing so I doomed Alithoras? Would you place such a burden on me all the days of my life?"

Lanrik held his ground. "The prophecy isn't certain. I don't—"

"Enough!" Aranloth stamped the end of his staff against the stone flagging. "You're both right. And you're both wrong. There's a third way."

They all looked at him. Even Hargil and Ruthark at the tower entrance glanced over their shoulders.

"There are too many of them to fight," Lanrik said.

"I don't intend to fight them."

Then how can we get out of here?"

"The tower has a basement," Aranloth answered. "The survivor that I spoke with told me there's a tunnel that leads deep into the woods. If we discover it, then we can elude Musraka and his men."

Lanrik thought about it. "Maybe so, but what about Erlissa? If we don't get the cure from the shazrahad, she'll die."

Aranloth smiled grimly. "Musraka knows much about the poison, but he knows little of lòhrens. Erlissa is strong in lòhrengai. The magic fortifies her body, and it will help her to resist it until we draw near to Lòrenta."

"But what's the good of that? There's no cure in Lòrenta?"

The lòhren shook his head. "It may be as Musraka says. No cure may exist north of the Graèglin Dennath. But in Lòrenta I'll find references to the poison in the Halls of Lore. There are many books on the subject, some from the Azan lands themselves. But what Musraka doesn't guess is this. The Letharn, that ancient race of men who once ruled much of Alithoras, long ago dwelt in the lands that he now calls home. They too were fond of poisons. They would have known of this plant, and the herb that worked as a cure. They imported such things from all over Alithoras and grew them in the Angle. Many such plants still survive there, growing untended in the wild, even if their names and uses are lost to memory."

Lanrik stared hard at the lòhren. "That was thousands of years ago. You're only guessing that the cure still grows there. And even if it does, it's still too far to retrieve in time."

The lòhren ran a hand through his hair. "No, we can't be sure the plant still grows there, and we don't have the time to go there, or anywhere else to get it. At least, that's what Musraka thinks. But he knows less about all of us than he thinks he does, and *nothing* of the power upon which Lòrenta is founded. The same force that protects the fortress from assault has other uses."

25

Erlissa raised an eyebrow. "The ùhrengai that wells up from the fountain?"

"Yes," Aranloth answered. "It has many properties. It does not heal, but it can preserve. Within the veil of its power you can lie down and rest. You will sleep, a sleep near to death perhaps, but you will not die. Should you be woken, the poison will progress as normal, but otherwise, we'll have the time we need to seek and find the cure."

The light from the flickering fire had grown dimmer as they spoke. It was now quite dark in the tower, but Erlissa's eyes gleamed with determination. She turned to Lanrik.

"That's what we'll do. It gives me a chance, and it saves the sword."

Lanrik stared back at her. He knew that she had made up her mind and would not turn from her decision. Still, he did not like it. It was a courageous choice, though some might call it stupid. But she always trusted to her luck, and perhaps Musraka himself had played a part. The shazrahad had held her captive for a time, and she would do anything she could to stymy his plans, even, it seemed, at the risk of her own life.

He looked back to Aranloth. "Very well. But if the tunnel leads to safety, why was there only one survivor from the attack on the Halathrin?"

The lòhren met his gaze squarely. "Apparently, many of the Halathrin fled that way. But none reached the safety of the outlet into the forest. They all died within the confines of the tunnel."

"What killed them," Erlissa sked.

"The survivor wasn't sure. He believed this, though. Shurilgar, who betrayed them, had learned of the tunnel's existence. He cast a great sorcery within it, and the survivor heard the screams of those who sought to escape that way."

Lanrik listened to the lòhren speak while he looked down at the flagging. He wanted to locate the trapdoor that led into the basement.

"Let's get started then," he said. "The sorcery must have worn off long ago, whatever it was. We should have more luck than the Halathrin."

Aranloth shook his head slowly. "You need to understand something, Lanrik. Sorcery may linger for many lives of men, and Shurilgar was very powerful. His trap, whatever it was, is still set. I can feel it now. The very earth beneath our feet throbs with its malevolence."

3. Flood of Fear

There was silence after his words, and Lanrik felt the air in the room grow heavy with dread. Yet there was no other way out.

"We'll just have to take our chances," he said.

Without further pause, he continued to look for the trapdoor. His matter-of-fact acceptance of the situation would set an example for the new Raithlin. They were not used to intense danger. Somehow, a difficult expedition had turned into something more perilous, and he hoped they could cope with it. He must lead by example and show them that it *could* be coped with. The last thing they should see were his own doubts, even if he had many of them. He had to conceal his fear. Likewise, he must hide the fact that the threat to Erlissa set him on edge, just as Aranloth's seeming self-assurance of finding a cure appeared to him to be overconfidence. Unless, of course, the lòhren knew more than he was telling. If so, it would not be the first time.

It was Erlissa who eventually found the trapdoor. It was directly opposite to the entrance.

"Over here," she said quietly.

In antiquity, the Halathrin would have used furniture or a rug to hide it. The elugs, however, had destroyed that long ago. What had kept it from view was the dust of countless years. Erlissa continued to brush it aside with her boot while the others approached. The stone flagging looked like any other, except that it had a metal ring set into its center to make it easier to lift.

Aranloth wasted no time. "Stand back," he said.

The lòhren slipped his staff through the loop and set its tip against the next square of flagging. With a quick heave the square of stone lifted, and Lanrik and Erlissa stepped in to ease it to the side. They were careful to make no noise. This was a chance to escape from Musraka, but it would be lost if he became suspicious.

Lanrik looked down into the gaping hole that the missing flagging revealed.

"What can you see?" Arliss asked.

"Not much except the top of a wooden ladder. It seems sturdy enough."

The timber was ancient, but it looked like it could still hold the weight of a climber. He tested it carefully, making sure it was solid before he went down into the pit.

The ladder remained secure under his weight, and he knew he should have trusted the craftsmanship of the Halathrin. It was dry beneath the tower, protected from the elements as the upper floors were not, and those conditions served well to preserve the timber.

He reached the bottom and waited in the dark. There was only a glimmer of light, and he could see little except vague outlines of massive stonework. He guessed it formed the foundation of the tower, but as yet he could see no tunnel, nor could he feel the movement of any air. He thought of making a noise, to see if he could detect by sound or echo how big the chamber was, but decided against it. He did not want waken whatever nameless sorcery Shurilgar had invoked.

Aranloth came down the ladder next, and the lighted tip of his staff cast a reassuring light. As the lòhren climbed lower, the shadows receded and Lanrik caught his first real glimpse of the chamber.

The great slabs were indeed foundations. They were neatly laid, and seemed large enough to support a structure many times greater than the tower that rose above. Still, Lake Alithorin was nearby, and the Halathrin might have feared movement from wet ground.

Beneath his feet were similar flagstones to those above. The chamber was round and smoothly crafted for work intended to remain out of sight. The great slabs ringed him, but on the opposite side, in the direction of the square, he saw a massive portal. Aranloth's light did not illuminate the tunnel that lay beyond.

Amid all his concerns, Lanrik felt a touch of amusement. They would escape beneath the very feet of Musraka and his men. When the shazrahad finally discovered the deception, he would be furious. Yet he was not stupid and would also realize that they had some plan to help Erlissa. Musraka could not possibly guess its nature, but that would not stop him from trying his best to hinder it and reclaim the sword.

Lanrik's amusement was short lived. Aranloth joined him at the bottom, and the lòhren's sharp gaze studied the tunnel while the next person began to climb down. His eyes, and his expression, showed deep uneasiness. If he was fearful of ancient sorcery, there was good reason for it.

"Do you have any idea what kind of trap Shurilgar set?" Lanrik asked.

"I sense the elùgai," Aranloth answered, "but I cannot deduce its nature."

Nothing about this is going to be easy, Lanrik thought. It was hard to prepare a defense if you did not know what form the attack would take.

The rest of the group soon assembled in the chamber. Ruthark and Hargil quietly pulled the stone flagging over the trapdoor and joined them last.

Aranloth gave everyone a searching look.

"There's danger ahead," he said. "I'll lead, but you must keep your eyes open. If something happens, remember this. Do not flee back here. There's no escape this way – not with Musraka above. And if his presence isn't good enough reason, consider this. None of the Halathrin made it back this way."

Without another word he turned and walked toward the portal. Lanrik agreed with the lòhren's assessment, but could not help consider what remained unspoken; the Halathrin had not escaped by pressing forward, either.

The dim light of Aranloth's staff now lit the tunnel on the other side of the portal, and they stepped through. Erlissa followed behind the lòhren. Lanrik went next, and the new Raithlin formed a guard at the rear. How long Musraka would wait, no one could guess, but sooner or later he would tire of it.

They moved through the tunnel. It was wide enough for several people, but they continued in single file. Aranloth went slowly, and though his eyes searched everywhere, Lanrik knew that he used some art of lòhrengai to try to locate the trap. He now felt something of the sorcery himself, or at least he sensed the magic in his sword stir in reaction to it.

The tunnel extended in a straight line. There were no bends or side chutes used for cellars or storage spaces, and there was no variation in the stonework. It was exactly what the survivor had told Aranloth: an escape route. How far it ran into the pinewoods though, no one knew. They had been walking for a while, and even at their slow pace they must already have passed beyond the square and the rest of the town. The forest grew above them now. Dark and brooding as it was, Lanrik wished he were there instead.

Ahead, Aranloth came to a halt. A long time he paused, and everybody waited in silence, but whatever he studied by the dim light of his staff no one else could yet see. Eventually, he moved on, but now each step was slower than ever.

In a few moments, Lanrik saw for himself what had caused the lòhren to stop. A body lay on the ground. It was ancient and decayed. Little remained but grime-coated bones and tattered remnants of white cloth, now yellowed and stained. A leather scabbard, cracked and warped by time, rested by its side.

The survivor's account, as it had been with everything else, was accurate. It appeared as though no one had escaped the raid. Lanrik paused to study the remains for some moments, but he could detect no sign of what had killed the Halathrin warrior. None of the bones showed evidence of breaks or notches that a blade might have caused. He did note one thing though; the man had not drawn the sword from its sheath.

Within a few paces more bodies came into view. They lay scattered across the floor. The bones rested exactly where the people had fallen long ago, unburied and untended. It made Lanrik picture the terror they must have felt.

The lòhren began to mutter something. It was little more than a whisper, and Lanrik strained to hear. After a few paces, he understood.

Eleth nar duril, the lòhren said repeatedly. Lie in peace, in the Halathrin tongue.

Soon the bodies of warriors gave way. Now, there were no swords or blades, no shields or daggers, no bows and arrows. The bones belonged to women and children. Lanrik felt his heart pound harder, and anger rose within him. But fear swelled with it. He tried not to look at the bodies as he passed, but it was hard not to. The fragile bones of children, some of whom had died in their mother's embrace, were everywhere.

The muttering of the lòhren grew louder, and Lanrik reached for his sword. Whatever had lain in wait for these people now waited for him. His hand touched the hilt, and he felt the power within the blade roil.

Aranloth led them onward. He held the staff high above his head, trying to see further into the darkness, but it achieved little except to reveal the horror about them in greater detail. Lanrik took long and slow breaths to calm himself. His sword reflected the lòhren-light and felt alive in his hand. He heard the movements of those who came after and wondered how they fared.

The Raithlin, he knew without looking, had drawn their own weapons. But ready as they were, they could not properly prepare for an attack without knowing the nature of what threatened them. Nor was it encouraging to consider that the long blades of the Halathrin warriors had done them no good.

At last the bodies of the women and children gave way to warriors again. They lay thickly all over the floor, and the travelers now had to pick their way carefully through a rubble of bones, skulls and discarded weapons.

A new scent tainted the air. Aranloth came to a halt and sniffed it, and Lanrik did the same. It smelled like disturbed mud at the bottom of a stagnant pond. There was also a movement of air, for the first time so far in

33

their underground journey, and it was this that carried the smell.

Aranloth did not move. His whole body went rigid, and the light at the tip of his staff wavered. Erlissa remained behind him. She had not yet earned her lòhren staff, but she stood straight and tall, her head tilted a little to one side and her arms out in front of her body.

The smell swiftly grew into a stomach-churning reek. It was fetid and putrid, as though the deep bottom of Lake Alithorin boiled upward and drove the decay of centuries toward the surface. The movement of air quickened into a breeze. It continued to intensify until it felt like the very air pushed against them in the narrow confines of the tunnel.

Lanrik gripped the hilt of his sword tightly, yet there was no enemy that he could see, and he felt helpless. Deep inside his heart, a shadow of fear darkened and grew. Distantly, he heard a rumble, as though the foundations of the earth broke their bonds and once-solid ground slid like mud. The forward press of air beat against him like a hammer blow. The wind swept dust off the stone flagging and drove it into his eyes. At the same time a thrumming sensation came up through the floor.

He turned his gaze to the lòhren. Aranloth's staff now pointed forward in a defensive position, yet still no enemy showed itself.

"It comes!" yelled the lòhren.

Erlissa moved to the lòhren's side. Her dark hair streamed behind her, and she held her arms higher, fingers pointing forward.

Suddenly, Lanrik heard a rushing noise in the dark ahead of them. It was the bubble and gush of water. Not the steady running of a stream, but the wild torrent of a

34

river in flood. Somehow the sorcery of Shurilgar had diverted water from Lake Alithorin into the tunnel.

A film of moisture sprayed across Lanrik's face. The gloom deepened, and the wavering lòhren-light faltered. A knee-high wave smashed into their legs. Cold water filled their boots.

The wave swelled around them, constantly rising, and it became hard to stand.

"Hold fast!" the lòhren cried.

Yet in moments the rush of water rose to their chests. White foam rode its scum-crusted top, and it smashed into their bodies. Lanrik went down in the torrent. His mouth filled with putrid water. He struggled to keep his head above it. Ahead of him, only Aranloth stood tall, unbent by the surging wave. Erlissa was lost from sight. He tried to struggle back to his feet, and heard a shout from somewhere behind him. The Raithlin had fallen too. Nothing could survive this flood, and now he knew how the Halathrin had perished. They had not escaped this sorcery, and neither would he.

4. The Light of Truth

Lanrik, his lungs full of water, sank to the bottom and his back came to rest against the hard flagging of the floor. Though the torrent raged through the tunnel, strangely, it exerted no force at the bottom.

A sense of peace settled over his mind. Death was certain, and no matter how many times he had fought it before, it was now inevitable. He closed his eyes. It was easier to surrender than to struggle without hope.

All about him was blackness. His thoughts swirled, and then like leaves blown away in the wind, they dissipated. He was at peace. There was no longer anything to strive for. Nothing remained to fight against. Now, there was neither good or evil, nor fear or happiness. There was nothing.

A lone thought drifted through the timeless oblivion. It disturbed his tranquility like a drop of water breaking the clarity of a still pond. He remembered Erlissa. A picture came to him of how she looked the first time that he saw her. Once more, he was in the shazrahad tent. The thick shadows pressed against him. Destiny lurked in the corners, unseen but all-powerful. The hangman's noose hung before her, intended to break her spirit. But once more he saw the expression on her face: alert, curious and ready for anything. The bloodstained rope had not intimidated her. He recognized this as the single moment in time that he had fallen in love with her. She was the drop of water, and he the pond. He wanted to tell her that it was so.

He felt emotion stir amid the calm. His eyes flicked open, and the press of water drove against them. All was still dark, yet he saw a glimmer of light. He concentrated on it. As he watched through the blur, it clarified and blossomed. In moments, it blazed brighter than the sun.

In the very heart of the light stood a dazzling form. The figure was tall and robed in white. Bright fire streamed from it. He felt warmth bathe him like sunlight on a winter's day. Suddenly, he remembered the scent of moist earth. He thought of green grass and air so fresh that it could be drunk like wine.

He breathed deeply . . . and spluttered. Scrambling to his knees, he gulped in the life-giving air. Ahead of him, Aranloth stood straight and tall. Silvery-white fire wreathed him, but swiftly faded. Erlissa crouched at his side, a pale green light flickering at the tips of her fingers.

Lanrik spun around and saw that the Raithlin were getting to their feet.

He turned back to Aranloth. "The water! What happened to it?"

"There *was* no water," the lòhren said calmly.

Lanrik looked about him in a daze. The bones of the Halathrin remained unmoved. How could that be? The force of the flood should have swept them along the tunnel.

He looked wide-eyed at Aranloth. "It was a trick?"

"Indeed," Aranloth said. "But a dangerous one. From the first moment we entered the tunnel, Shurilgar's sorcery commenced to work. It wrapped around us, entwined itself through our thoughts. It sapped our will and brought to the fore our weaknesses, but most of all it deluded us. It used all our senses to give shape to its

37

purpose. It made us aware of Lake Alithorin. Then it built its lies, step by step, on that foundation of fact. We believed its whisperings, and the illusion became real. The mind is a powerful thing."

Lanrik understood now. The sorcery was gone. His garments, which should have been dripping, were not. He ran his hand through his hair, and it was dry.

"No sorcery is stronger than self-deception," the lòhren added.

Erlissa raised an eyebrow. "But no enchantment is more potent than self-belief."

Aranloth inclined his head. Lanrik was still trying to regain his breath, and he wondered how they could philosophize at a time like this. He went to check on the Raithlin. They seemed shaken and subdued, their drawn swords held in white-knuckled grips.

Arliss rallied and gave him a quick grin when he approached. "I was due for a bath, I guess."

"It's been a long journey," Lanrik said. He could not help but admire her resilience.

She sheathed her sword and brushed her hands together.

"It's a pity that make-believe water doesn't clean like the real stuff," she said.

Ruthark and Hargil chuckled. They sheathed their swords as well, and Lanrik thought they would be all right. It was a hard introduction to the life of a Raithlin, yet it was the sort of experience that no training could simulate. It was molding them, tempering them into what they needed to be in order to serve Alithoras. And at the same time, it was giving them the skills they needed to survive.

Erlissa called out from ahead. "Time to go," she said. "The sooner we're out of here the better."

They began to walk once more. Aranloth led them quickly now, his strides long and fast and the light of his staff a steady reassurance.

"The sorcery is gone forever," the lòhren called back to them. "Our survival destroyed it, for like any lie, it cannot withstand the light of truth."

The tunnel did not change as they progressed. It must have required an enormous effort for the Halathrin to build, and how long it had taken, Lanrik could not guess. Being immortal had its advantages, he supposed. They were people with the time to achieve their goals.

He thought of the bodies that lay behind them. Immortal or not, blades and sorcery still killed them. For a long time the Halathrin had defended Alithoras from elug invasions. They paid a high price for it. Still, they had their own reasons and motivations. Not everything they did was solely for the protection of Alithoras.

Aranloth slowed his pace. For the first time since their descent, the tunnel changed. It suddenly veered to the left and began to drop at a steep angle. It was strange, but the Halathrin knew what they were doing. Everything in a construction like this served a purpose, whether it was obvious or not.

"I can smell the pine forest above," Erlissa said.

Lanrik could not, but women had a better sense of smell than men. It was one of the advantages of employing female Raithlin. The ability to detect smoke, or other odors, could save lives in the wild.

He kept on walking, glad that they were coming to the end of this stage of the journey. It was still a long way back to Lòrenta though. At least they would soon be able to retrieve their horses and ride. The Raithlin he had left with them were disappointed at his decision. They had wanted to play a greater part in things than serve as horse guards, but their time would come. Had he known that Musraka would attack, he would have brought them along. But stealth was what he had wanted at the time, and horses and additional people would only have worked against that.

A new thought came to him. How exactly had Musraka found them? Ebona might have helped initially, but after that the Azan must have followed them for some time. If so, they would know of the Raithlin left to guard the horses. Had they attacked their camp before riding to the Halathrin settlement? There were six Raithlin; enough to make life difficult for the Azan, but not so many, or well enough trained, to long repel a concerted attack.

Aranloth came to a halt. They had finally reached the end of the tunnel. Stone and mortar surrounded them. The blank wall they faced was solid, and without any obvious exit, but it leaned at a slight outward angle. A great chain fashioned of inch-thick links was imbedded in the wall, and the other end was strung to a massive pillar set into the floor. The chain was taut and evidently under a great strain of weight. A pin, thick as a man's forearm, pierced the last link, which was an enlarged circular ring. The metal bar ran right through the center of the pillar, and its end was visible on the other side.

On top of the stone post, shoulder high to Lanrik, rested a hammer. It was made of iron, thick and heavy, with a short, oaken handle. Rust pockmarked its surface, and it had no doubt lain exactly where it was, untouched and unseen by hand or eye, since before the destruction of the settlement.

"How exactly are we supposed to get out of here?" Ruthark asked.

Lanrik reached for the hammer. "With this," he said. "I guess it'll only take one stroke."

He took the handle in both hands. It felt like it was made of lead, and his muscles bulged and strained with the effort of holding it.

Aranloth looked closely at the wall, and then came back to the group. "The Halathrin leave little to chance. But the escape route has been untended for centuries. It's possible that trees have grown in the way, and the wall may not collapse as intended."

"There's only one way to find out," Lanrik said.

He was sick of this underground place, and the sooner he got out of here the better. It would be just fine by him if he never had to go anywhere like it ever again.

The lòhren gestured with his staff and everyone stood back. Lanrik positioned himself behind the pillar so that the loosened chain would not hit him as the wall collapsed – if it did. He made a few practice strokes of the hammer, and then took a deep breath and swung a mighty blow.

There was a great ring in the narrow confines of the tunnel, a clang of metal as the pin drove through the stone and clattered on the flagging at the base of the pillar's far side. At the same time, the end wall of the tunnel dropped like a drawbridge. The massive chain slammed into the floor, and then ran forward. A vast boom sounded, and natural light filtered through the dust-filled air.

Lanrik waited a few moments before edging forward to look outside. It was still daylight, but for some reason it appeared dimmer than he would have expected, even for the forest. He drew his sword, and then stepped out over the toppled wall. It remained intact, though he could see metal bars holding it together wherever the stone had fractured. He did not look back, but heard movement behind him and knew the Raithlin were following.

He looked about him in the gloom. Tall pines towered about him. Their straight trunks and leafy branches blocked most of the light and obscured his view, but he saw through the occasional gaps that they were in a steep-sided dell. It made sense, he supposed. The Halathrin had built the tunnel as an escape route, and when they exited they would want to do so in a place that hid them from the enemy and muted noise. The dell was a good location for that. Scouts would have next ascended to the rim, ensured they were clear of the enemy, and then guided the fugitives out and away. At least that's what would have happened. They had not counted on Shurilgar's treachery.

He signaled the others to join him. He did not know exactly where they were, but the horses and remaining Raithlin were on the west margin of the wood. It would be less than an hour's walk to reach them. At least the wolves would not be able to track them by scent, and they would likely be prowling about the city and watching Musraka's men anyway. The tunnel, at least now that they had survived it, had proven fortuitous. Both of their enemies were behind them. At least for the moment.

Lanrik moved ahead. Ruthark and Hargil melded into the forest on either side, just as they had on the way in. The sides of the dell were rocky and steep. At times, it was more a matter of climbing than walking, but they eventually reached the top. Lanrik paused and studied the surroundings.

It was still dark beneath the trees, and he could not see the settlement nor any smoke from the burning pine.

But he could smell it in the air. It seemed strongest in the direction that he took to be east, and so he turned west and commenced walking toward their camp.

They would not arrive back at exactly the same spot where they had entered. That, thought Lanrik, was a good thing. It would give them a chance to come up to the camp by an unexpected angle and investigate it closely. There was no way to know how many men Musraka commanded. They could have captured the Raithlin and left a contingent there. He did not want to walk back into a trap.

Lanrik set a faster pace on the way out of the woods than he had on the way in, but stealth was still important. Wolves need not be the only danger that lurked in the trackless gloom. Yet they reached the eave of the forest without any difficulty. Late afternoon light slanted through the thinning trees, and Lanrik signaled the others to wait while he went forward on his belly, using the Raithlin crawl, until he looked out beyond the world of trees.

The yellowed light of day's end revealed the flat grasslands that stretched west of Lake Alithorin. To the north, he thought he saw the land begin its gradual rise toward the mountains of Northern Alithoras. Southward, he studied the forest margin carefully. He saw only the long line of marching trees, but that was all he expected. The Raithlin would stay within the cover of the timberline and out of view. So too would Musraka's men if they had overrun the camp.

There was little light left, and that suited Lanrik well. He went back to the others.

"I know where we are," he said. "Our camp is less than half a mile to the south."

"Did you see the others?" Arliss asked.

43

"No. I saw no sign of them." He sat down on the ground. "The only way to find out if Musraka has already been there is to go ourselves. It'll be dark in a few minutes. We can rest briefly, and then head out onto the grass."

The others sat down. They seemed restless to be on their way, obviously fearful of Musraka catching up to them, but Lanrik knew that even a few moments of rest would do them good. Assuming they eventually found the other Raithlin unharmed, it would be a tiring ride back to Lòrenta. And no doubt the shazrahad would sooner or later give chase. They needed to pace themselves, for such a pursuit would be unrelenting.

Long shadows glided through the forest when the sun set. An owl hooted somewhere deep amid the trees, and Lanrik stood.

"Time to go," he said.

He led the way, and as ever, Ruthark and Hargil flanked him. It was dark on the plains, the border of the forest just a black shadow, but the bright stars provided enough light to travel by.

The grass was short and their strides long. They quickly reached the vicinity of their old camp. Halathgar, the constellation of the Huntress, glittered palely.

Lanrik went ahead for the last hundred paces by himself. He stepped slowly, his every movement hushed, and all his senses acutely alert. He approached along the margin of trees so that the lighter western sky would not silhouette him.

When he peered into the camp he knew that something was wrong. There was no fire or noise of any kind, not even the quiet stamp of a horse's hoof or the swish of its tail. He remained perfectly still, taking in the sight and allowing his eyes to adjust to the darker

44

shadows of the forest. He caught a glint of metal, the barest flicker, and waited. Nothing happened. The blade did not move, nor did anyone reveal their presence by sound or movement.

Moving slowly, and drawing his cloak tighter about himself, he stepped forward. The blade was clearly visible now. It lay on the ground. A little to the side was the body of a Raithlin. Durnlath's pale face looked up at him with sightless eyes, and Lanrik's spirits sank. Had he known that things would end this way he would never have brought the Raithlin. They were his responsibility, their presence in this place at his command, but he was not here when they needed him the most. It was one thing to put himself at risk, but another to place someone else in jeopardy. He felt the crushing weight of leadership.

But what of the others? He saw no sign of the remaining five Raithlin.

Quickly, he scouted the camp. The horses were gone. The body of one of Musraka's men lay under a tree, a Raithlin arrow in his chest. Had Musraka taken the Raithlin prisoner? Lanrik considered it. He did not think so. The shazrahad would have used them as a bargaining point when they met in the settlement. But would that necessarily be the case? He might have withheld that information. It was always better to hold something back in negotiations for later use. The Raithlin might, or might not, have evaded the Azan.

Lanrik called the others into the campsite and explained the situation.

"If they escaped, where would they go?" Aranloth asked.

"Into the trees," Lanrik offered. "There's cover there, and a few men with bows might hold off Musraka's men."

"Maybe," Aranloth said. "Or we may find only dead bodies and that our horses have been stolen."

"Perhaps," Lanrik agreed. "But we had better go in and look. And let's hope they survived, not just for their own sake, but because without the horses Musraka will soon find us."

5. The Jealous Dead

Lanrik led the way into the forest. If it had been gloomy during the day, it was now a pit of shadows. Nor was it silent anymore. The limbs of the trees creaked strangely, and shallow roots muttered as they rubbed against one another. There were shuffling noises, high-pitched cries and angry hisses. The entire forest seemed alive, from the thick layer of dry needles that covered the ground, up the trunks and high into the topmost boughs.

It was a grim place to get separated, and Aranloth caused a faint light to glimmer at the end of his staff, which helped to keep them together. Lanrik led by instinct rather than sight. It was impossible to track anybody, so he put himself in the Raithlin's position. He tried to feel what they felt when Musraka's men attacked, think as they would have, and then intuit how they reacted.

Outnumbered and shocked by Durnlath's death, they would have been scared. That would make them retreat. But where to? Would they run blindly into the forest? No, he had trained them better than that. They would seek a defendable place to regroup. Somewhere close, so that he and the others could find them. So far so good, but what terrain offered the best protection in a forest?

He knew the answer as soon as he thought of the question. The grasslands to the west were fairly flat, but there were hills and ravines in the forest. Though he could not see it, he sensed with his every step that at his left the land rose. He turned that way. The steeper the ground grew underfoot, the more confident he became that he was on the right track.

Someone approached him from behind. He knew it was a Raithlin by the quiet tread of their feet.

"I smell smoke," Arliss whispered.

"Where's it coming from?"

She hesitated. "Just ahead, I think."

They went on. In moments, Lanrik smelled it too. He slowed his pace, and the light at the tip of Aranloth's staff faded and went out.

It was hard to tell in the gloom, but this seemed just the sort of place the Raithlin would choose to defend themselves. The slope was increasingly steep, and the trees grew thickly. He moved ahead. Flickering light soon began to show where a fire burned. But why was there a fire in the first place? Would the Raithlin light one? Or was it lit by Musraka's men?

He paused, uncertain how to proceed, and a voice boomed out of the dark from his left.

"Halt or die!"

Everyone went still, and Lanrik cursed himself. The fire was a trick. Its purpose was to lure them forward while the people who lit it hid elsewhere.

However, he thought he recognized the voice.

"That's a good ploy," Lanrik said. "The fire had me. And to think I fell for something that I taught you myself."

There was movement in the shadows. The light of Aranloth's staff glowed again, and from the dimness between two trees the gray form of a man emerged. He held a bow, an arrow notched to the string.

48

Lanrik faced him. "No need to shoot, Feldring. Killing your own Raithlindrath, although an achievement, will likely hurt your career."

Feldring lowered the bow and slipped the arrow back into its quiver.

"It's good to see you, Lindrath. We've had some problems . . . "

Lanrik saw strain on the man's face. He also saw it lift, even as he watched. Feldring was the most senior of those left behind. Now that his leader was back, he was unburdened of responsibility. Lanrik did not hold that response against him. He was, in fact, quite pleased with the man's efforts in a difficult situation.

"I know. I found Durnlath. What of the others?"

"We all survived," Feldring said. "But it was a close thing."

He gave three sharp whistles, not so loud as to carry far, but loud enough to bring the other Raithlin. They came in from different directions, one even dropping from a nearby tree.

There were some quick greetings, but Feldring wasted no time. He explained what had happened since they parted that morning. The Azan had attacked, seemingly more interested in stealing the horses than anything else, but when that failed they did not push their advantage of numbers home. They left swiftly.

Feldring glanced toward Erlissa. "Did you get the book?"

She patted her backpack. "We got it."

Lanrik told him of the confrontation at the tower, Musraka's poisoned knife, and their escape through the tunnel.

49

"It's time to go," he said when he was done. "The Azan know where you're camped and they'll come here first."

Feldring led them a little further into the trees where the Raithlin had tethered the horses. Lanrik's stallion and Erlissa's chestnut had once belonged to the Azan. They were fine horses, and he knew why they wanted them back. Just as well that they had not got them though. It was a long way to Lòrenta, and he feared Erlissa would soon be in no position to walk.

Aranloth led them out of the forest, the light of his staff helping keep them together. They led the horses by hand, Hargil taking not only his own mount, but Durnlath's as well. The two of them had been friends, and Lanrik decided to watch him closely. It was hard to deal with unexpected loss, and he would be questioning everything he knew at the moment. He would hide the pain he felt, but that did not mean it was not there.

They moved out of the trees and onto the grass. Aranloth extinguished his light, and pale starlight glittered on pieces of exposed harness.

"What now?" Aranloth asked. "Shall we rest, or ride?"

Lanrik studied the Raithlin. They were tired and scared. But they were not injured, nor had they reached their limits. Of Erlissa and Aranloth, he had no doubt. He had endured this sort of thing with them before and knew they could cope.

"We'll ride until midnight," he said. "The Azan can't track us at night, and that should give us an advantage over them. They'll find it hard to catch up."

He urged his alar stallion into a canter. Just as they did on foot, Hargil and Ruthark flanked him, and as ever, Arliss guarded the rear.

They moved at a steady pace across the grasslands.

"Be careful," he called out. "Night riding is always risky, but the horses are surefooted and the terrain flat."

That the Azan would pursue, he knew without question. And in truth, it did not matter that they could not be tracked at night. Musraka would guess their likely destination. But it would slow them down somewhat, and it would make the Raithlin feel more secure.

Sometime before midnight, Lanrik slowed a little and eased to a walk beside Hargil. He gestured toward Durnlath's mount. "Shall I take the reins for a while?"

The Raithlin shook his head, but did not answer, and they rode in silence for a little while. Lanrik knew Hargil was trying to come to terms with things, but some things, death especially, could never be worked out or explained. They must just be accepted. Or not. But the latter approach kept the pain alive longer than need be, and it got in the way of remembering what was important about a person who was gone. But mourning was vital too. It should not be put aside, or hidden.

"Durnlath was a good man," he said eventually.

"The best," agreed Hargil.

"He was the first of Lòrenta's Raithlin to fall," Lanrik said. "But he left a mark on all of us – one that will last through the years."

"That he did. But why did he die? I mean, he was better than I was, better than some of the others. Why him and not me?"

Lanrik pondered the question. "I'm not sure if there's an answer to that. The misfortunes of the world are many, and ill luck abounds. He was in the wrong place at the wrong time. It could just as easily have been me. It might be any one of us next time." He paused and then went on. "Do you think it would have stopped him from becoming a Raithlin if he knew how dangerous it would turn out?"

Hargil shrugged. "Maybe, but I don't think so. He knew there would be risks. He probably just didn't expect to meet them this early in his career."

"No," Lanrik said. "I guess that even when we're expecting problems they always seem to catch us by surprise."

"That's true enough."

Lanrik hesitated, and then spoke again. "I'm going to miss him," he said.

Hargil looked at him sideways. "Me too."

"I know."

Silence grew again, but it was companionable. After a little while, Lanrik took a tighter hold of his reins. "I better go up front again."

"No problems," Hargil answered. "And thanks for not trying to tell me that everything is going to be alright."

Lanrik nodded. There was no real answer to that. Hargil understood the truth of things as well as he did. He would get over his friend's death in time, but that was not what he needed to hear now. What was necessary was that he mourned first.

The alar stallion responded smoothly when Lanrik nudged him forward and took him out to the front once more. Bright Halathgar was riding higher in the sky, and midnight was nearing. It had been a long day, but rest would soon be at hand. At least a temporary one.

Another few miles went by before he called a halt. He and Aranloth had a good arrangement. In day-to-day matters he was in charge, making these sort of decisions. There were other times when only the lòhren's expertise would serve, and they seemed able to swap back and forth easily. It was a good relationship. The lòhren valued his skills, and Lanrik, for his part, respected the lòhren. Even if he did hold back information.

There was more going on with the poison than Aranloth had said, but trust was part of their relationship. The lòhren would reveal the full truth when he was ready. But that did not mean that Lanrik could not try to prod it from him.

They set up a fireless camp beneath an isolated clump of straggly oaks and shared a cold meal.

"I'll take the first watch," Lanrik said.

The travelers settled into whatever comfortable places they could find to sleep. Lanrik walked around at first, making sure that he stayed awake. The night was not cold, but the Raithlin, wrapped in their cloaks, were near invisible.

Their current way of life was new to them, he supposed. But he had lost count of the number of times that he had camped in the wild just like this, without even a fire for warmth. At least there were people with him now. Not that he minded being by himself. He enjoyed solitude, but it was better to have company. It was fulfilling to pass on all the skills that he had. The Raithlin were learning fast. Their abilities increased day by day, month by month. And this current situation would harden them mentally. The physical skills of the Raithlin were important, but a calm and dauntless attitude was even more vital. It was also something that no one could teach them. They would either develop it, or not.

He walked over to the tethered horses. Some of them picked at the grass from time to time, but they mostly stood quietly, thinking about whatever was important to horses. That they actually *thought*, he knew. No one who was close to horses believed otherwise. And they had personalities, just like people, once you got to know them. He gave his black stallion a rub and scratched its ears, then headed a little way from the camp to keep watch.

The night grew old. Halathgar glittered coldly above, and then began its downward slide across the nighttime sky. A breeze quickened from the north, cold and sharp. It came from the mountains, either Auren Dennath or Anast Dennath. He wondered what they were like, and his old yearning to travel, to find and explore new lands, woke in him. Suddenly, he wondered how Erlissa felt about that. Did she share his love for it? Or would she travel only where she had to go as a lòhren. He knew her well, but not so well as he had once thought.

After a while, he woke Arliss.

"Your watch," he whispered.

"Is there any sign of the Azan?"

"Nothing," he said. "It's as quiet as an inn without ale."

She tossed her hood back and grinned.

"If people can't drink, they usually find something else to do."

She gave a throaty laugh and walked away before he could reply.

He lied down, and a dreamless sleep came swiftly. He knew nothing more until Ruthark gently woke him the next morning. And morning it was, for though the grass was still wet with dew, the sun was a roiling globe of fire that climbed the rim of the world.

There was activity all about him. The horses had been fed a ration of grain, and a small fire, set in a slight depression and smokeless, was being readied to cook breakfast. He felt embarrassed and rose swiftly. All this had been done without him and while he slept. He must be getting older, for hard as yesterday was, he had never slept this late in the past.

He walked to the edge of the camp and looked back over the ground they had covered last night. There was no sign of the Azan. Not much of the forest was visible either, but he saw a few dark smudges where it reached out beyond the tight clump of trees that hugged Lake Alithorin.

"Breakfast!" Aranloth called.

That the lòhren was the best cook among them everyone knew. He gave them each a slice of bread, several days old and quite dry now, but he had transformed it by warming it and smearing it with wild honey from the high fells of Lòrenta.

He offered some to Erlissa, but she shook her head.

"No thanks. I don't feel like anything but water this morning."

Aranloth looked concerned, but did not try to force her to eat. His glance strayed to Lanrik and they both knew what the other was thinking: the poison was beginning to work.

They swiftly finished breakfast.

"Let's go," Lanrik said. He was the last to wake but the first on his horse, and he led them off at a good trot.

The grass was long and green, for spring had come even to northern Alithoras. There were few trees, meaning little cover, and though Lanrik was confident that Arliss was watching for any sign of pursuit, he still checked for himself from time to time. He stopped when she started to roll her eyes at him.

It was good to have other Raithlin with him. That was rarely the case on Galenthern, and though it was true that the Raithlin of Esgallien had been better skilled, these new recruits had handled themselves well in difficult situations.

At noon they found the Great North Road, which the Halathrin had built. It served not just the settlement at Lake Alithorin but other places where once they had dwelt in the north of the land. It was strange to think that armies had marched along the same route that he now rode, even though that had been before the founding of Esgallien. The Halathrin needed to respond quickly to war, and this road brought them into the southlands swiftly. It was disturbing to think, however, that since the Halathrin had withdrawn to their forest home in Halathar, this same road would serve to bring the enemy quickly into northern Alithoras if they ever broke through the league of the free cities, Esgallien and Camarelon.

Lanrik led the others onto its smooth surface without hesitation. It might be older than the city of Esgallien, but the Halathrin built to last. Even now it was free of potholes, the gentle slope from a slight rise in the middle running water off into the fields by the side. The grass grew shorter on the hard and dry surface, and he nudged his mount to a faster pace. The great stallion responded with ease, but he was mindful that the other horses could not match him either for sped or endurance, so he did not push the pace too hard.

He bent low to the horse's withers and scanned the ground as he rode. He saw no sign that the Azan had beaten them here. That did not mean much, for Musraka might cut in front of them at a later point. But he thought they had a lead, and he intended to keep the pace up to ensure it stayed that way.

When the other horses showed signs of tiring, he called a halt. They tethered their mounts and ate another cold meal. The horses picked at the grass, the sound of their grazing a comfort to someone who had grown up with it, but Lanrik knew they could not long maintain the pace he was setting. Still, Lòrenta was not that far away, and horses could be hard ridden for short periods without hurt.

"The sooner we get home the better," Aranloth said to him when they were a little away from the others.

Immediately, Lanrik shifted his gaze to Erlissa. She looked pale and subdued.

"The poison is taking effect, isn't it?"

"I think so." Aranloth leaned on his staff. He looked the veritable picture of an old man, but that did not fool Lanrik. The lòhren was strong, both in body and in mind.

"What do you really know about the poison, Aranloth?"

The lòhren did not move. He continued to gaze at his student.

"Not much that I haven't already spoken of."

"What about the cure, then? I know you haven't told us everything."

Aranloth straightened and shifted his gaze to Lanrik. After a moment, he shrugged.

"You've become more perceptive since you've wielded the shazrahad blade. Lòhrengai can do that."

"True enough," Lanrik replied. He held the lòhren's gaze and waited.

Aranloth did not say anything further at first. Lanrik was not sure if he would answer the original question at all, but then the lòhren broke his silence.

"Long ago, the Letharn used the plant that Musraka calls *King's Poison*. That much I already told you. They were fond of such things, and assassinations were not

57

uncommon. They favored it for that purpose due to the same properties that Musraka listed. Although I doubt that he is aware that it has healing properties too, under certain unique circumstances. The Letharn learned much about it. One thing that they discovered was that when the leaf of the plant is dried and ground into a dust, its potency is multiplied. To inhale just a few grains of it, or to get it onto your hand where it can then swiftly be transferred to the face and enter the body by the eyes, nose or mouth, is more lethal than entering via a wound."

Lanrik nodded but did not speak. He did not want to interrupt the lòhren.

"All that was in the far past," Aranloth continued. "But not so long ago you were on the very threshold of the place where the Letharn used it more than anywhere else."

Lanrik frowned. "Where was that?"

"At the origin of the Angle. Do you recall where we climbed the escarpment and stopped at a monument halfway up?"

Lanrik remembered the place well. Mecklar had pursued them there, but they had rested momentarily in front of a tunnel that ran into the side of the escarpment.

"I know the place you mean. You translated some of the writing on the monument."

Aranloth nodded. "I'll repeat what it said." He tilted his head as if in thought, and then spoke again.

"Attend! We who mastered the world are become dust. We possessed the wealth of nations. Gold adorned our hands; priceless jewels our brows; bright were our swords. The world shuddered when we marched! Now, our glory lies unheeded in the dark of the tomb. Servants mutter secret words as they walk the hidden ways. Death and despair take all others!"

The lòhren looked at him gravely, and Lanrik wondered how sharp his memory was to repeat that, seemingly word for word. Or did he know it for some other reason? Had it been imprinted on his mind by some great event?

"The Letharn meant those last words literally. All the wealth they possessed was buried with them, but even in death they were jealous of it. All the gold and jewels are covered with a layer of King's Poison. It rests upon it as a thick dust. To breathe it in, to touch their treasure, is to die."

Lanrik thought about it. "That says a lot about the Letharn, and a lot about the poison, but what about the cure?"

"The tombs needed attendants," Aranloth said. "Whenever a Letharn was interred, new treasures were brought in. The attendants came and went often, performing a multitude of ceremonies, and inevitably accidents occurred. A mere brush against the dust might kill them. So in addition to cultivating the poison, they also grew the cure. Many fields were devoted to it, and though it was from the dry south it grew well even in the wetter climate of the Angle." Aranloth paused. "This much I indicated in the tower, and what I said was true, yet it will be difficult to find it now. It does still grow there, for I've seen it. But it might take weeks, or even longer, to find it."

Lanrik was thinking while the lòhren talked. He guessed where this was going.

"If the attendants used the cure they would want a supply that was close to hand. It was kept in the tombs, was it not?"

Aranloth nodded. "Yes, it was stockpiled deep inside them and far away from the living."

"So, the quickest way to retrieve it will be to go there. But how can you be sure it survived through the years?"

"The poison and the cure were both used as a dust. The tombs are dry, and I know the poison still retains its power. I believe the cure will retain its virtue as well."

"Well, that makes it simple then. We'll go there and come back all the sooner instead of looking around the Angle for weeks."

Aranloth studied him. "It's not quite that simple. The tombs are a dangerous place. There are many perils – the poison is just one. If you recall, not even the Halathrin entered and came out alive."

Lanrik cast his mind back. He remembered what Aranloth had told them about the Halathrin who had gone inside. Then he thought of his conversation with Erlissa afterwards and knew what disturbed Aranloth.

"Now I see," Lanrik said. "The best place to find the cure is the one place that Erlissa made me promise never to go."

Aranloth nodded. "What exactly she foresaw, I don't know. She didn't tell you then, or me afterward. But I think it was your death. She won't want you to go there, even to save her life. But to save it, I'll need your help. You must break your promise and challenge fate."

6. Time is Your Enemy

They rode all that afternoon and into the evening. It drained them, even Lanrik, who was used to pushing himself hard. But the new Raithlin, though obviously tired and sore, made no complaint.

Aranloth looked as resilient as usual. Erlissa, though she made no comment, was greatly taxed. She became increasingly quiet and withdrawn. Not only did she contend with the rigorous journey, but she also fought an inner battle. Her command of lòhrengai might help her, but it was evident that at best it would only delay the inevitable. Yet that could mean the difference between life and death.

Their first goal must be to reach Lòrenta. They could sort everything else out after that. Reluctantly, he called a halt, and everyone wearily dropped from their mounts and carried out the tasks of setting up camp. It was a subdued evening, with little talk and less laughter.

Lanrik hoped that it would be their last night on the road. By this time tomorrow they should reach Lòrenta, and there would be time enough then to consider his next course of action. How much faith could he put in the ùhrengai of the fountain? Could Aranloth really use it to place Erlissa into some kind of enchanted sleep? He had his doubts, though given the things that he had seen in the lòhren's company, he supposed that he should

61

not. Aranloth would do exactly as he had promised. But that, by itself, would not save Erlissa. Nothing but the cure could do that.

He wondered if it was too late to come to an arrangement with Musraka. He was willing to give up the sword, regardless of the consequences, and he felt that sooner or later the shazrahad would catch up with them. Yet he could not disregard Erlissa's decision. If he gave the weapon to Musraka, it would place a burden on her. One that would be hard to live with, and that would worsen every time the enemy attacked Alithoras. She would see any success they had as her fault.

The night grew old, and a new day eventually dawned. He rose early and studied their backtrail before breakfast. There was no sign of the Azan. That only served to make him uneasy. If they were not behind, they might be ahead. That Musraka would never give up was beyond question.

Erlissa was pale and weak. She ate no food and her face was haggard. Nor did she speak. It seemed to take all her remaining strength just to get in the saddle and commence riding.

During the morning Lanrik eased back and rode level with her.

"How are you feeling?"

"I've been better, Lan."

"Is there anything I can do?"

She gave him a faint smile, but did not answer.

"I wish I could do something."

She looked at him fondly. "Just get us to Lòrenta. After that, what will be will be. I have a feeling things will work out, though not in the ways we expect. You'll just have to trust to fate."

"I can't do that. I don't have your temperament."

"No, you don't. We're very different. And yet also much the same."

"I don't know what that means."

She laughed at him, and for a moment shrugged off her sickness. But the change did not last long. Almost immediately the color drained again from her face. She withdrew into herself and once more took up her battle against the poison.

He moved back to the front. All he could do was what she had asked: get them safely to Lòrenta.

They rode the rest of that day, stopping for regular but brief rests. The horses were tired and their pace lagged, but they followed Lanrik's black stallion determinedly, and the riding was still swift along the Halathrin road. However, by midafternoon, the wild Hills of Lòrenta rose to their right, and Aranloth came up to Lanrik.

"We'll have to leave the road soon," he said. "There are many ways to the fortress, but some are quicker than others. I know a trail through this side of the hills that'll serve us well."

Lanrik studied the bedraggled group behind him. They looked tired, and Erlissa seemed less than secure in her saddle.

"It'll be a long night," he said. "But I think we better ride through it."

Aranloth did not disagree. He pointed with his staff and spoke again.

"See the two hills there? The higher one on the right overgrown by heather, and the lower one on the left covered in pines?"

Lanrik nodded. "I see them."

"We need to reach the valley between the two."

Lanrik gave a low whistle to get everyone's attention, and then led them off the road.

The grass was longer and the ground less flat. He slowed his pace, but only a little.

The afternoon wore on. They climbed ever higher, and the hills grew closer. The grass dried out and turned a straw color. There was plenty of rainfall in the hills, but the soil was not fertile. It was a strange land: high, remote, and as wild as any place that he had ever been. The open fells to the right looked barren of life, though he knew that was far from the case. The birch forests to his left were dark and secretive. Ahead, he took a path leading to the valley that Aranloth indicated. It was clear of trees, and though the ground was steepening quickly, it remained good riding country.

Lanrik had explored the hills often, and he remembered being here before, but Aranloth's knowledge of this land was unsurpassed. As night fell, bringing a swift darkness to the valley, he took the lead. Once more a light glowed at the tip of his staff, and they followed the spark amid the dark of the crowding valley sides.

The lòhren led them truly. Tarns and sedge-lined gullies were frequent, but the paths he chose were always swift and sure. He kept them on solid ground, although the dangers of spongy earth and rocky ledges were never far away.

They penetrated deep into the hills. It grew cold. They were now much higher than on the grasslands, and though spring had come to this part of Alithoras, winter had not yet fully loosed its grip.

The air was still, and their path took them between hills that grew increasingly higher and steeper. Fog and cloud hugged the crests and high ridges, which glowed eerily in the dim starlight. Ice crusted the edges of the willow-rimmed tarns, which lay dark and silent in the deep shadows.

The night wore on, and they stopped every hour to walk the horses and rest them briefly before riding once more. Erlissa did not walk at these times. Lanrik helped her onto Durnlath's mount and led her mare by hand.

He rode close beside her now. Several times he stopped her from falling, until at last he lifted her like a child and placed her ahead of him on the black stallion.

The night seemed to last forever, but eventually dawn came, gray and chill. A late frost turned the dry grass silvery. There was no ice in the middle of the tarns, but mist rose from their blackish surfaces like sluggish steam.

In the distance, Lanrik heard the yelp of a fox and from the high fells the calls of grouse and quail.

The riders emerged from a stand of birch, and there stood Lòrenta. It was no more than a mile away. They approached from its side rather than its front gate. Its ramparts of white marble dazzled the eye.

Aranloth sighed. "Here at last."

Lanrik took one of Erlissa's hands in his own.

"We're here," he whispered. But her hand was limp and she did not answer. For a moment he feared she had died, but then he heard her cough and mutter.

What she was trying to say, he did not know, for he heard at the same moment a cry from the left. He turned and looked straight at the Azan. There were more than he had seen at the Halathrin settlement. Twenty horses steamed in the cold air, and sweat lathered their coats. They had been hard ridden, and were galloping still, their riders bent low over their backs.

"Follow me!" Aranloth commanded.

The lòhren nudged his roan forward and raced ahead. The travelers followed him closely. He led them around the side of the fortress and toward the front gate. Lanrik thought he knew why. That entrance was always attended, and they should be able to get in quickly and have the gates closed behind them. Still, it would be a race, for the Azan were not far behind.

Arliss fell back a little, and Lanrik did not know why. Did she have some plan? Whatever it was could wait. They had a lead, and unless something went wrong they should reach the gates ahead of their enemies.

He yelled back over his shoulder.

"Arliss! Catch up!"

She hesitated, and then nudged her mount forward at a faster pace. It quickly closed the gap.

The wind rushed in Lanrik's ears, and dirt thrown up by the horses in front sprayed into his face.

They drew near to Lòrenta's portcullis, and he spotted movement on the ramparts.

"Open the gate!" Aranloth yelled.

The lòhren stood in his stirrups; his white robes whipping about him, and he lifted high his staff.

The portcullis opened as they approached. The tunnel beyond was narrow and shadowy, but they raced inside without hesitation.

There was a rush of hooves behind them as the Azan neared, but the gate dropped down with a boom. At the same time arrows fired from the ramparts struck the earth and made the horses shy.

The travelers rode through the dim tunnel and into the bright yard beyond it. They drew to a halt. Musraka, remaining stationary on his mount and seemingly unafraid of the arrows, hailed them from outside.

"I can wait," he said. He was a dark shadow behind the metal bars, and there was no sign of his men.

"Time is your enemy," he said. "But it's my ally."

He rode off then, and true though Lanrik felt the words to be, he quickly put them out of his mind.

Dismounting, he carefully pulled Erlissa onto his shoulders. She was unconscious, and he wondered if they were too late.

He gestured to Ruthark. "Make sure the horses are looked after." He glanced at Aranloth. The lòhren said nothing but turned and strode ahead. Lanrik followed him through the winding corridors of the fortress. From time to time startled students scurried out of their way. Twice, lòhrens offered to help, but Aranloth waved them away. It took Lanrik a while to realize that someone was following them. He turned and saw Arliss.

She shrugged. "I thought you might need me."

Lanrik did not answer. He went on as fast as he could. He did not know what the lòhren was going to do, so maybe Arliss could help. Strange, considering that she and Erlissa barely spoke to each other, but he was not going to refuse her offer.

By the time they reached the great courtyard at the center of the fortress, Lanrik's legs ached.

"Straight to the fountain," Aranloth instructed.

Lanrik stumbled after him as fast as he could. He paid no heed to the green grass, nor the flowerbeds and gardens. He had eyes only for the sparkling white-granite basin, and the great statue that was its centerpiece. The stone lòhren, with his staff extended, and the shooting column of water, from which drifted a mist that canopied all around it. Lanrik felt a sensation of peace. It was the power of ùhrengai at the heart of the fortress, but it did little to dispel his fears.

"Over here," Aranloth said. The lòhren indicated one of the stone benches that ringed the fountain.

Lanrik laid Erlissa down gently. Her chest rose and fell with her breathing, but she seemed unconscious. Her head lolled to the side, and he took off his Raithlin cloak, folded it neatly, and placed it behind her neck.

Her eyes flickered open, and she summoned the last of her strength to speak.

"Be careful . . . Lan. Don't do anything stupid looking for the cure. Musraka will seek you out, and it's not worth the risk to the sword."

"I don't care about the sword," Lanrik said. "I only care about you."

She closed her eyes. "Don't argue with me, Lan. You have responsibilities . . . to Alithoras. That comes first."

"I don't give a damn about my responsibilities." He would have said more, but Aranloth approached and looked at her closely.

"There's little time," he said.

"What can I do," Lanrik asked.

"Stand back. Whatever happens, don't interfere. And don't touch her."

Erlissa closed her eyes while Lanrik and Arliss moved away.

The lòhren went to the fountain. He extended the tip of his staff deep into the pool of water that filled the basin. Lòhren-fire spurted beneath the surface. The water roiled and swirled. A seething mist rose into the air. Sunlight caught it and made it sparkle like a cloud of diamond dust.

Tentatively, Arliss reached out with her hand and took Lanrik's. The ground trembled beneath their feet and he felt a change in the air. He sensed the ùhrengai that lay dormant in the deeps of the earth. It woke and

68

surged upward. Tendrils of power whipped though the courtyard, and all at once he had a sense of the vastness of time. He knew that his life, and even the legendary fortress, were nothing compared to the ùhrengai's antiquity. It had been here since Alithoras rose from the waves; it would be here when the land sunk once more. Both man and fortress were less than a pebble on the side of a mountain.

Aranloth left the basin and paced slowly toward Erlissa. Lòhren-fire dripped like water from the tip of his staff. He swirled it slowly through the air, and the white mist from the fountain gathered about it and thickened. He passed it over Erlissa's still form, again and again. Mist rose from the ground and settled out of the air above. It enveloped the bench.

Lanrik thought it was beautiful, and then he realized that it was shaped like a coffin. He shivered, and Arliss squeezed his hand.

Without warning, Aranloth struck the ground with his staff. There was a bell-like ring from the rocky deeps in response. Suddenly, the swirling vapors stilled, and the lòhren-fire died. The white mist was now solid. It encased Erlissa like a block of crystal: cold, remote and untouchable.

"It is done," Aranloth said. "She is caught in a moment of time." He walked forward, but stumbled and fell to one knee.

Lanrik and Arliss ran to him. They helped him to stand.

"Is she still alive?" Arliss asked.

"Yes. But only just. All that she was, all that she is, all that she might yet be, is bound to the ùhrengai. She cannot see or hear us, she cannot think. She cannot even dream. She will sleep in oblivion until we return with the cure."

The next morning was bright and clear. Lanrik, well rested but troubled, looked out over the battlements. Below was a clear space and then the birch wood. Nothing moved in the open or within the trees. He remembered Elù-Randùr, who had attacked the fortress with elùgai last summer. He had escaped, though his brethren had not.

Lanrik looked for a different enemy now. Musraka was someone else from his past, another unresolved issue. But there was no sign of him. He considered sending out a group of Raithlin, but rejected the idea. Musraka was cunning. He would not be easy to find. And what then anyway? It would only lead to a fight. No, there was no point in that. Durnlath was already dead; there was no need for others to suffer.

He and Aranloth had arranged to leave that night anyway. Musraka would never discover where they were going. Aranloth told him that even Ebona could not guess their destination, for she had little knowledge of the Letharn. They were safe from the shazrahad.

But did they really need to go to the Angle? There was another way to obtain the cure Erlissa needed. Musraka possessed the antidote. Lanrik knew he could track and find him. He believed he could do it unobserved. But what then? He would have to steal into their camp, find it, and then slip away undetected.

The danger of a mission like that was great, though he had once gone into the midst of an enemy army. That gave him confidence that he could actually succeed, but there was an unavoidable weakness to the plan. Musraka would know that he might make such an attempt. After all, the shazrahad had commanded the same army that he had infiltrated. The Azan would be waiting for him, which the army had not been.

Reluctantly, Lanrik gave up on the idea. He was willing to risk the danger, but the plan was less likely to succeed than the alternative of going to the Letharn tombs. He hated the idea of leaving Erlissa imprisoned by some sort of enchantment. He wanted to see her walk again, to smile at him and to see the flash of her eyes. But patience would serve best now. The long road was the surer path.

It occurred to him that he had made many of these choices and been in the same situations before. It was almost as though history was repeating itself.

His hand rested on his sword hilt. He felt something in the weapon react to his touch. That he and the blade were linked, he knew. But this felt less like lòhrengai and more like some kind of recognition. Not of him, but his thoughts. It was as though the blade *agreed* with him. He realized that, in a way, the sword was central to everything that had happened. Its lòhrengai had run through his body and become one with him, but he had never tried to become one with it. Another thought came to him. There was elùgai in the blade too, and even the lòhrens did not fully understand exactly what the sword was capable of, or its purpose. That was disturbing.

He heard footsteps behind him and turned. It was Arliss.

"Aranloth wants to see you," she said.

"Where is he?"

"I'll tell you, but promise me something first."

Lanrik heard determination in her voice. "What's that?"

"Take me with you."

71

He shook his head slowly. "Aranloth and I have already made our decision. We're going by ourselves, and we're going tonight. There's no need for anyone else to risk themselves."

"Don't you think my skills are good enough?"

He looked at her and considered the question.

"Of all the new Raithlin in Lòrenta, your skills are the best. But it's not about that. I just don't intend for any more of you to die."

"You take too much onto yourself. Durnlath knew what he was doing. I know what I'm doing. I'm not stupid. There'll be risks, that much is certain. But this is certain too. You *will* need help."

Lanrik shook his head. "I think Aranloth and I can manage."

"I don't think so. The unexpected always happens. If you take me with you, you'll be better prepared for it."

He knew she had a point. Her skills were good enough, and something might happen that neither he nor Aranloth anticipated.

"I'll think about it," he said.

She grinned suddenly. "You'll agree in the end."

Without another word she turned and led him away. He followed her through Lòrenta's maze of corridors. Aranloth waited in one of the many small meeting rooms. It contained only a round table and several plain wooden chairs. The lòhren, still looking tired from his efforts at the fountain, slumped in his chair. His staff lay across the top of the table. Arliss left the room and closed the door behind her.

"Bad news," the lòhren said without preamble, and rubbed his face. The skin of the back of his hands was pale, and his speech listless.

"Musraka is no longer our only worry. A wandering lòhren returned from his travels this morning. He brought unsettling information."

Lanrik had a bad feeling. "What did he say?"

"He told me that soldiers from Esgallien are on the move. Twenty of them – and well north of Caladhrist."

"There could be several reasons for that," Lanrik said hesitantly.

"Maybe. But you know in your heart what it means."

"You're probably right. King Murhain hasn't given up. He wants the sword. Musraka wants it too. It seems as though everybody wants it but me."

Aranloth sighed. "That's true. And that makes you the best person to keep it. Yet it might be best to leave it in the fortress while we seek Erlissa's cure. It's safe here, but out in the wild it could get into the wrong hands."

Lanrik thought about it. He had another sword, one that he could wield with pride – the Raithlin blade that Gwalchmur had given him.

"I agree," he said. "But on the other hand, you've already suggested that Ebona is involved. And what if Elù-Randùr has something to do with all this? We might need to defend ourselves against sorcery and witchcraft. I trust in your skills, but you can't be everywhere. Our mission must succeed, or Erlissa is lost. I won't allow that, so if that means risking the sword, I'll take my chances."

Aranloth looked like he might argue, but in the end he just shrugged. "You may be right."

"There's another thing," Lanrik said. He felt uncomfortable mentioning this concern, but he thought Aranloth should know.

The lòhren sensed his change of mood and looked at him sharply. "What is it?"

"I don't think all of this is a coincidence."

"What do you mean?"

"Does it feel to you like we've been down this path before? It's not the first time that Musraka has pursued us. It's not the first time that we've gone to the Angle. Nor is it the first time that Ebona has helped our enemies."

Aranloth frowned as he thought about it, but did not interrupt, so Lanrik continued.

"I think the sword has something to do with it. Do you remember what you once said? That it's an embodiment of prophecy, and that the elùgai in it works to bring Assurah's foretelling to fulfillment."

Aranloth's frown deepened, but he still made no move to speak.

Lanrik went on. "I think I can feel it. When I touch the hilt, I sense the elùgai stir. Or maybe the prophecy itself. But I feel *something*. It sings out like a call to arms."

Aranloth rolled his staff back and forth on the tabletop while he thought.

"It might just be," the lòhren said at length. "But if so, there's nothing we can do at the moment. All the more reason to leave it here, though."

Lanrik shook his head. "I can't do that. But when this is done, I think we should destroy it."

Aranloth let go of his staff and sat back.

"Perhaps. I've been thinking about the problem since we first learned of the prophecy. It might be the answer in the end, but we'll have to wait and see."

Aranloth looked as disturbed as Lanrik had ever seen him. After a while, he raised his eyes and fixed him with a troubled gaze.

"You realize that if what you say is true, the sword might draw our enemies to us in the wild."

Lanrik had not considered that. He still was not sure if his feelings were imagined or not.

"Maybe," he said. "But there's a risk no matter what I do."

Aranloth did not answer. Lanrik knew the lòhren would not try to convince him again to leave it behind. Nor would he encourage him to take it. It was his own responsibility to decide, but it was clear that whatever choice he made would be a dangerous one.

7. Carist Nien

Shadows groped down from the high fells. They smothered the fortress and dulled the white marble of its walls. All was still, and the world momentarily hushed during those few moments when the newborn promise of night was freshest.

Inside the fortress of Lòrenta, however, not everything was motionless. A group of people, though quiet and subdued, gathered near a secret exit at the base of one of the walls.

Lanrik sat astride his black stallion. The shazrahad sword hung in its scabbard by his side. He would take it on this quest, for Erlissa meant more to him than anything. Yet he was mindful of his responsibilities to Alithoras. He would protect the blade. He would fight to keep it out of the hands of those who would misuse it, or, merely by possessing it, set in motion a prophecy of dark destruction.

He had not made the decision lightly, but the sword's capacity to help outweighed its potential for harm. At least, he hoped it would be so.

He glanced at Aranloth, who slouched in the saddle of his roan. He appeared unaffected by the dangers that might lie ahead. Lanrik wondered how many times the lòhren had left the fortress on a quest. How many dangers had he faced and survived? He had done all of this before, and it showed in his relaxed attitude, yet even so, there remained an undercurrent of nervousness. Lanrik had learnt to recognize the near invisible signs: a slight narrowing of the eyes, and the tight grip of his hands on the oaken staff.

Lanrik had made another decision besides taking the shazrahad sword. It too was unsettling, but it was his job to make these choices, and he would not shirk them. Arliss was beside the lòhren. She was mounted and prepared for travel, for he had agreed to let her come. That she would be of help, he knew. But her life would be at risk also, and that disturbed him. But her presence meant a greater chance of saving Erlissa, and thereby helping strengthen the lòhrens who protected Alithoras. That was what the new Raithlin were for, and Arliss fulfilled that purpose.

They were not alone. The rest of the Raithlin, Hargil and Ruthark at their front, had gathered to see them off. They stood nearby, their faces showing a mixture of disappointment that Lanrik had not chosen them to go, envy that Arliss had been, and relief that they would remain in the safety of the fortress.

Lonfar stepped forward and shook his hand.

"Good luck, Lan."

"Thanks." Lanrik said. He shook his uncle's hand warmly. "You'll look after the new Raithlin while I'm away?"

Lonfar winked at him. "I'm only a librarian. But I'll keep an eye on them, if you like."

Arliss nudged her mount closer. "They respect you, old man. They've all heard the stories about you. They don't care what you are now – they know what you can still teach them."

77

"Well, thanks . . . I think," Lonfar said. "How about you leave out the old man comment next time, though."

She grinned at him. "No reason to be offended. Some girls like older men."

Lonfar's face reddened and he turned to Lanrik.

"You'd better watch this one Lan – she's full of cheek."

"I've noticed that myself."

Arliss looked from one to the other, and tried unsuccessfully to suppress a grin.

"Don't pretend you don't like it."

Lanrik did not answer. He *did* like it. But no good would come from letting her know that.

"Time to go," he said.

"Yes, Raithlindrath," Arliss answered with mock formality. Then she smiled at Lonfar. "Goodbye, old man."

"Goodbye, Arliss." The older Raithlin pointed at Lanrik. "Look after him, will you?"

Arliss looked serious for the first time. "I'll see what I can do."

The three of them dismounted to pass through the narrow tunnel that led to the other side of the wall. When they reached the end, Aranloth opened the door. A massive panel of stone pivoted at the mere touch of his hand, and beyond was a rocky slope that led away from the fortress.

The lòhren closed the door and when the slab pivoted back into its normal position, nothing could be seen of it anymore. The wall looked just the same as it did at any other point of the fortress.

"Quietly now," Aranloth whispered. "Noise travels far over rocky ground at night."

Lanrik went to the front, and they led the horses by hand for a little while. After some minutes, the slope lessened and the rocks gave way to earth and grass. They mounted and commenced to ride.

There was no sign of the Azan, nor did Lanrik expect there to be. Ebona might, or might not, be aiding them, but even her witchcraft could not pinpoint their exact location. Not with Aranloth present, anyway. The lòhren had assured them he would prevent that.

The night air grew cold, and Lanrik pulled his Raithlin cloak tightly about him. He wore one of the newly made garments intended for recruits, but he missed his old one that had been with him for years.

Aranloth pointed southward with his staff.

"We'd better go that way, Lanrik. I have a plan to get us to the Angle quickly."

Lanrik veered in the direction that Aranloth indicated. He had not explored the south of Lòrenta well, for the land grew wet and boggy. He wondered what idea Aranloth had, but now was not the time to ask.

They rode quietly through the night. Fog rolled down from the brooding hills and thickened all around them. The trail was mostly silent. Occasionally, they heard foxes yelp or owls hoot within the dim tracts of the many birch woods.

The fog grew heavier until it was like a blanket cast over the whole land, and the silvery trunks of the slender birches gave way to willow trees. There were not many, but they were massive and gnarly – ancient samples of their kind that seemed as old as the hills themselves.

The travelers rode deep into the night before stopping. Their camp, positioned beneath one of the great willows, was as dry as they could expect under the influence of the fog, and though the overhanging branches would have diffused smoke, Lanrik lit no fire. They were too tired to wait for food to cook.

"We'd better keep a watch," he suggested, chewing on some fresh bread.

"I'll take the first," Arliss said. "I'm not sleepy."

They spoke little more. Aranloth lay down near the gnarled and twisted trunk, and Lanrik wrapped his cloak about himself and tried to sleep.

The horses stayed where they were, tethered to some young saplings that grew outside the shadow of the willow. They swished their tails occasionally and quietly stamped their hooves in order to deter mosquitoes. Other than that, it remained quiet except for the slow drip of water from the ends of the fog-wetted leaves.

After a time Arliss got up and moved away from the camp. Lanrik knew that it was hard to stay awake during a watch, and moving around often helped.

He drifted into a deep sleep. Sometime later, Arliss gently shook his shoulder to wake him. The fog must have thickened even further, for the night was black as a pit, and he could barely see her pale face.

"Anything happening out there?" he asked.

Arliss pulled her hood up. "No," she whispered. Without another word she moved away from him and Aranloth to find a spot to sleep.

Lanrik thought that something was disturbing her, for she was not her normal self. He wondered what it was, but his mind soon turned to another question: where exactly was the lòhren taking them?

He still had no answer by the time dawn came. The morning was gray, and the fog deep and impenetrable. But the air was full of bird calls, and though the sunrise was not visible, the east was shot through with silver light.

Lanrik lit a fire for breakfast. The willow tree would disperse most of the smoke, and the fog would conceal the rest.

When they were finished eating, Lanrik broached the subject of their destination.

"Why are we heading south, Aranloth?"

The lòhren chuckled. "I knew you'd be wondering about that. You can't guess the answer?"

"I've tried," Lanrik admitted, "but I can't work it out."

"Well," continued Aranloth, "the main idea is to get to the Angle as fast as we can, isn't it?"

"Of course, but there's nothing faster than horseback, and —"

Lanrik stopped, and Aranloth grinned at him.

"Now you've got it," the lòhren said.

"Boats!" Lanrik said. "I should have guessed. It makes sense – the headwaters of the Carist Nien must be nearby. I just didn't realize that the lòhrens traveled that way."

"If it didn't occur to you, we can hope it doesn't occur to Musraka, either."

Lanrik nodded in agreement. "What about the horses?"

"They'll be all right. We often use the river because it's a quick way to travel southward. There's a little settlement of fishermen at the headwaters who help supply the fortress with food. They'll look after the horses for us."

The fog hung in the air, thick and unmoving, as they rode through the dank morning. The ground grew dangerous, full of bogs and moss-covered boulders. Springs seeped water onto the hillsides and rivulets were plentiful. By midmorning, the sun had burnt away most

81

of the fog. It clung to the lowlands and the tops of the fells, but where Aranloth led them it became ever clearer. There were few trees, and as they crested a hill the fishermen's settlement lay before them.

There were scores of cottages. Large racks, made of long poles and wicker, faced the sun, and countless fish dried upon the framework in the open. Smoke rose from chimneys and formed sluggish columns in the still air. The scent of fish and smoke was strong.

Each cottage had a large vegetable garden and many of the larger fenced yards contained sheep and cattle.

The travelers neared the settlement and the villages who worked the fields waved. Aranloth saluted them with his staff.

The road through the settlement was muddy, but the little cottages were neat and tidy. Laughing children ran before and after them, but they stopped and went back into the village when the travelers passed through its center and continued until the road descended a steep slope. At its bottom was a long shed, and beyond that, a creek.

"It seems like a small start for a great river," Arliss said.

"It doesn't look impressive now," Aranloth answered, "but the river grows wide and deep soon enough. All the hills for league after league drain into it, and many small streams and creeks contribute to its flow. Not that far away from here it's a thunderous flood as it descends some rapids, but after that, it's a smooth ride to the Angle."

Aranloth dismounted and carefully knocked the tip of his staff against the shed's wooden door. They waited until an old man, his hair silvery white but his skin nut-brown from decades of sunlight, emerged. His face split into a gap-toothed grin when he saw Aranloth.

"Careth Tar! Great father!"

Aranloth shook the man's hand and the villager grinned even more broadly.

"Come inside," the old man said. He popped his head back through the doorway and called out. Two young boys quickly appeared and took the horses' reins at his bidding.

"Look after them well," Aranloth said.

The boys did not answer but shyly bobbed their heads in acknowledgement.

The travelers followed the old man into the shed. It was not as dark as Lanrik expected. The roof was high, and several windows and doors allowed plenty of light to enter. Tools of many types hung all over the walls, and root crops lay stacked high at one end. The opposite side contained a half-built boat, but it was different from anything Lanrik had seen in Esgallien.

The old man observed his gaze and grinned yet again.

"It's called a shuffa," he said. "We build them more for speed than fishing, but we use them for that sometimes, too."

"It looks fast," agreed Lanrik. He studied it carefully. It was a dozen feet long, quite narrow in the middle, and pointed at both ends.

"It looks like some intricate craftsmanship goes into making them."

The old man looked prideful. "My Dad taught me how to build them, and he learned from his in turn. All our forefathers from time out of memory were boat builders. They're simple things really – little more than a bit of light timber. It's putting them together right that takes all the skill."

"We'll need to use one of them," Aranloth said.

The old man gestured them toward a wide doorway on the far side of the shed, and they went through. Outside, the ground dropped quickly into a steep bank. The villagers had cut stairs into the earth and lined them with stone. Beyond that, a simple jetty struck out into the creek, and many boats were tied to oak posts at its side. Some were shuffas, while others were much broader and probably used for fishing instead of travel.

"Take your pick," the old man said. "When do you leave?"

"Right now," Aranloth answered.

The old man looked at him keenly. "Urgent business, is it?"

"Indeed," the lòhren said. "And dangerous business too. There are Azan in the hills – a group of twenty men. They might track us here, so you'd best prepare the village."

The old man grinned. "We're always ready for a fight."

Lanrik looked at him anew. He was old, but the veins in his arms stood out from the lean flesh. Once, he was strong. Maybe he still was. But it was the glint in his eye that made him look ready to live up to his words. If the village had enough men like him, they would repel the Azan if it came down to a physical confrontation. And they likely had weapons too. Most villagers had an old sword hanging behind their front door and a long spear leaning in a corner somewhere. They would be taken down and sharpened now, and a keen lookout kept for any sign of trouble.

Aranloth shook the old man's hand.

"We'll leave straight away."

The villager gave them all a friendly wave.

84

"I'll pass the word around about the Azan. We'll be ready if they come."

Aranloth picked out a shuffa, and Lanrik helped Arliss inside. They sat down carefully, but the boat seemed relatively stable. Neither of them were used to this kind of thing, but the lòhren stepped in after them and untied the mooring rope swiftly.

"Take a paddle," he said, "and let's get going. You'll get used to things quickly."

They each picked up a long pole with a broadened end and mimicked Aranloth's actions to start the shuffa moving. Soon they were in the middle of the creek. After that, the current took them, and they used the paddles more for steering than anything else.

They gathered speed and moved at a steady pace along with the water. The river grew as they progressed, soon widening, and the banks receded further away. It was an uncomfortable feeling for Lanrik, whose training had rarely involved boats, nor was he a good swimmer. However, he soon grew confident in the sturdiness of the shuffa, however light it was, and began to enjoy the scenery as they drifted along.

The banks to either side were overhung by many tress, mostly willows, and up and beyond them the hills rose and steepened into heather or fog-shrouded heights.

So the day continued until they pulled up at a shallow bend of the river and drew the boat onto a shoal of sand in order to rest for lunch.

"We're a good way from Lòrenta now," Lanrik said. "I think I'll risk a fire."

Arliss collected some driftwood from nearby, and they established a camp. Although they did not use the fire to cook any food, it was comforting and gave them a sense of ease and rest. The sandy shoal, quiet and secluded, was just the sort of place that Lanrik loved. But soon the river called to him again and the urgency of the mission drove him on.

"Time to move," he said.

They followed him back to the boat, but before he reached it, he stopped suddenly.

"What is it?" Aranloth asked.

By way of answer, Lanrik pointed.

Far away up stream were six boats. And though they were half a mile away, the current of the river was bringing them swiftly to where the travelers stood.

"Could it be fishermen from the village?" Lanrik asked.

Aranloth stamped the end of his staff angrily into the sandy shore. "No," he said. "They rarely come this far downstream. The Azan have somehow managed to find us – again."

Lanrik strode to the shuffa, and with the help of the others he pushed it into the current once more. They stepped in and paddled quickly, aiming for the center of the river where the current was strongest.

When the flowing water took hold of them properly, Lanrik turned around and studied the enemy.

"They've gained on us," he said. "But things should even out from now on."

Arliss spoke up from the back of the boat. "Do you think they can catch us, Aranloth?"

The lòhren did not pause in his paddling. "Not anytime soon," he said. "The current is doing most of the work here, and that's the same for both of us. But we have another problem."

Lanrik looked back to the front. "What's that?" he asked.

The lòhren kept his attention focused forward.

"This is a big river, and it gets bigger as it goes. But we're still in high country here, even though Lòrenta is behind us. By this afternoon we'll reach a kind of escarpment. The river drops down it through the rapids that I told you about."

"Can we get through them?"

Aranloth looked back for the first time. "They're dangerous. The current is swift and unpredictable. Not only that, there are many boulders and rock ledges that could rip a shuffa apart in moments. No one ever risks it. Instead, they carry the boats down a track in the escarpment."

"How long does that take?"

"Several hours," Aranloth said.

"Damn!" Lanrik cursed. "They'll leave their boats behind and catch up to us."

"Most likely," Aranloth admitted.

"We could leave the shuffa behind," Arliss mused, "but it's a long walk to the Angle, and the Azan will still be close behind us."

"How did they find us so soon?" Lanrik asked.

Aranloth ran a hand through his hair. "I don't know. There's something wrong. I know this, though. It wasn't because of Ebona. They're getting help from some other source."

Lanrik looked back over the river again. The Azan had stopped gaining on them, but they were close enough that he could distinguish Musraka. The man had made a promise to chase him to the ends of the earth, and he was fulfilling it.

"They must have attacked the settlement," he said.

Aranloth looked worried at the suggestion. "The villagers had warning, so I think they would have been prepared. More likely, the Azan just stole the boats, but they would not have got them without some kind of fight."

Arliss spoke up from the back again. "So, what are we going to do? It seems that we've outrun our luck. We can't use the river much longer, and going on foot is just as dangerous." She directed her next comment at Lanrik. "You might have to give Musraka the sword. It's the only way out of this mess."

Aranloth grunted. "That's not really an option."

"But you said yourself that we're stuck. What other way is there?"

The lòhren turned around and looked at them both.

"There's one other way," he said.

"What's that?" Lanrik asked.

"We'll have to do what no one else ever has, and what I don't think the desert-dwelling Azan have the stomach for."

Arliss raised an eyebrow. "Which is?"

"We'll risk the rapids."

Lanrik felt the blood drain from his face. "I thought you said that it couldn't be done?"

"No," the lòhren replied. "I said it *hadn't* been done, not that it *couldn't* be. But it will be very dangerous. There's a chance that the shuffa will be destroyed and we'll be thrown into the raging waters."

Aranloth looked back again. "The choice is yours, Lanrik. Return the sword, or trust to our luck."

Lanrik thought about it. "How long do we have?"

"Not long," the lòhren replied. "Look downriver."

Lanrik did as instructed and realized that Aranloth was right. He saw the escarpment ahead. The river dropped and twisted over it in a spray of white froth and spume. The prospect of trying to get through that nearly paralyzed him with fear.

It seemed that each choice he made lately only brought increased danger. Perhaps Arliss was right: the only way forward might be to give the sword back. But that filled him with as much fear as the rapids.

He closed his eyes and calmed himself. There was no time for the deep and proper thought that he would like to give to the problem. He must do as Erlissa did, and trust to his instincts.

When he opened his eyes, the rapids were nearer. But he had made his decision.

8. A Shadow of Life

Erlissa woke from a dreamless sleep. She sensed that little time had passed, and that disturbed her. Lanrik could not yet have found her cure, and Aranloth had assured her that until then she would rest in oblivion.

The last thing she remembered was the lòhren. The power and skill that he had invoked at the fountain awed her, and the risk he had taken on her behalf was humbling. For though he had never said anything while they traveled, it became clear to her by the end that his attempt to save her jeopardized his own life. Had he made the slightest error, or misjudged the forces at play, the ùhrengai would have consumed him.

But it had not. And she felt a bond of loyalty between them. One that had not existed before, but that was now unbreakable.

She thought of her training as a lòhren, and the time Aranloth had invested in her. She had always known that his skill and power far surpassed her own, but now she realized how vast was the gulf that separated them. Yet he was always a kind and patient teacher.

She recalled his comment that her sleep at the fountain would be one of total oblivion. How then had she woken?

All about her was blackness. It was a dark so deep that it denied the existence of light itself. Nor could she feel or sense anything. She began to panic, and that disturbed her more, for all she felt was the *emotion* of panic: there was no racing heartbeat, no sweaty palms. There was nothing but an agitation of her mind.

She reined in her scattered thoughts. That something was wrong was obvious, and yet she sensed no threat. She was safe within the protective force at the heart of Lòrenta. She sensed it all around her. It seemed to have no beginning or end. It had no purpose, at least none with her, but she was now linked to it and it to her. The enormity of that joining threatened to overwhelm her, for it seemed to encompass everything in the world, all that had happened and everything that yet could. She had a feeling that here, in the fathomless depth of the powers that moved and substanced the world, anything was possible. The immensity was too much for her to grasp, and she felt panic rise again. She shied away from it and concentrated on the ordinary instead.

Her thoughts turned to Lanrik, who was anything but ordinary; yet picturing his face was calming. At least until she remembered that Arliss was with him at the fountain. How could he be so smart about some things and so stupid about others? It was obvious that the girl wanted him, but he seemed unaware of her feelings. That would not last, not now that Arliss had a free hand to act on her desire.

Erlissa realized that she should be jealous, that other girls would have been, but she had always been different. Lanrik would make his own choices, and things would turn out one way or the other. It was out of her control, although she regretted her coolness to him lately. He thought their different responsibilities were drawing them apart, and they were, but it was also her reaction to Arliss. Perhaps she *did* get jealous after all.

Somewhere in the deeps of the great dark she heard a voice. It was not Lanrik's. It was a female; and though she could not grasp the meaning of the words, they resounded with power and determination. Unexpectedly, the dark spun around her. Where there had been nothing before, there was up and down, left and right, and an unnerving sensation of falling.

Light blazed into her eyes. Noise drowned her ears, and sensations racked her skin like a thousand cutting knives. She screamed, and her lungs emptied of air, but she knew that she was alive again, out of the great dark, and yet her feeling that something was wrong only grew.

Her eyes adjusted to the light, and she realized that it was not bright at all. About her was the gray of dawn. She felt green grass on her back, lush and thick, and she sat upright. It was then that she saw the speaker.

Ahead of her, standing on a turf-covered mound, was the Guardian of Enorìen. The muscles beneath her bare skin flexed and rippled at her slightest move. Dark hair fell in waves from her proud head, and her green-brown eyes, alert and wary like a wild animal's, scrutinized her.

"You answered my call," the Guardian said.

Erlissa sat up. She was dizzy but found her voice.

"What's happening, Carnona? Why am I here? *How* am I here?"

Carnona stepped off the mound and walked close.

"How I summoned you does not matter. You are here. That is the only thing of importance."

The Guardian hesitated, and a look of uncertainty covered her face. When she spoke again, it was with a softer tone.

"Perhaps I should tell you. It will help you to understand what I want."

Carnona frowned, looking like she was deep in thought or trying to find words for ideas that she guessed were beyond Erlissa's grasp.

"Aranloth joined you to the ùhrengai of Lòrenta, and I know why he did so. Little happens in the land that I am unaware of, for some things I see before they happen, and much else is obvious to those who open their minds and think. And just as you can walk, step by step from Lòrenta to these hills, the ùhrengai of the land is linked. It all has one source. If one part of it is touched, the disturbance will travel through the whole just as ripples cross the surface of a pond after a pebble is cast into it." Carnona gazed at her intently. "You *are* that pebble."

Erlissa stood up. It was good to feel the earth beneath her feet, but she realized something unnerving.

"I cannot be in two places at once. So if I'm the pebble, the real me is still at Lòrenta." She gestured at her body. "This is just the ripple."

The Guardian studied her with unblinking eyes.

"Few among your kind would understand that. Aranloth chose you wisely. You are indeed the ripple, a shadow of life. And not even ùhrengai can long keep you here, for you are also still in Lòrenta, and nature will draw you back to your true self, just as water seeks lower ground."

Erlissa was wobbly on her legs, but she felt her shadow-body fill with strength at her every breath and movement. The forest of Enorien ringed the grassy glade in which she stood. Ancient trees leaned over it, as though listening. She sensed it was a place of power, and she could feel the ùhrengai of the land pulse and flow beneath her feet.

"Very well. I understand how I came to be here, but *why* am I here?"

Carnona looked at her with expressionless eyes.

"You made a commitment when Aranloth retrieved the mistletoe berries. Now, listen carefully, for time slips away. I am ready to call on you to uphold your promise. But just as I said then, I will say also now. The decision is yours whether or not you will fulfill the task I set you. I cannot force you, nor would I in this matter even if I could. If you deny my request, I will return you to Lòrenta, and you will sleep in oblivion until Aranloth returns and wakes you. *If* he returns with the cure for the poison that ails your true body."

Erlissa felt a stab of fear. She did not like Carnona's implied observation that the others were in danger. But that was out of her control now.

"Tell me what you want," she said.

The Guardian gazed at her with intent eyes, as though weighing her up and examining the stuff of which she was made.

"The situation is simple. Ebona is, as you would say, my sister. We were both born of the world at the same time. Once, our realms were wider than they are now." She swept a hand around in an arc, and the skin of her arm glowed nut-brown at the touch of the morning sun. "But my heartland is here, just as hers was far to the west. Yet after long ages, when Men multiplied and swarmed across the land, she chose to influence them, and she gathered power from their worship and sacrifice. When they migrated eastward, she abandoned her realm and followed them. I stayed true to my nature. I guarded my heartland from the ravages of civilization and nurtured it."

Erlissa nodded. "Aranloth has told me something of your origin and past. I know more of his overthrow of Ebona. It seems her avarice betrayed her, for she lost both the lands of her birthing and her influence over mankind."

Carnona gave a curt nod. "That is so. She became much diminished. Yet she would be again what she once was. Moreover, she has the ability to achieve that goal."

Carnona shivered and her eyes burned. Whether it was with fear, hatred, or some other emotion, Erlissa could not tell.

"I have paid her little heed," Carnona said, "until now. For this winter she began an attempt to usurp my heartland, to make it, and the ùhrengai that sustains it, her own. She would replace what she once lost, and combine it with her influence over Men. Her sway over Esgallien grows apace, and now also her long arm reaches out to Camarelon. In this, she is assisted. The elùgroth who assaulted Lòrenta aids her."

Erlissa shuddered. *Elù-Randùr.* She knew him. Despised him. And feared him too. He had escaped the destruction of his brethren at Lòrenta. But his words had burned her. He had said that she was a sister to his kind. There was truth in his accusation, or there would be if she was not careful with her power. She took it as a warning: it was her responsibility to ensure it never came true.

Erlissa frowned. Something did not quite seem right.

"Surely, here in your own heartland, you are stronger than Ebona. You can repel her."

"Yes. And I have done so for many months. But her strength ever waxes. And the power of the elùgroth upholds her while I weaken. I can hold her off. But it is increasingly hard. One day, one day soon, she will prevail."

"And what are the consequences of that?"

"Her power will mature. She will gather armies and ravage the land with war. She feeds on death, and combined with Elù-Randùr, many realms of Alithoras will fall. By the time they become jealous of each other's growing power, they will have destroyed much of the land."

The sun rose over the tops of the trees and birdsong swelled through the forest. Erlissa felt the power and beauty of this ancient land, untouched by the hand of man. The feeling was at odds with Carnona's fear.

"Very well. I understand your predicament. But what do you want with me? I'm the least of the lòhrens. In fact, I'm only a lòhren in training. I haven't even earned my staff yet. Nor will I be a lòhren until I get it."

Carnona smiled. Her face was as changeable as the weather in spring. "Aranloth has not told you?"

"Told me what?"

"A lòhren does not earn their staff. It is not given after passing a test. It is found. Its nature is determined by the need of the land."

That was news to Erlissa. She wondered why Aranloth had never mentioned it.

"With or without a staff, how can I help you?"

"You can do what I cannot. You can leave this land, you can travel to where Ebona lairs with the elùgroth and break the source of her power."

Erlissa felt her heart sink. She could think of nothing for which she was less suited, or that filled her with more fear. But she owed it to Carnona to hear her out.

"And what exactly is the source of her power?"

"I will tell you that in time. For now though, you must understand something. Alithoras is in great peril. I can aid you a little, but only you can defeat Ebona and the elùgroth. There is no one else. I am weak if I leave here. Likewise, the form you now wear is but a shadow of yourself. It will diminish over time. Each day that passes you will fade a little more, until your shadow-self flows back to Lòrenta. But in the meantime, if you are hurt, or killed, your true body will likewise suffer."

Carnona gazed at her, revealing nothing of what she thought.

"Will you accept the quest?"

9. Like Many, but Trust Few

Lanrik gazed at the upcoming rapids. White froth and foam rode high on the water, and a growing roar filled his ears. He yelled in order for the others to hear him above the tumult.

"Onwards!"

He did not need to say anything else. Aranloth glanced back briefly and gave him a curt nod. The lòhren's face was hard to read, but he seemed to approve of the decision. Arliss muttered behind him, and he knew she was less happy with the choice, but she made no attempt to talk him out of it.

The shuffa gathered speed, and the banks of the river sped past in a blur. Lanrik had a vague impression of rocky slopes on both sides and a twisted trail that descended the tree-clad ridges on the left.

He looked back. The Azan were guiding their boats away from the middle of the current and toward the sluggish edge of the river. They had come to a near standstill. After that quick look, he only had eyes for the river ahead.

They plunged down the first rim of the escarpment, and a cold spray of water slapped his face. The sudden drop through the air made his stomach heave. Before he was ready for it, they crashed into the river again with a jarring splash. The shuffa bobbed in the water for a few moments, and then the current took hold of it once more.

They sped along and Aranloth used his paddle to steer the boat away from a massive boulder that rose up like a giant from the riverbed. The shuffa missed it, but it loomed close, and Lanrik, though seeing it for a bare moment, noticed every detail from the green moss that grew all over one face to the sharp and jagged surface that reared above them. Had they hit it, it would have blasted the boat to splinters and flung them into the raging waters.

Aranloth got better control of the boat, and they copied the way he hung his paddle into the water like a rudder to try to slow their progress. Lanrik was not sure if it worked, for they shot forward anyway like an arrow released from a bow. Arliss yelled from behind him, and then laughed. Whatever her first misgivings were, the wild side of her nature reveled in this mad rush of exhilaration and terror.

A series of boulders appeared on the other side of a veil of water-spray, and Aranloth desperately used his paddle to try to guide them through a gap in their middle. The shuffa turned unsteadily, and then shot forward again. There was a jolting bump and a scraping noise as the light timber of the boat ground against the side of one of the rocks. The boat tilted, and they bounced away from it. Aranloth nearly fell overboard because of the sudden shift, but his hand gripped the top lip of the boat, and at the same time he braced his legs against the inside. The boat righted itself, and he sat upright again.

Lanrik glanced quickly over at the side of the boat. The stone had scratched an ugly scar in the timber, but it had not broken it.

The current took them again. White water was all around them. It frothed and churned about a jumble of smaller boulders. The shuffa spun wildly, and for a moment they faced back toward the direction they had come from. Just as quickly the water swirled them about again. They floated in a deep pool now, the water slightly less fast.

Aranloth used his paddle to adjust the direction of the shuffa.

"Hold tight," he called. "The worst is next."

The river gathered up the shuffa again and thrust it forward once more. Lanrik felt ill to the pit of his stomach, and his face dripped river water and cold sweat.

They raced ahead and without warning passed over the lip of a great drop. The shuffa hung in midair, and then its front dropped. A moment later they speared into a pool of swirling water and nearly capsized. There was a scream. Lanrik turned, but Arliss was gone. He swung his head around wildly in all directions, but there was no sign of her anywhere.

"Arliss!" he yelled. There was no answer except the roar of the water. The shuffa shot forward again, and they plummeted over another ledge, but it was less steep than the first.

"We have to stop!" Lanrik yelled.

The lòhren turned. "I'm trying! We're nearly at the end!"

Within a few minutes they had managed to guide the shuffa to the left bank. The rapids were gone and the river flowed calmly. Lanrik looked back and stared in disbelief over the mile or so of raging torrent that they had come through.

They drew the boat up to a sandy shoal. "Did you see her?" Lanrik asked the lòhren.

"No."

"Could she have survived?"

"It's possible. If she managed to swim to the bank quickly. Too long in that icy water would kill her."

Lanrik knew the lòhren was right. He flicked his hood up over his head and forced himself to face the reality of the situation.

"It'll take the Azan hours to bring their shuffas down the portage trail. I'm going back for her, even if it's only to find her body."

"I'll stay here," Aranloth said. "She'll need the warmth of a fire if she's still alive."

Lanrik turned to go, but Aranloth spoke again.

"One more thing."

Lanrik faced Aranloth again. The lòhren's expression was grave.

"Think on this. The Azan have found us wherever we go. And it has not been Ebona's doing. That means someone else must be helping them, but only the three of us knew we were coming this way."

"What are you suggesting?"

"You know what I'm suggesting."

Lanrik shook his head in denial. "Arliss would never betray us. And even if she wanted to, how could she? She has no means of talking to the Azan"

Aranloth spoke softly. "None that we know of. But many things are possible, and I'm suspicious of her."

Lanrik stood his ground. "You're a better judge of character than I am. But in this, you're wrong."

"I hope so. But a wise man told me long ago the motto that he lived by, and his advice still serves me well. *Like many, but trust few.*" The lòhren paused. "Think on it."

Lanrik did not answer. He strode up the steep path that lined the bank of the river. He knew Aranloth was wrong. There must be another explanation. Perhaps he was mistaken about Ebona. It was not the first time that he had misjudged her powers.

He studied the rapids while he thought, searching for a body washed down stream, but saw nothing.

Sweat trickled down his back and sheened his face. It was hard work walking up the winding track, but Aranloth was right about one thing: the water was icy cold, and if Arliss was still in it she would be dead by now. He had to hope that she had made it to the bank quickly enough. Even so, the cold might still kill her anyway.

He went ahead. The path twisted back and forth. Boulders and rocky ledges forced it to veer often, and stands of stunted trees, mostly some kind of cedar, threatened to choke the trail. But there was a way forward.

It would be hard going for the Azan to carry a boat through here, but he did not doubt that they had already started doing so. Musraka would never give up, and it was yet another reason to find Arliss quickly.

He paused in the deep shadow of a stand of cedar. Something had disturbed him, and it took him a moment to realize what it was. And then he knew. Over and above the crisp scent of the trees he smelled smoke. Could the Azan have gotten down this far so quickly? Or was it someone else?

He continued carefully along the path. It was quiet. There was no sound except the hum of insects and the rush and gurgle of water from below. Keeping in the shadows, he peered beyond the trees.

Ahead of him lay a small glade. The river rushed by on the left, and on the right another stand of trees closed it in. Beyond that, the path continued up onto a ridge and twisted out of sight.

Lanrik only had eyes for the clearing. A fire burned in its center. Clothes were stretched out on a small outcrop of rock beside it. They still dripped water. Just as he saw them, he felt something at his back. He leapt into the glade and rolled, and then surged up with the shazrahad sword in his hand.

He looked straight into the eyes of Arliss. A sword was in her hand. Her short blond hair was wet. The clothes on the rock were hers, for she stood naked before him, her only adornment a small silver medallion. Her skin was pale except for the slight scar on her face and others across her arms and stomach. Droplets of water still clung to her, and she shivered. Nevertheless, she laughed loudly.

"Do you always raise a sword against naked girls?"

Lanrik clumsily sheathed the shazrahad blade. "I wasn't expecting someone behind me. I wasn't—"

"Hush. Just admit it. I got the better of you."

Lanrik turned his back to her. "You *definitely* did that. Your Raithlin skills are good – better even than I realized."

"That's no way to offer congratulations, you know. Wasn't it you who told me never to turn your back on someone carrying a drawn weapon?"

"It sounds like good advice. But how about this? Put on your clothes, and then I'll face you."

She gave her usual throaty chuckle. "But my clothes are *wet*. I can't put them on, even if I *am* cold."

Lanrik turned around. She stood unmoving before him, except for her shivering. Quickly, he took off his Raithlin cloak and wrapped it around her. Her bare skin felt like ice, so he picked her up in his arms and strode to the fire. He laid her down close to the flames.

103

She looked up at him, her eyes dark, and her expression unfathomable.

"*That's* how you treat a lady. I knew you had it in you."

Lanrik shook his head. "Stay close to the fire. I'll get some more timber."

He quickly retrieved a few dry branches and added them to the flames. Smoke rose in a column, but it did not matter. Arliss needed the heat, and the Azan already knew where they were.

Arliss rubbed her hands together, but he saw that she shivered less and that color had returned to her skin.

"You were lucky to get out of the river when you did."

"Lucky? Luck had nothing to do with it. I'm a good swimmer." She paused. "And I don't give up. Not ever. Not if I want something badly enough."

"Well, I'm glad you made it. In truth, I didn't think I'd find you."

She looked at him seriously. "It's nice to know that you came looking anyway." She gave him a sly glance. "I see that Aranloth didn't come. Just as well – he might have got a bigger shock than you."

Lanrik looked away and tried not to grin. "Yes, I think you'd have surprised him. But he stayed behind to build a fire."

She turned her palms toward the flames of her own fire. "I'm happy just as things are at this one."

"We can't stay here, Arliss." Lanrik said. "We have a lead on the Azan, and we'd better keep it that way."

He stood up and offered her his hand.

She seemed reluctant, but rose and gathered her clothes.

"They're still damp, and the boots are wet," she said.

"The life of a Raithlin is hard," he answered. "Put the boots on and let's go."

"You want me to walk around in the forest, naked except for a pair of boots and a borrowed cloak?"

Lanrik grinned at her. "You won't get far without the boots. The cloak is optional."

She punched him playfully, and he turned around. She pulled on the boots, and when she was done he faced her again. She was a strange sight, but the fire and cloak had done their job. She seemed warm.

"That's better," he said.

She ran a hand over the cloak. "Is it really?"

He shook his head. "Let's just go."

"Yes, *Sir.*"

They moved back into the trees. It was quicker going downhill, and they made good time back to the bottom of the escarpment.

The shoal near where Lanrik had left the lòhren was close.

"You'd better get changed here," Lanrik said.

He stepped a few paces forward and kept his back to Arliss.

"Don't you want your cloak back?"

"When you're done changing will be soon enough."

Arliss placed it over his shoulder anyway, and she laughed at his refusal to turn around. Nevertheless, she changed quickly into her half-dried clothes while he refastened the cloak about his shoulders with its pin.

She walked past him when she was done with another laugh.

"Come along then," she said, and glanced back at him.

He caught up and they walked into the clearing together. Aranloth leaned on his staff near to the fire he had built. He looked to be deep in thought as they approached.

"Why so glum, Aranloth?" Arliss said.

"Ill fortune has that effect on me," he answered. "But I wonder *why* our luck has turned on us."

Lanrik knew where this conversation would end up, and he wanted no part of it. He refused to believe that Arliss would betray them, even if she had some means of communicating with the Azan.

"Arliss made her own fire," he said. "So we won't need this one."

Aranloth kicked sand into the flames and looked at her steadily.

"You're quite resourceful, aren't you?"

"I've been well trained," she said.

Lanrik walked over to the boat. "Let's go. We have a lead now, and I don't intend to lose it."

The other two said no more. They pushed the shuffa back into the water and guided it toward the middle of the current again. It took hold of the boat, and they glided downstream.

The afternoon wore away with little talk among them. There was no sign of the Azan; it would take them many hours to carry their boats down the portage trail.

At least the quiet gave Lanrik time to think. He had not known that Arliss was attracted to him. That much was now obvious, if nothing else. It just made Aranloth's suspicion of her all the more ludicrous. But what was he going to do about her feelings? That he liked her in turn was just as obvious. She was the complete opposite of Erlissa in many ways, and in so many ways more suitable for him. She was brash and eager, courageous to a fault, and willing to try anything. She was also a planner. She left nothing to chance if she could avoid it, but when circumstances altered she could adapt. She could be kind too, and he admired that quality above all the others.

Erlissa, on the other hand, could not be more different, except for her kindness. And yet there was no doubt of the love that he felt for her. They had each risked their lives for the other, and the bond between them was unbreakable, even if it had been strained the last few months.

He thought of Erlissa as he had last seen her, laid to rest almost like it was a funeral. The thought of never seeing her smile again, or hearing how she spoke his name, was unthinkable. He knew he would listen for her voice all the days of his life.

The dying rays of the sun struck yellow-pink lights off the glistening surface of the Carist Nien, but they did not stop their journey. Their quest pulled them forward, and their enemies drove them on. Night fell. It deepened around them until all they could see was the glint of starlight above. River noises grew loud. Water slapped against the light timber of the boat and gurgled over stones along the riverbank.

Lanrik stretched his legs often and moved around as much as he dared. He did not want to rock the boat, but he was getting sore all over.

"There's a good place coming up where we can rest," Aranloth said.

"We need it," Lanrik agreed. "But maybe we should just keep on going anyway. We can take turns to guide the boat."

"I expect the Azan will stop for the night," Aranloth said. "They're not good with boats, as there isn't much water in their homeland."

"We can't be sure of that," Lanrik said. "If we stop, they may catch up to us, even get ahead in the dark without either of us knowing that they've done so."

"That's true," Aranloth said. "What do you want to do?"

"Let's keep going."

Aranloth nodded. "I'll take the first watch, then. See if you can get some sleep."

There was little free space in the shuffa, but Lanrik and Arliss managed to lie down. They could not get comfortable though, even using their Raithlin cloaks as pillows. But they managed to find positions where they could at least try to sleep.

They did not speak. Nevertheless, Lanrik felt at ease with the silence. He was glad that he had made the choice to bring her. She had good skills as a Raithlin, and she was always humorous company. Both were important attributes under stressful situations. Aranloth's suspicion of her was unfounded, and yet it *did* disturb him that the lòhren was suspicious. Lanrik believed his earlier assessment that Aranloth was a good judge of character, but he was wrong to doubt Arliss. She was many things, but a traitor was not one of them.

He remembered the first time he had met her in Red Cardoroth. He and Aranloth sat at a small table in an inn. It was a rough place: the drink watered down, the food poor and the patrons rowdy. But they were not interested in any of that. They had learned earlier that day of a knife fighter, of a girl who had no equal with a short blade, who frequented the *Crimson Hand* tavern. And they had come to find her.

They were told also that she had no living family, and that she was young and courageous. Lanrik thought she might be suitable as a Raithlin. They watched her for a long time, seeing how she drank with friends and strangers alike, and spared a good-natured word for all. He saw that she was fast witted and easy going. She had rebuffed many of the men who approached her with a self-effacing joke or a deft change of topic. She did it with practiced ease, and Lanrik admired that she managed it without causing offence. Many of the men who had sought her favor at least thought that they had found good companionship, rather than disdain.

Yet one man was not turned aside by kind words. Drunk and insistent, he had clinched her arm and tried to pull her away. She grabbed his hand and twisted the wrist back, using her body weight. The man screamed and reeled away. That she could have broken bones, Lanrik knew. Instead, she let him go, but when he spun to face her again a knife glinted in her hand. She held it with the firm but relaxed grip of an experienced fighter. The blade hovered between them. After a moment, the man spat on the floor and staggered out of the *Crimson Hand's* door and into the wintery night.

Lanrik rose and spoke to her, impressed enough to offer her a job immediately. She had accepted with her usual speed of decision. He had known at the time that he could train her, but she had turned out even better than his expectations.

It occurred to him that it was when they returned to Lòrenta with Arliss that he first noticed the distance between him and Erlissa. Had she seen something of the future? Did she guess that Arliss had an interest in him? Was she jealous? He tried to put these thoughts away, for they would only prevent him from sleeping. He would think about them another day, though he doubted that he would ever figure things out.

The steady thrum of the water as it passed beneath the boat was more lulling than he realized, and he soon slept.

10. The King's Men

The river was quieter, and the night old and dark, by the time Aranloth placed a hand on his shoulder.

Lanrik was a light sleeper, and the instincts of his Raithlin training were honed to a sharp edge. He woke swiftly, immediately assessing his surroundings. There was nothing out of place, and after he realized that, another thought occurred to him. It seemed to him that all his life was spent this way: sleeping outdoors, pursued by enemies and dogged by danger. He did not like it, and just as swiftly as he had woken, a melancholic mood swamped him.

Aranloth did not speak. The lòhren lay down, hastily drawing his white robes about him, and Lanrik had a clear view of the river ahead. He could not see far, but there was enough light to ensure that he could guide the boat and keep it to the center of the current.

Long hours passed, and he had time for serious thinking. His life had not turned out as he had once thought. And yet, he could not complain. For all the problems and hardships that he had endured, there were unexpected pleasures too.

Erlissa came to mind. She was remarkable, and he had a feeling that when she came into her own as a lòhren, she would achieve great things. He was not certain that he would still be with her when that happened. Just at the moment, he was not sure if she would even live, or if she would remain trapped in the ùhrengai of the fountain. There was much that was uncertain, and he hated that. But he could not plan for everything. Arliss was living proof of that point.

He glanced back to where she slept. He could see little more than a gray outline, but he pictured in his mind her ready smile and the way her quick humor lit up her face. There was a dark side to her as well, rarely seen, but he knew it was there. Everyone had secrets, he supposed, but in her case he sensed that they were a burden. But even as they weighed her down, they also shaped who she was and what she stood for.

When it was time, he shook her shoulder and woke her. She sat up and took his place guiding the boat, and he stretched out on the smooth planks of the hull and went swiftly to sleep.

There was little change in their routine for the next several days. There were endless hours of riding the river, interspersed with brief periods on land. Tension simmered between them, and they spoke less than was their wont. Arliss knew that Aranloth suspected her of treachery; she was astute to other people's moods. Aranloth, for his part, remained aloof. And though he said little, his speculative glances at her did not go unnoticed.

Lanrik was caught between them. He trusted them both implicitly, and it was disturbing that they no longer trusted each other.

They saw little of the land as they passed down the river, for the overhanging trees along the riverbank blocked most of their view. Nevertheless, he could tell that the land was changing. It was growing flatter and lower. The river widened and the current, though it continued to sweep them along at a steady rate, had slowed.

112

One morning there *was* a change to their routine. The sun was warm and bright. Far away and high in the sky, vast flocks of ducks circled and wheeled. There were wetlands ahead. The slowing of the river indicated it, and the ducks confirmed it. Lanrik thought that they must be large, for even in the swamps of Galenthern he had never seen so many birds clutter the sky at the same time.

He was watching them when something lower on the horizon caught his attention. First, he noticed a flash of color, and then as he studied the area that it came from he saw a figure run down the right bank of the river. It dodged between shrubs and momentarily disappeared behind a thick belt of trees, and then appeared again right at the bottom of the bank. The figure was a man, and he splashed his feet in the water as he wove his arms high and furiously, trying to get their attention.

Aranloth saw him too. "Do you think it's some kind of trap?"

Lanrik studied the man, and realized that he was a youth.

"I can't see how. It looks like he needs help, and I just don't see how the Azan could have gotten here ahead of us."

"I think you're right. He looks pretty anxious about something."

Aranloth raised a hand and waved back at the youth to signal that he had seen him.

"There's only one way to find out what's going on," the lòhren said.

They angled across the river, and when they drew near to the shore Aranloth stiffened.

"I know him," he said.

"Who is he?"

"He belongs to a family that lives by the river. There are several such groups in small villages along this stretch. Some people would call them poor, and while it's true that they have little money, they live very well off the land. They raise stock, tend well-watered gardens, hunt and of course they fish. They don't trade much, for they produce nearly all they need themselves. There are people like them all over Alithoras."

The youth waited for them as they approached. When they bumped up against the bank he helped them pull the shuffa higher onto the sand, and though he was young his arms were tanned dark by the sun and corded by hard muscles.

"Hello, Caldring," the lòhren said.

The youth seemed shy in the presence of the lòhren, but looked him in the eyes at the greeting.

"Aranloth," he said quietly.

"I can tell something's wrong. What is it?"

Caldring went white, and Lanrik thought he would faint, but the youth clenched his fists and forced himself to speak.

"They killed my family, Aranloth. They killed everyone."

Aranloth went suddenly still. "Who killed them?"

"Men from the south. We've never seen them before, but one of the other families said they were from Esgallien."

Lanrik felt dizzy and he gripped the hilt of the shazrahad sword. It was warm to the touch, and he was momentarily taken back to when the Royal Guards pursued him for the blade and he had to kill their leader. He felt the power of the sword stir, and he no longer had any doubts about what he had considered in Lòrenta.

History was repeating itself. And the sword was at its center.

Caldring wiped a tear away from his face, but then he straightened and determination etched his every feature.

"I saved myself by hiding in a pigsty. It was there, crouched in mud and filth among the swine, that I overheard their leader, and I know why they came. They know you're coming down the river, and they've set a trap for you. That's why they took the village – so that you wouldn't have warning of their ambush."

Aranloth hissed through his teeth. "They will pay for that, and the king of Esgallien after them."

"Revenge would be good, but it won't bring my parents back."

"No, it won't. But evil must be fought wherever it is found. Otherwise, it grows."

Lanrik stepped forward. "Why are you warning us? You realize that you're still in danger? You've taken a risk for us, when you could have hidden until everything was over."

The youth shook his head. "Aranloth has often helped us, and I'm in less danger than you think. I can run faster than the soldiers can, and I know these lands as they never will. Even if they saw me, they would never catch me. Not outside the village, anyway."

Lanrik did not answer. He liked the youth's confidence, even more so because he had backed it up by his actions. Not only had he skillfully evaded the soldiers, but he had also shown character by risking himself to help a friend. He might make a good Raithlin, and without his family, he would need to feel that he belonged somewhere. The Raithlin might offer him exactly what he needed.

Aranloth tapped his staff with a finger while he thought, and then looked up at Caldring.

"Which side of the river are they on?"

"Both," the youth said. "And they're in the middle too."

Aranloth nodded slowly, but Arliss looked puzzled.

"How can they be in the middle as well?" she asked.

Aranloth glanced at Lanrik briefly, and then shifted his cool gaze to Arliss.

"Just ahead the Great North Road crosses the Carist Nien. There's no bridge, but none is needed. The water is only a few feet deep, often shallower in summer. And though there's no man-made structure, there *is* an island. It's only small, but it would provide sufficient cover to conceal a group of soldiers."

He turned to Caldring. "I take it the soldiers are armed with bows?"

"Most of them," the youth answered. "It's a complete ambush. If you continue ahead, even knowing where they are, they'll still get you."

Aranloth grunted. "Maybe. But if we wait until nightfall, they'll find it difficult."

Caldring shook his head. "You know the crossing Aranloth. Even at night it'll be risky."

"We don't have much choice, lad. There are enemies behind us too. The only way for us is forward, and we'll just have to take our chances one more time."

Caldring looked at the lòhren earnestly. "There's another way. I can guide you."

Aranloth raised an eyebrow. "You mean through the swamp?"

"Exactly."

The lòhren considered the offer for a moment, and then shook his head.

116

"No. We can't go that way. It's a maze in there, and it's a dangerous place too. You know that better than I. It'd take far too long, and we'd have to leave the boats behind."

Caldring stood straighter. "It *is* a dangerous place, and most people would get lost trying to cross it. But not me. I've known it all my life. I've hunted there, and fished, and explored it when I had nothing else to do. I know all its tricks, all its trails - the false and the true. I can lead you through, and no one would be able to follow. And I could do it quickly."

Aranloth looked at him long and hard. "I don't think so, lad. Thank you for the offer, but you're too young to get mixed up in this. We'll give you a little food, and then we'll go on our way. You'd best make your way to one of the other villages."

"I don't want to live in another village. It'd be too much like my home. Please don't send me away."

"I'm sorry," Aranloth said. "What we're doing is too dangerous—"

"Wait," Lanrik interrupted. "I have an idea. Walk with me for a moment, Aranloth."

Lanrik strolled a little way along the bank and the lòhren followed reluctantly. Arliss remained with Caldring and put an arm around his shoulder. She spoke to him, but Lanrik could not hear what she said.

"It's not safe for him to join us," Aranloth stated.

Lanrik did not disagree. "I know. But he's not safe by himself either. I don't think he's got any intention of going to another village. He came here to warn us, and after that, I think he might go back to his old home."

"His home is gone," Aranloth said. "The soldiers are there now."

"Exactly."

Aranloth let out a long breath. "You don't think he would try something? He couldn't take them on."

"I think that's precisely what he's thinking about. And he'd get some of them, too. He's got obvious skill. He hid from them after all, and I don't think that was as easy as it sounded. And he made it here to warn us afterward. Everything he did took skill as well as courage. I don't think he's got a definite plan, but I'm sure he's thinking of it."

"Maybe so. But what we have to do next, and after, if we make it through, is still too dangerous. I'll talk to him. I think I can convince him to give one of the other villages a go."

Lanrik looked over at the youth while he spoke.

"He said it himself, Aranloth. He doesn't want that. He's just lost his home. But he could have a new one. He might become a Raithlin in a few years. We need people like him, and just now, I think, he wants us. He needs a sense of purpose rather than a place to go where people will feel sorry for him."

Aranloth gazed at the ground while he thought and tapped his fingers absently against his staff. After a while, he sighed.

"You may be right. Anyway, you're the Raithlindrath, so it's your decision."

The lòhren walked back and Arliss dropped her arm from Caldring's shoulder.

Lanrik did not hesitate, even though his decision was a great responsibility. He knew that whatever choice he made now would shape the youth's future for the rest of his life. He understood that better than Caldring did. None knew better than he that a small change in the present could have a massive effect on the future. It was only by looking back that a person understood the

118

significance of their choices. The youth would learn that for himself in time.

"You know a way through the swamp?"

The youth looked at him earnestly.

"I do."

"And you understand that there's danger behind as well as ahead?"

Caldring shrugged. "Tell me someplace where there isn't danger – sooner or later."

Lanrik felt sorry for him. He had learned a fact of life that many only discovered when they were older. He held out his hand.

"Then you're welcome to join us."

Caldring shook hands with him solemnly, and Lanrik thought he detected a sense of relief. The boy knew well enough that he was going to be in danger, even if he did not grasp its exact form or extent. But he also realized that he was getting away from something worse.

"When we've got to the other side of the swamp," Lanrik said, "I'll give you another choice."

"What's that?"

Lanrik pointed to the Raithlin symbol on his cloak.

"Do you know what this represents?"

The youth peered at it thoughtfully.

"A trotting fox looking back over its shoulder. Sure, I know what it means. Everyone does. You're a Raithlin."

Lanrik nodded. "Yes. And I want you to come with us, even after the swamp. If you're willing, I'll take you on as an apprentice. I'll teach you how to be a Raithlin. If you succeed, there'll be a place for you in our band. Would you like to try that?"

Caldring seemed surprised. "I can't say I've ever thought about being a Raithlin. It just never occurred to

119

me before. But there's nothing for me here. I'm willing to try, if you're willing to teach me."

"Then it's a deal."

The two of them shook hands again. Lanrik could almost see tension lift from the boy's shoulders. He had a future again, even if it was one that he had never thought of before.

"Now, how far away is the trap?" Lanrik asked.

"Only a few miles."

"Right then. Where do we leave the boat? Is it worth going on for a little while, or should we start for the swamp from here?"

The youth did not hesitate. "Leave the shuffa here. The swamp is close, and the sooner you reach it the sooner you'll be free of your enemies."

"That's good enough for me," Lanrik said. "But we won't just leave the boat in the open. Help me take it up onto the bank so that we can hide it."

The two of them lifted the shuffa. Lanrik was surprised anew at just how light it was. The villagers upstream possessed a great deal of skill to craft it. The old man had made light of it at the time, but it was strong enough to withstand the rapids and light enough to lift easily. That was no easy feat. He could even have moved it by himself. That was impressive, and he wondered what use the Raithlin could put such boats to. It was a question for another time, but he would not forget.

They reached the top of the bank and eased the shuffa into a ditch overcrowded with tall ferns. They placed it upside down, in order that water would not gather at its bottom and rot the timber. Someone might retrieve it for use at another time.

A few patches of timber still showed and Caldring gestured toward them.

"Should we hide the last of it with some broken off ferns?" he asked.

Lanrik pursed his lips. He might as well start the training now.

"We could. But we don't know how far our enemies are behind us. If they collude with the king's men ahead, and realize that we haven't gone along the river, they'll come back and search for where we left it. That might take them a day or two, assuming they come here at all."

Caldring considered that. "So the broken off branches would wilt, or even turn brown. Then they'd stand out among the greenery even more than the patches of timber."

Lanrik nodded. "Good thinking. That's exactly right."

He picked up an old tree branch. It left an imprint in the soil from lying there for weeks.

"Do you see the mark that's left?"

Caldring looked at the ground and nodded.

"Remember this. Anything that you move or touch can leave a sign. When I'm done, we're going to put the branch back in exactly the same place."

"What are you going to use it for?"

"Watch and see."

They walked back down the bank. Aranloth and Arliss waited in silence. They did not even look at each other, and the tension between them was tangible.

"Up to the top," Lanrik said.

They followed his direction without speaking.

Lanrik turned to Caldring. "Now stand behind me and watch what I do. I'm trying to remove any sign that we left the river here. Nothing I do now will totally hide our passing, but it'll deceive the casual observer."

121

Using the branch, he smoothed over the marks on the sandy bank, particularly where the boat had been run aground. He worked slowly and methodically, always keeping an eye on the river to make sure the Azan were not in sight.

Eventually, they reached the top again. "That should do it."

He handed the youth the branch and they walked over to the spot where it came from, taking care to leave no tracks on the harder ground. Caldring replaced it carefully.

"Good. That's exactly as it was."

They joined the other two and Lanrik placed a hand on Caldring's shoulder.

"You'd better take the lead," he said.

"Wait," interrupted Aranloth.

The lòhren ran a hand through his hair and looked hard at the youth.

"There are rumors about the swamp. I've never been in there myself. Are they true?"

Caldring shrugged. "You mean the monster?"

"Yes, the monster."

"I've never seen it. My uncle saw it twice though. That was a long time ago. He said it mostly kept to itself, and I guess it's probably dead by now. At least, I don't think anybody has come across it since then."

Aranloth did not look convinced, and Lanrik shook his head. Was nothing they did ever easy?

11. Sacrifice

Erlissa was scared.

She was afraid that she would never wake from her sleep, worried that Lanrik and Aranloth had imperiled themselves on her behalf, and fearful that Ebona was an enemy beyond her power. Yet she felt a calling too.

Somehow, this was her destiny. She felt deep inside her that the quest was inextricably linked to her future as a lòhren. She could see no good end for any of it, and yet she could see no good end if she did nothing, either.

"I'll do it," she told Carnona.

Her body felt strong, and her command of lòhrengai was growing. She would give herself up to the chances of fate, as she always did. In a world where luck ruled everything, fortune favored the bold. Sometimes.

Carnona gazed at her implacably. If the Guardian felt gratitude, she did not show it. Probably, she had no expectations and just accepted things as they came. The two of them were, in their own way, kindred spirits.

The Guardian *did* incline her head in a slight acknowledgement, however.

"You will be my emissary. I am strong in this land, but weak outside of it. Also, Ebona would sense my approach. Yet you might surprise her, and the elùgroth with her. But it will not be easy." Carnona paused, as though assessing the truth of her own statement, and then continued. "Your lòhrengai is no match for them, but it would be fitting for you to carry a token of this land, and its power, with you. We shall see if it offers one."

Erlissa wondered what that meant, but she had no time to ask.

"Come," Carnona commanded.

The Guardian turned and strode away. Erlissa followed, hurrying to keep up, but she was always a few paces behind.

Carnona moved among the trees like a fleeting deer. She found trails where none were visible, leaped gracefully over fallen logs and strode ahead when the ground was level.

The forest was dark and dim, and to Erlissa, the Guardian was often little more than a gliding shadow ahead, but she managed to follow. Where they headed, she did not know, but over a period of hours she sensed a change in the land. They were climbing higher.

The slope grew steeper and the trees thinned. From time to time glimpses of the great forest that spread out beneath them came into view. It was a land of hills and valleys, dry ridges and nighted hollows. Most of all, it was a land of trees. But as they reached a flat plateau, the ever-present forest gave way to a grassy top. Yet the crest was not completely bare.

A lone tree, gnarled and ancient, grew at the summit. It was slightly taller than Erlissa. Its leaves were ragged, swept by spring winds that drove along the hilltops but left the valleys untouched. The bark was dry and fissured. It grew in little more than rock, the ground about it cracked by the ice and blasting sun of a thousand seasons. Yet still, it was a thing of power.

Erlissa studied it, and the Guardian waited in silence. It was, perhaps, a walnut tree. Here and there, hanging from its ragged twigs, were green husks that encased growing nuts. The tree seemed as old as the hills themselves, and though battered by the passing ages, it thrummed with vitality.

"What is it?" Erlissa asked.

"It is a tree," Carnona replied. "No more, and certainly no less. It is one of the oldest in my realm. And this is a land full of old things. Long it has stood here, and many times have I visited it. It is one with the earth, or the earth one with it. It is all the same thing."

"What do you want me to do?"

Carnona glanced at her curiously. "You need not do anything."

"Then why are we here?"

"You are here to see the tree. After that, what will be, will be."

Erlissa did not understand, but she sensed this was a situation where it would do little good to ask questions. The Guardian had already told her everything she was going to, or everything that she could.

Erlissa realized that she must follow her instincts instead. She closed her eyes.

Deep below her, she sensed the ùhrengai of the land. It coursed up through the tree as well. It had looked old, and she felt that it was just as enduring as the rock of which the hill was made.

She walked over to the tree. A passing cloud dimmed the sun as she placed her hand against its trunk and tried to sense more about it. It quivered like a thin sapling at her touch, and she sensed burgeoning life all about her. All at once she was the wind passing over the crest of the hill, the cold fog that settled deep in shady hollows, the

125

play of dappled light over the leaves of countless trees. She sensed the running water of creeks, the dry soil of ridges and the slow grinding of rock against rock deep under the piled weight of the earth.

And then she sensed Ebona.

Far away and faint, she discerned the witch's power. It strived against Carnona's, and it pressed against the land of Enorïen ceaselessly. It was a tainted force, and she felt something unnatural about it, but even as she tried to understand what caused that, the sun broke out from behind the cloud, the wind flurried, and once again she stood at the crest of the hill, before the ancient tree, her palm pressed hard against its trunk.

The tree stirred. She felt sap flow beneath the bark. Its leaves shivered, and something moved beneath her touch.

She did not take her hand away. The trunk slowly swelled. Bark split. The rent exposed dark timber. Sap, thick like old honey and full of the life of the land, ran down from the sides of the wound.

The trunk groaned, and the split ran along its length from where Erlissa's feet shuffled nervously to where her eyes gazed upon it. Her hand was now inside the wound, in the trunk of the tree itself, and she felt something. The timber was smooth and slippery. Instinctively, she grasped it with her hand and pulled. From the living tree she drew forth a staff. The wood, dark with a rippled grain, was warm, and it felt right in her hand. The tree had given it to her. *Enorïen* had given it.

The ancient walnut sagged. Bark flaked off and fell to the ground. The leaves withered and blew away in the breeze, falling like tears. The branches drooped, and the tree stilled. It became a stark pillar against the sky.

Erlissa turned to the Guardian, and the staff throbbed in her hand when she spoke.

"Now I understand. The land chooses a lòhren's staff. It's a gift, and in return we give our service to Alithoras."

Carnona nodded curtly. "It is different for each lòhren, and I understand why Aranloth did not tell you. It would only cause you to seek for what you could never find, only be given."

"Did you know this would happen?"

Carnona shrugged. "I knew it might. I did not know that it would. The land makes its own choice. And I serve, even as you. But I hoped."

Erlissa looked at the staff. It was growing duller to her eye, and unexpectedly the dark wood reminded her of the wych-wood staffs that elùgroths carried. And yet it did not feel like them. It was resonant of life, of the land, and especially of sacrifice. The land had given of itself. The staff represented everything that elùgroths were not, and everything that she must strive to uphold. Deep in her heart she understood, and accepted, that it was now her responsibility to ensure the sacrifice was not wasted.

She turned again to Carnona. "What must I do? What is the source of Ebona's power, and how shall I try to break it?"

Carnona indicated a patch of grass. "Sit," she commanded.

Erlissa settled down and cradled the staff in her lap. The Guardian squatted next to her, but when she spoke she kept her gaze fixed on the view over the tree-clad hills.

"When Ebona left her birthing lands, she forfeited much of her heritage. In its stead, she drew on the power of mankind: men, and women, worshipped her. They sacrificed others in rituals to sate her. She grew to greater

127

power and wider influence. At one and the same time she was a creature of the old world and a part of the new."

The Guardian paused, as though in thought, and Erlissa wondered if she herself had been tempted to follow her sister's path.

"You know this already, but what you don't know is that death rips the veil between this world and the otherworld. The two become joined, and in that moment there is power. Ebona drinks this in just as a thirsty man drinks water. To her, death becomes life."

The sun beat down on the hilltop and sweat beaded Carnona's nut-brown skin. She absently wiped it from her face and continued.

"The men of Esgallien fall ever deeper under her sway. They have begun to sacrifice to her, and her power increases. The king allows it; though in truth, he has little choice. Others control his realm. But they are resisted and a quiet battle rages."

Carnona glanced at her to emphasize the importance of her next words.

"So, in trying to save Enorien, you will also help save your own land."

Erlissa understood, but she did not interrupt.

"Ebona has found a place that helps her," the Guardian said. "The valley of Caladhrist is an old, old place. Men have died there. Many men, over a long period. It is a place where the veil between the worlds is already thin. She uses this. A cave in the valley-side is now her home. Caladhrist is partway between Esgallien and Camarelon, and she would make it the center of a vast realm of power."

Carnona grew silent, seemingly lost in thought.

"How does the elùgroth help her?" Erlissa asked.

"He is a meddler, that one. For a long time he has stirred up trouble in Alithoras." The Guardian turned to Erlissa. "And he hates Aranloth. Hates him with a burning passion. Those two are bitter enemies. One day, one of them shall prevail, but the time of their confrontation is not yet."

The Guardian turned the discussion back to the matter at hand.

"The elùgroth found something for Ebona. Something that she lost long ago, when men first began to worship her. How he found it, I do not know. It was hidden in the old lands, far to the west of the Halathrin. But he gave it to her. It is a cauldron, small, but carved with scenes from the far past. You will know it when you see it. He adds his power to it, and she adds hers, and the blood of their sacrifices mingles in its basin. This is the source of her current strength. Break the cauldron and you will break her assault on this land."

"And how can I break it?"

Carnona gazed at her for a moment. "I wish I knew."

"What do you mean? You're not telling me that you're sending me on this quest without even know what I'm supposed to do?"

Carnona shook her head slowly. "I do not know what you're supposed to do. But I trust to fate, and to the land. And I trust you. You were born for this task, and you can do it. The how, I have not discovered, though I expect you will learn something about your staff. I think it will be the key, but I could be wrong."

Erlissa stared at the Guardian, and Carnona stared back, unabashed and unapologetic. It was infuriating. And yet it made sense, in its own way. Carnona had told her nothing new. She had felt she was destined for this quest, though she did not know why. She also thought the staff was vital. It was more than her passing the threshold into becoming a lòhren. It had a significance beyond that. Nor did she even consider herself a lòhren. Her training had been far too short, her powers not yet properly understood or developed. Yet she had used power of a kind for a long time, although that was not going to be enough for her to contend with Ebona, and possibly, an elùgroth.

On the face of things, she had no chance at all of succeeding in this quest. Yet her feet had been placed upon her current path for a reason. What would be, would be.

She shrugged, and for the first time saw Carnona smile. It was fierce and bright, there one second and gone the next.

"We have a long way to go. This is near the heart of my realm, and we must reach the western borders soon. Time runs swiftly. You will feel strong now, but soon you will begin to weaken. When that happens, do not be afraid. But do not forget either that you must achieve your quest before you fade completely. Or all is lost."

"How long will it take?"

Carnona raised her muscled arm and pointed out over the hills. Erlissa followed the Guardian's movement, and her gaze passed out over the sunlit ridges, over the sleepy hollows of Enorìen, and into the haze that blurred the horizon in the distance.

"You must travel swiftly. Caladhrist is not close, and though you know the way, it will take you five days. Do not linger on the journey, for you have only enough time to reach there. No more."

Erlissa sighed. "Then I had better get started."

Carnona glanced back at her. "There is one other thing."

"What's that?" Erlissa did not like the new note that had crept into the Guardian's voice.

"You know that you are but a shadow of yourself. You will not need food, nor even water. That will speed your travel."

"But?"

"But even as your shadow-self has come here to Enorien, your coming has opened a veil between the worlds, just as does death. I sealed the gap as swiftly as I could, but even so, some creatures broke through. They roam Alithoras now. I cannot say where, but they will sense you. They wish to be part of this world, and they are evil. They will try to kill you."

"Why?"

"Because if they can do so before you fade and return to your true self, the veil will be forever weakened. If you returned, they would be drawn back with you and the rent healed as though it had never existed."

Erlissa felt a fresh tremor of fear run through her body.

"So let's get this straight. I'll be hunted before I reach Ebona, and even if I get there I'll have to find a way to destroy the cauldron that even you don't know."

Carnona did not flinch. "I told you that it would not be easy."

12. Dark Counsels

Musraka let go of the silver mediation. Its chain bit into the skin of his neck, and the disk remained warm against his chest. He did not like using it. He distrusted magic, and he doubted Ebona, who had given it to him, and its matching twin that he in turn had given to Arliss. But regardless of his misgivings, the gifts had proven useful, as had the witch's counsel.

It was Nurhaq who spoke first. "Well, what did she say?"

Musraka did not like him. The man was scrawny, yet whatever he lacked in stature he made up for in courage and cunning. He was usually silent, and always hard to read. That made him dangerous though, and Musraka sometimes wondered if that cunning would ever be turned against him.

"Our quarry continues to travel south. They still head for the Angle, but they have left the river. The lòhren learned of a trap ahead."

"Whose trap?"

"Men from Esgallien."

Nurhaq spat. "The king still wants the sword. And Ebona is not our friend. I think she helps them just as much as us. What does she care who wins the blade in the end, so long as it works against the North."

There was a rumbling of agreement from the other men.

"That is true, and yet she still *does* help us. We must play our own part though. The sword is mine, and I shall have it back."

One of the other men spoke. "We're a long way from home, shazrahad. How can we compete with the king's men? They outnumber us, and they know this land. It seems to me that they'll kill Lanrik and the lòhren before we catch up to them."

Musraka slowed his breathing and lidded his eyes. There it was again – the faint stirring of rebellion. It had grown over the weeks; it was almost in the open now, and he would have to do something, once and for all, to stop it. These men were his to command. Their opinions counted for nothing, and he would remind them of it.

"What do you suggest, Rhamon? Should we return home? Should we just give up?"

Rhamon looked uneasy. He was fat, and his greasy skin paled. He must have realized that he had crossed a line, but he also knew that some of the others supported him. That would buoy his confidence.

"No one likes giving up. But the sword will work the prophesy, whether it is in your hands or possessed by the king of Esgallien. Nothing has gone right for us since that accursed Raithlin stole into our camp and took it from your tent."

Musraka smiled. It was not how he usually reacted to insults, but he could wait. It was a fact that Lanrik had taken the sword from his tent, but for Rhamon to remind him of it *was* an insult. But the moment of truth was coming, and the fat man before him, growing ever more confident, was oblivious to it.

"So, do you think we should return home?"

Rhamon stood up. He had lost weight over the last few months, but his stomach still bulged underneath his thick beard.

"Of course. None of us has been warm for a long time. It's bitterly cold here. And dangerous. We're out of place and sooner or later we'll be discovered – even living in the wild."

Musraka stood up slowly. He made his expression appear as one of thoughtfulness. He stepped closer, bridging the gap between himself and Rhamon. When he was close, he acted.

Swiftly he drew the elug scimitar that he had used since Lanrik had stolen his own sword. It was a mark of his shame, but he had vowed to use it until his own blade rested in its sheath by his side.

Rhamon staggered back. The big man tried to draw his own weapon, but he was too late. The scimitar struck him on the neck. Bright blood spurted, and he fell to his knees.

Musraka swung again. This was *more* humiliation. His former blade was sharp. It cut silken thread floating in the air, but the scimitar was as blunt as a peasant's table knife.

He hacked at Rhamon's neck. Again and again, until the head toppled from the fat body.

He looked at his men over the corpse. They had scrambled back. He lifted his sword, blood dripping from its notched edge.

"We will not turn back. The shazrahad sword is mine, and I have a plan to retrieve it. I know where Lanrik and the lòhren go. I believe they will elude the men from Esgallien, and I will be waiting for them when they reach the Angle. Or when they return from it. And know this: if anyone else here has an opinion, they will find the same fate as Rhamon. I command here, and you will obey. Or die."

The men around him were silent. They could think of no answer, or dared not answer, which was all the same to him. He looked at each of them in turn, staring into their eyes until they looked away. Only Nurhaq held his gaze. It was infuriating, and worse, for he could not read the little man's expression. He saw no anger, no shock, no fear, no disrespect. He saw nothing, and that was what worried him.

Musraka kicked Rhamon's body and rolled it over onto its stomach. He used the man's clothes to clean the blood from his blade before he re-sheathed it. When he looked back, Nurhaq still watched him.

The shazrahad made a decision. The little man would soon die. He would be next to serve as an example to the men of who was in charge, and that orders must be obeyed without question. He glanced once more into the little man's eyes and reminded himself to be careful. Nurhaq would not easily be caught by surprise, and for all his scrawny frame, he would not die easily either.

"Let's go," Musraka commanded.

They walked over to their boats and pushed out into the river. Without another word they were on their way. There was still some chance of catching the Raithlin before he made it much further. But if he got past the trap set for him by the men from Esgallien, it would be time to come up with another plan.

He might have to split his forces, for Lanrik had a knack of avoiding pursuit. It might be better to wait for him in a place that he was likely to go. That meant either the Angle or Lòrenta. Or both.

One thing was certain: sooner or later he would kill him and reclaim the sword of his forefathers from the man's dead hand.

Brinhain was displeased. It irked him that he must lie on cold and wet stones. His bones ached, his muscles were sore, and he was bored. He hated the river; he hated the wild, and most of all he hated the deprivations entailed in being away from his tenement home in the heart of Esgallien city.

The Carist Nien gurgled past on either side of the little island where he lay. He hated that noise too. And he hated having to watch ahead, being unable to move freely while he and his men waited for a boat to come downriver.

More than anything, he hated dealing with Ebona. If he could, he would have delegated the task to one of the other Royal Guards. But he could not. He *dared* not, for no matter how much he feared her, he knew also that he must please her. If the king was dangerous, the witch was triply so. He had no desire to end up as one of her sacrifices.

Even as he thought of her, the fear of her presence grew on him. He suddenly sensed her all about him, and he shivered.

The current of the river swirled and eddied. Bubbles rose to the surface. The water foamed and churned, first one way, and then the other.

Suddenly, a figure of water staggered up from the river, swathed by white froth and riverweed. Brinhain felt the fear of Ebona strike like a dagger into his heart. She swayed, nearly toppled, and then surged fully upright, high above him. Water dripped onto his face. The men nearby cowered and backed away. He would have done the same, but her eyes held him. Her watery mouth spoke and words gurgled out.

"Lanrik has learned of us," she hissed. Water ran from the frothy ends of her hair as she spoke.

"You did not kill all the villagers. One escaped and gave warning of your ambush."

Brinhain trembled. "No, My Lady. We killed them all. I promise."

"Fool! I don't need your promises. I need you to carry out instructions. If I tell you that a boy escaped, a boy escaped!"

Ebona towered over him, and he felt cold beneath her shadow.

"Do you understand me?"

"Yes, My Lady. I understand."

"Very well. You may yet have a chance to redeem yourself, for I know where they are headed."

Ebona looked down at him. He felt the chill stare of her gaze and knew that death was near. And yet he also knew that if he served her well there would be no limit to the rewards he could claim.

"Where shall I take the men, My Lady?"

"Your quarry is headed for the swamp."

Brinhain thought about it. "We have no way to find them in there. The swamp is vast, and even if there is a way through it, we don't know it. We'll have to pick up their trail wherever they leave it."

Ebona stepped up from the river and onto the island. Water filled the deep tread marks that she left in the pebbled bank.

"But if I asked you to, you would go into the swamp, wouldn't you?"

"Yes, My Lady." Brinhain answered without hesitation.

137

Ebona studied him carefully. "So quick to agree. Too quick, I think. It makes me wonder if you really thought about it, or if you just chose to tell me what you believe I want to hear."

"My Lady—"

Ebona interrupted. "It does not matter. You will obey me, or you will die. It's that simple." Her voice became softer. "But I'm not a harsh taskmaster. Serving me has its benefits, as you have discovered, captain, and as you will continue to discover. And as it happens, you need not enter the swamp."

She leaned over him and spoke quietly. "They have no horses, so they will travel slowly. And yet they are in need of haste. I know where they will travel through the swamp, and I will tell you where to wait for them to exit."

She straightened. "Take the men and head southward. Skirt the swamp and when you have reached the right spot I'll give you a sign."

She looked at him coolly. "Do not disappoint me, captain."

Brinhain shook his head. "I'll be waiting for them. When they come out of the swamp, I'll kill them and take the sword."

Ebona smiled at him, but it only served to make him feel icy cold all over.

Without warning the water that formed her figure dissolved. It fell to the ground with a heavy slap, and then slid back into the river.

Ebona was gone, but the fear of her remained, and Brinhain doubted he would ever be free of it.

He turned to his second in command. "Gather the men. We ride, and we ride now. We have somewhere else to be, and someone yet to kill."

13. The Watcher in the Dark

It was a dark trail, a slippery trail, a trail over corrugated logs set into stinking mud. The swamp was alive all around them, full of unseen life and unidentifiable noises. Nameless creatures lurked and called from the shroud of dimness that blanketed the world. It was not like the wetlands of Galenthern, for it was filled with strange trees and a sense of watchfulness unfamiliar to Lanrik.

He was glad to have a guide, and no matter that Caldring was a youth, he led them with confidence and assurance. He trudged ahead, surefooted on the damp logs, his gaze seeming to take in everything from the path at his feet, to the scum-topped pools of water and the deep pits of mud, to the tops of the lichen-crusted trees.

Lanrik followed close behind, and after him came Aranloth. Arliss, as always, guarded the rear. They moved swiftly and silently, and had already journeyed far into the swamp.

Caldring came to a halt, and Lanrik saw why.

"We might as well rest for a while," the youth said.

Lanrik pointed ahead to where the log-trail ceased abruptly.

"Is this as far as it goes? Or are there other log tracks that we can use further along?"

Caldring slapped at a mosquito on his arm.

"This is it. My village only ever built one trail. Over the years it was extended, but they never got further than this. From now on, it gets dangerous. The heart of the swamp is ahead. And though I know the way, the path is still hard to find. We'll have to go slowly. Be sure to step only where I do."

They sat down on the logs to rest. Damp as they were, it was the driest bit of land they would find for some time, and Lanrik knew it.

"It's time to ask some hard questions," Aranloth said.

Caldring looked at the lòhren curiously, but Lanrik knew exactly what he was talking about. He explained the situation to the youth.

"They keep on finding us. Both Musraka's men, and now the king's men."

Aranloth's sharp gaze bored into Arliss. "The question is how?"

Lanrik looked away into the swamp. "I don't know, Aranloth. But I trust Arliss. Otherwise, I would never have brought her."

"Trust is sometimes misplaced."

Arliss stood up. "I'm right here, you know. Don't talk about me as though I'm not."

"Do you have an explanation for how they keep finding us?"

Arliss stared at the lòhren. "No, I don't. But if you want me to leave, I'll go right now."

"You're not going anywhere," Lanrik said. "I need you."

He turned back to Aranloth. "It *must* be Ebona."

Aranloth shrugged, but did not answer.

"I know you don't think so," Lanrik said. "But she's found us before with her witchery."

"I underestimated her then. Now, I don't. I use lòhrengai to mask our presence as we cross the land. But she has not even tried to find us. If she had, I would have felt the touch of her mind as she sought us out."

Aranloth laid down his oaken staff beside him.

"I'm not suggesting that Ebona isn't involved. I don't doubt for a moment that she's helping all our enemies. And it means nothing to her which one of them finds and tries to kill us. She just wants to see us dead."

"We're at an impasse, then," Lanrik said. "I trust your skills, and if you say that she hasn't found us herself, then I believe you. But I trust Arliss too. With my life. There must be an explanation that we haven't yet considered."

Aranloth shrugged once more. "Perhaps. Time will tell. But for now, we'd better rest. There's a long way to go, and it'll all be on foot, so the sooner we do that, the sooner we can be on our way again."

There was no further conversation, and Lanrik was grateful for it. Aranloth had made up his mind, but he was not one to foist his views on others. The lòhren had said what he had said, and now it was just a matter of waiting to see who was right. Lanrik knew one thing for certain though: something was wrong. Their enemies *were* finding them too easily, but he knew in his heart that Arliss was no traitor. But if she was, his support of her might make her think twice. He knew little of her background, but her life had been hard and she valued loyalty. She would find it difficult to betray someone who supported her.

There was little rest to be had in the uneasy swamp. Flies and mosquitoes were a constant source of irritation, as was the sense of something that watched them. It was a common feeling in the wild, and Lanrik was used to it, but here, in this swamp, he felt it more strongly than he ever had before.

Caldring led them on again when they were done resting. They went slowly, following carefully in his footsteps, and being sure to test their footing before they put their weight down.

For two days he led them. The swamp grew darker as they proceeded, until it was in a perpetual state of evening. The smells grew worse, as did the flies and mosquitoes. They never saw them, but Caldring told them that there were vast bodies of water nearby. Certainly, the deafening calls of ducks and other water birds, and the whoosh and drum of their unseen wing-beats as massive flocks flew high above, proved it.

Caldring assured them that they were nearing the edge, but the feeling of being watched only grew stronger. The trail they now followed looked like many people had been here over the years, and that they had beaten a wide path. Their pace increased, but only slightly.

The trail dipped down briefly and became mud slicked. They were about to begin the upward climb when Lanrik stopped suddenly. He was a tracker, used to keeping an eye out for any sign, but even Caldring saw the marks ahead of them.

The youth produced a knife and Lanrik drew his sword. He heard the hiss of a blade from its sheath a moment later as Arliss drew her own weapon, but he knew her attention would now be solely on their backtrail. She trusted him to warn of danger from the front, and he trusted her to guard against any surprises from the rear.

He bent over and peered at the tracks for a long time. They were like none that he had ever seen before.

The deep imprints looked like those of a barefooted man, only they were massive. Sometimes, tracks in mud swelled, the weight of the person or beast pushing the soft material outward, but he did not think that was the case here, for the stride length was also large. He did a quick calculation and decided that whoever left those tracks was at least eight feet tall, probably more.

Caldring shuffled nervously beside him.

"The monster is alive," he whispered.

Lanrik moved ahead, taking the lead. He did not sheath his sword, nor did he speak to the others. The tracks, and his drawn blade, were the only warning they needed.

Frogs croaked and insects chirped. Strange noises rose from stagnant pools and water-lizards plopped into unseen ponds as the travelers went forward.

The others stayed close behind Lanrik. They made no noise, and he heard nothing out of place, but something disturbed him. He came to a stop.

For a long time he stood there, perfectly still, unsure of what worried him. Then he realized what it was: something smelled out of place. It was a sharp and acrid odor, almost a reek, and it was growing stronger.

The smell came from somewhere ahead. The dim trail led that way, overshadowed by a thick tree-canopy that formed a tunnel. There was nowhere else to go except forward or back. Backward was not an option, and so he took a tentative step ahead.

One pace was all he made. The swamp now seemed silent all around them and on the dim trail a form appeared. It was a great creature that strode on two legs. Fur, or matted hair, tumbled all over its long limbs and the reek grew stronger.

A massive head atop the creature's thick neck turned from side to side, studying its surroundings as it walked. Long arms swung at each stride. There was power enough in those arms to tear a man apart, and Lanrik took a firm grip on his sword.

The creature spotted them. It came to a standstill, the massive body suddenly motionless, the great eyes in its head peering at them. There was no fear there, but there was intelligence and wariness.

Lanrik's heart raced and he heard a gasp from behind him. The creature watched them for a long while, undecided as to what to do, then as swiftly as it appeared it turned and walked back up the trail. Its strides were long and fast, and in a matter of seconds it was gone. All that was left was its scent on the air, until that too faded away into the usual stench of the swamp.

It was Aranloth who broke the silence. His voice held a strange note to it.

"A carethgar," he whispered. "Few of them are left in the world."

"Are they dangerous?" Lanrik asked.

"If roused, I guess," Aranloth answered. "But mostly they avoid people, as this one just did."

"That fits," Caldring said. "It hasn't been seen for many years, but it's remained here all this time, avoiding us."

"And just as well," Arliss said. "I've heard rumors of such a beast, though I took them for nothing more than legend."

Aranloth did not look at her. He kept his gaze focused ahead.

"We lòhrens have a saying." His voice grew soft and he began to chant.

Many things lie
Beneath the sky
Beyond the ken
Of mortal men

He said no more, and no one answered him.

They waited several minutes, being sure to give the creature a chance to get well ahead of them, before they started again.

Lanrik led them forward but the carethgar was gone: disappeared into the deeps of the swamp that was its home.

As they progressed, the ground firmed and the smell of the swamp receded. The trees changed, and it became more like a normal wood.

"We're nearly there," Caldring said.

Lanrik stayed in the lead. The path was clear, but it was his job to sense any danger that might lie ahead.

Somewhere to the left the Carist Nien ran its course, but it was miles away. Once they left this swamp there would be nothing between them and the Angle but league after league of hard walking.

The trees thinned and the light of late afternoon shot through the increasing gaps in the foliage. Lanrik moved ever more carefully, wary of coming out into the open as always.

They reached a point where the path widened and had obviously been trod frequently over the years. Lanrik did not like it.

"It's time to leave the path," he said to Caldring. "It's too predictable for my liking."

Caldring nodded in understanding and took the lead again. He went into the trees, still being careful of where he stepped, although the ground was now for the most

145

part dry. He took them several hundred paces into the woods, and then led them parallel to the path.

It was slower going. Shadows grew thick about them, but they reached the end of the woods and a verge of green grass that stretched away in the gray light of evening.

Lanrik studied what lay ahead. It was something to their left that caught his eye though. He did not know what it was at first, but then he saw it again. It was the swish of a tail. Soon, he made out the shape of a horse concealed on the edge of the trees where the path they had earlier followed emerged from the trees.

Lanrik let out a slow breath. Now that he was looking that way he saw more and more horses. There were at least a dozen, tethered in the eaves of the wood. And where there were horses, there were men. In this case, they would be the Royal Guards of Esgallien.

He stepped back into the deeper shadows and spoke to the others.

"We've been found again," he said. "The Royal Guards must know that we're no longer on the river, and they're waiting for us where the path comes out of the swamp."

Aranloth grunted but did not speak.

Arliss frowned. "It's nothing to do with me."

"They don't seem to know exactly where we are," Lanrik added. "That's something at least."

"It'll be night soon," Arliss said. "We can slip away during the dark and leave them here, waiting for us, while we get on our way."

Lanrik hesitated. "That's true. But I have another idea."

14. Paths Already Trodden

Erlissa walked briskly. The turf of the old Halathrin road felt firm beneath her feet. The sky was clear, and the sun bright, yet a shadow chilled her heart and dimmed her eyes to the beauty of the land.

She worried about Lanrik. She tried not to, for she needed to concentrate on her own problems, but her thoughts and fears for him all seemed to have a will of their own and would not be constrained.

Her own dilemma was never far from her mind though. She must somehow defeat Ebona, a creature of far greater power than herself; and she had no idea where to start.

It was thinking of Lanrik that gave her direction. What would *he* do? He had ventured alone into an army of enemies, rescued her from imprisonment, and then escaped. He had achieved the near impossible, and though luck had played a role, most of it came down to his courage and planning. He was a man who left as little to chance as possible, and she must learn from his example. She would have to think her way through the task that she had accepted and use her strengths rather than dwell on her weaknesses.

What, then, were her strengths? For a moment she thought she had none, but then her pride asserted itself. She was not without resources. Her lòhrengai was no match for Ebona, but that did not mean it was not useful. If she could not challenge the witch directly, she must find a way to use her power differently. Stealth and deception were possibilities that she must explore. Also, the witch would not be looking for her. Her focus would be on her struggle with Carnona, and that was an advantage, for though she was winning the contest, it would constantly sap her powers.

Erlissa mused over those thoughts for a while. Something else was in her favor: would the witch understand that she was only a shadow of herself, that her real body lay in a death-like sleep beneath Lòrenta's fountain? That might prove useful before the end. The witch would undoubtedly sense something strange, but she might not understand its cause, and that could make her hesitate.

Stealth, secrecy, and surprise must be her focus, and she would think on that as she walked and try to formulate a plan.

A breeze blew across the downlands that surrounded her. She felt the air on her skin, saw the green grass growing over the long slopes and the tree-lined creek banks at their bottom, and yet she felt that something was wrong. She was here, but it seemed to her that she was not really part of it. She focused on why that would be, and the more she did so the more she sensed the connection to her own body, her true body, in Lòrenta.

Erlissa understood what was disturbing her. It was a problem without solution, for she did not really belong here. Only the summoning of Carnona and the power of ùhrengai had made her presence possible, but her body called her back, and the pull was growing stronger. It would continue until finally she could no longer resist it.

She hastened forward along the still road. Her stride was quick and unwearying, one of the benefits of not being real, she supposed, though if her body did not tire as much as was normal, her mind and strength of will certainly did.

She remembered the road well, having been here with Lanrik and Aranloth, and it felt strange to her to walk its length without them. She was alone and unaided, but then she felt the warmth of the walnut staff in her hand and realized that she was not quite alone. Something of the forest had come with her, even if she did not understand it.

She attuned her mind to it, but her powers were not as sharp as Aranloth's. She could sense little about the staff, but as she did so, her seeking mind detected something else, and she cast her perception further afield. Somewhere to her left, still a fair distance away, but coming toward her, she sensed a creature of power. It felt somehow akin to her. She did not know what it was but soon realized that it was not human. She felt waves of hate emanating from it. And fear as well.

It took her a moment to decide what it was. One of the creatures that Ebona had warned her of had sensed her, even as she had sensed it, and it was coming for her. For a moment she despaired; it would reach her before she made it to Caladhrist, but she hardened her resolve. The witch was beyond her powers, but this creature, if it attacked her, she had a chance of defeating. At least, if it was alone. She had a vague feeling that it was not.

Erlissa gripped her staff more firmly and walked on. Her long strides ate up the miles. To her left the woods of Alonin loomed, a green and inviting fringe of trees. She had been there before, when the hounds of Ebona had pursued her. Strange how things seemed so familiar

149

to her, how the past kept on bubbling up into the present.

Another thought occurred to her. Aranloth had led the hounds into the woods, and the Halathrin ruins, for a reason. Not only had the walls offered partial protection, but creatures of ùhrengai did not like civilization. The pattern of roads and buildings confused and weakened them. Perhaps not by much, but maybe by enough to make a difference.

She did not have to walk much further before she found the place where they had turned off. She stood there a long while, thinking if she was doing the right thing, wondering if it was right to go down paths already trodden, but she sensed the creature closing on her and made up her mind. One place was as good as another to die.

She gripped her staff tightly. Going into the woods would not slow her down much, and she would still reach Caladhrist in time - if she survived.

Her feet turned, almost of their own will, down the trail that she had taken before. Soon the road led toward a mass of jumbled stones. The old ruins loomed before her, just as she remembered, only now, in the light of late afternoon, they looked like what they were: the grave of a long-dead city and not the mess of boulders and jagged stone that she had taken them for the first time.

The pattern of streets was easily recognizable, as were parks where trees grew thickly. In the center was the overthrown tower where they had taken shelter, and she hurried toward it. Her boots moved silently over cracked flagstones and like a ghostly shadow she glided down the darkening street.

Scattered all about the foundations of the tower was a ring of fallen and shattered stones. The wall on the far side was partially intact, and formed a half moon.

She looked around, remembering the fight that had taken place here. She thought of Lanrik's bravery, of how close they had all come to dying, of their excitement at living, and wondered if she would survive to feel like that again.

She turned her back to the wall, faced the open, and waited. Soon she heard a strange and guttural grunt. She did not know what to expect and wished that she had asked Carnona something more about the nature of the otherworldly beasts when she had the chance.

Shadows flitted through the ruins. She kept her back to the stone wall and held her staff high.

A dark form lumbered into the half-light before her. It was man shaped, but a huge thing of grotesque muscle, bare skin and tufts of coarse hair. Its hands worked the air, gripping and tearing at nothing, even as its sharp-nailed toes scratched and clawed against the cracked flagstones. Its mouth, a gaping pit filled with saw-like teeth, slavered while the lips retracted spasmodically.

The beast grunted. The sound was loud and heavy, reverberating off the broken stones of the ruined city. The deep-throated call filled the night, and a howl of high-pitched screeches came in answer from a half dozen lesser creatures that scampered out of the shadows and cavorted around it.

The little creatures were only as tall as a young child, but their skin was leprous green and their teeth pointed and sharp. They clapped and jumped and scrambled over the flagstones, working in concert to spur the massive beast on.

The great creature ignored them and studied her. Its dome-like head, free of the tufts of black hair, was tilted in thought, and the eyes that bored into her seemed like pits leading to another world.

And then it lumbered forward.

Erlissa waited. She remained still, though her heart raced in her chest. When the creature was twenty paces away she summoned lòhrengai. It burned like fire in her body, and it sprouted like a shooting fountain from the raised tip of her staff.

Flame, blacker than the night but glistening with the light of a million stars, smashed into the creature and sent it sprawling back. It stumbled, a great arm of grotesque and bulging muscle rose up over its head in protection, and it went to its knees. The imps about it scattered and fled; those that could. Some writhed on the ground, burning and smoking things, turning to ash.

Erlissa shifted the spray of fire. It flashed to one side, and then the other, scorching more of the creatures. They howled and screamed.

The great beast grunted again, the bark of a wild animal, though it glared at her with hatred. It stood, and lumbered forward.

Once more Erlissa struck it with lòhren-fire. It staggered back, but this time merely bowed its head and plodded toward her again.

Erlissa was growing tired quickly. The flame sputtered, and then went out. She leapt up to the wall on the left side of the broken-down tower. She was certain that if she allowed the creature to close with her, she was dead.

It came closer. The tufts of hair on its body smoldered. Of the imps, there was no further sign. She straightened, prepared to try another blast of lòhrengai, and then felt something grab at her ankle.

Pain shot through her flesh as taloned hands, sharp as knives, dug deep into her flesh and ripped. She lost her balance, tottered and fell forward within the ruins of the tower.

Something smashed onto her back, and then sharp pain slashed across her shoulders. Small but strong hands gripped her throat, trying to tear and shred.

Erlissa flung herself about on the ground, attempting to loosen the thing that gripped her, but its clutch was unshakable. She felt blood drip down her neck and did not know what would kill her first - the severing of an artery in her neck or the hammer of blows from the great beast.

She let go of the staff and reached back with both hands. The imp on her back tried to avoid her seeking touch, but she clasped it anyway. It felt strong and sinewy. It resisted her touch, but she did not try to pull it off.

Lòhren-fire erupted from her fingers. The imp screamed and let go. It leaped off her back, but burst into flame even as it hit the ground. It disappeared in a stench of smoke and burning flesh.

Erlissa grabbed desperately for her staff, rolled to the side, and surged up. A great foot smashed into the flagstones. Stone-dust and debris flew out from the newly-pitted ground. The creature swung a mighty arm, but she ducked it and stepped back.

The two combatants looked at each other. Their situations were now reversed. The creature had the stone wall at its back, and she was in the open. But she did not think any imps were left. She had but one opponent, and yet she wondered how she could beat it.

The creature stepped toward her. Erlissa thought she was going to die, but if so, she would go down fighting. She stepped forward too.

A flicker of doubt crossed the beast's face. It hesitated a moment, and then stepped forward again.

Erlissa drove the end of the staff deep into its abdomen. It grunted, a massive hand swept down at the wood, but before it touched it Erlissa summoned all her power, all her desperate need to survive, and lòhren-fire erupted from the tip. A torrent of black flame slammed into the creature and it staggered back. Erlissa followed, the staff pressed relentlessly against it.

The black fire intensified. The creature slammed into the remains of the wall. The great stones shook, several of them toppling from the jagged rim above.

The beast reached down again and swatted the staff. Erlissa thought it would be knocked from her grip, but she hung onto it and pressed it back where it had been in less than a heartbeat. The creature screamed: a horrendous thunder of sound that filled the ruins. Flesh burned. Smoke spiraled into the air. Blood seeped from the wound and boiled and sizzled over blackening skin. The staff sank deeper and a writhing mass of flame erupted inside the otherworldly creature.

Erlissa leapt back. The beast tore at its own flesh, trying to pull out the lòhren-fire that burned inside it. Flame burst from its mouth, and it smashed into the wall behind it as it thrashed uncontrollably. More stones toppled. Suddenly, the wall collapsed and cascaded over the creature. It screamed silently, a long stream of flame shooting from its mouth as it went under.

Impossibly, the beast started to rise, flinging stones upward. And then its flesh withered away. Its arms went first, and then its head exploded with a sizzle and flash of red light.

The creature was dead. Erlissa, sick to her stomach, began to gag, but she was too tired to escape the stench.

She fell to the ground and lay there, exhausted.

A long while she remained still, neither awake nor asleep, caught on the verge of death. But her hand still gripped the staff. She thought of Enorìen, of its wild hills and forests, of mists in the valleys and the cool breeze against her face on the hilltops. She thought of the ancient tree, whose gift she touched even now, and she knew she could not give up. She owed it to Enorìen, to all Alithoras, to struggle on.

She rose to her knees, and using the staff as a prop, she stood. Her strength was returning, and with it an awareness of her surroundings. The creature was destroyed. That much she knew, but something new nagged at her until she concentrated her thoughts. There were more creatures. They were far away, but coming for her nonetheless. They approached from the west, from somewhere beyond Caladhrist.

She used the staff as a walking stick and began to make her way back to the Halathrin road.

It was still quite some way to the valley, but she must reach it before those that hunted her. She did not think that she could survive another encounter like this.

15. Thunder in the Night

There was no chance that the Royal Guards could hear him, but Lanrik whispered anyway. Being careful was a habit.

"We need horses," he said. "It's a long way from here to the Angle, and a long way back again once we have Erlissa's cure."

Aranloth scratched his head. "That's true, but there are no more villages between here and where we're going. Unless you mean to—"

"Yes. That's exactly what I mean to do."

Caldring looked from one to the other. "*What* do you mean to do?" he asked Lanrik.

Arliss was the one who answered. "He means that we need horses and that he knows where to get them." She made a sideways gesture with her thumb, indicating the direction of the Royal Guards.

Caldring looked bewildered. "You can't be serious, Lanrik? There'll be soldiers everywhere. You couldn't get anywhere near those horses."

Lanrik winked at him. "You'd be surprised at what a Raithlin can do." He pulled up his hood and drew his cloak tightly about his body. "Besides, the situation isn't quite what you think. There are plenty of soldiers, but they're guarding the track coming out of the swamp. The horses are behind them, out of sight and far enough

156

away that they wouldn't be heard by anyone coming up the path. At least, that's what I'd have arranged if I were in charge of the ambush. So there'll be few, maybe even no guards, with the horses."

"It's still dangerous," Aranloth said.

Lanrik knew that it was, and he knew that he could not hide that from the lòhren.

"True enough. But it's what we need, so it's worth the risk. I can't stand the thought of Erlissa staying trapped in the ùhrengai of the fountain any longer than she has to. And the faster we can reach the Angle and return, the less danger for us, too."

"He's right," Arliss said. "Being stranded on foot with enemies hunting us is asking for trouble. Between the two of us, we can pull it off. The guards probably won't even realize what we've done until dawn."

Lanrik shook his head. "No, Arliss. I'm doing this by myself. The rest of you can go out onto the grasslands and get some distance between yourselves and the guards. I'll bring the horses to you. That way, if I get caught, you'll still be able to escape."

"I'm going with you," Arliss said firmly.

He smiled. She had nearly stamped her foot in frustration at the thought of being left out.

"No, Arliss. This is a job for one person. More than that isn't needed and would probably just increase the chances of getting caught."

"But—"

"No buts," Lanrik said.

Surprisingly, she agreed. A little too readily for his liking.

He turned to Aranloth. "Keep an eye on her. I don't want her coming to help me when it's too late to send her back."

157

This time she *did* stamp her foot.

Aranloth nodded in agreement. The lòhren did not try to convince him the task was too dangerous. He knew as much as Lanrik that they needed the horses. But he did give him a meaningful look, a glance that said to be careful.

Lanrik gave his blade to the Lòhren. "The shazrahad sword mustn't get into their hands," he said.

"You can't go into their camp without a weapon," Arliss said.

"I'll have my wits."

Arliss raised an eyebrow. "That's not enough."

"I'll have my knives, too."

"That's not enough either."

She unstrapped her own sword and handed it to him. He hesitated, unsure what to do.

"Take it," she said. "You need it more than I do."

He took the blade and strapped it on. It felt different from the shazrahad sword, but he was glad to have it.

"Thank you," he said simply.

"Thank me when you return," she said.

Lanrik was not sure how to answer that, but she seemed to need no reply, for she looked away as though considering something more important.

Lanrik spoke briefly with the lòhren, telling him his plan, and Aranloth soon led Arliss and Caldring away onto the grass. They headed for the riverbank a mile further along. That way Lanrik would know where to find them later on.

Night had fallen. It was dark and quiet – the perfect environment in which to put his Raithlin skills to use. The only thing that he did not like was that it was still early in the evening. If any soldiers had remained near the horses they would still be alert. It would have been better to make the attempt after midnight, but waiting that long was a luxury he did not have.

He walked out onto the grass himself, but he did not go far. All he wanted was to put himself in a position so that he could approach the camp from the opposite side to the track that emerged from the swamp. That was the direction the soldiers would be least wary of.

It was a time to walk silently. It was also a time to walk quickly. Speed was important here, for later on he would have to move with extreme care, and that would be slow.

He continued on until he was a few hundred paces from where he thought the camp was situated.

There had not been any guards visible during daylight, but that did not mean that they had not been there, or that their commander had not established a night watch. He waited, listening carefully and scanning the dark smudge of the horizon that was the line of trees.

There was nothing to be seen or heard. He looked behind him, assessing the light on the horizon and how likely the chances that he would be silhouetted. The sky was clear, but the stars had not yet begun to shine brightly. There was little light, but even so, he would soon have to get down on the ground and crawl. But not just yet.

He edged closer. After some twenty paces he stopped and listened. He heard only the distant sounds of the swamp, and so he repeated the process. He did this several more times.

There was still nothing. But he knew he must be getting close now, and so he waited a little longer, sure that he had judged the distance correctly. He must be very near the camp.

At length, he did hear something. What noise it was, he could not tell. But it was enough to make him wait longer. He sat down and closed his eyes, sharpening his sense of hearing.

The minutes passed. Frustration was growing on him, but he let it go. Now was not the time for a mistake. He needed to hurry, but the greater need was to avoid getting caught. He slowed his breathing and waited some more.

A soft thump drifted to his ears. And then he heard it again, even louder. He smiled in the dark, for he recognized that sound. It was the stamping of a hoof. Probably the mosquitoes were annoying the horses.

He did not stand up. Instead, he used the Raithlin crawl to move forward across the ground. His palms rested on the earth, and he kept his elbows close to his trunk for support and to reduce the chances of being seen. The weight of his body was mostly on his hands, forearms and one leg at a time. He brought the free leg forward, low to the ground, and moved forward in that manner. It was slow going, but not as slow as it could have been. He was skilled in the technique.

He made no noise as he went and that enabled him to listen carefully for any sign of the enemy. He relied on that, on hearing or seeing them first, as his main defense against someone spotting him. Should somebody be nearby, he would hunker low and stay perfectly still. His cloak and the darkness should conceal him.

He kept going. Mostly, he kept his head down so that the white of his face would not make him visible, but from time to time he paused and looked intently ahead.

For what seemed a long time he saw nothing. But eventually the woods became distinct. He could pick out taller trees and smaller shrubs. The sound of the swamp, of frogs and insects and the splash of water came to him ever more loudly, but nothing further of the horses. Yet he knew he was now close and slowed down.

He heard it again soon. The stamp of a hoof and from somewhere nearby another horse shook its head. He was very close.

He moved forward once more, only going a few feet this time, and waited again. He saw movement now, dim, but recognizable as horses. More and more became visible as he watched. There were ten that he could count, but he saw no people, and that worried him. There would likely be at least one guard, no matter how many men the commander had sent forward to wait in ambush.

He waited some more, but there was no other sound or movement than the horses. Time was running out, but that was no reason to be careless. He moved to the left, being sure not to get any closer to the camp. He was looking for a different angle to see things.

The smell of the swamp drifted to him, but he still saw nothing alarming. The saddles were piled carelessly in a heap on the fringe of the trees, but he ignored them. If there were no guards *near* the horses, it was possible that they were *above* them.

The tree line was dim, but the trunks and branches, by virtue of being higher than the grassland, were placed in a better light by the afterglow of the setting sun. He studied each tree, each branch, looking for a sign that someone was there.

He saw nothing.

It was time to move in closer. He did not like that he had not found a guard. It would have been better if he had done so, and then disabled him. But there was none in sight, and perhaps they were using every man for the ambush.

He inched forward. If there were no guards, he would have an opportunity to saddle the horses. That would make their trip to the Angle easier.

The saddles lay in a jumbled pile and he veered in their direction. The night seemed particularly quiet, but he was quieter still. He moved to the closest saddle and looked around again. The horses remained still and ignored him. There was no movement anywhere.

He rose to his knees, took hold of a saddle, and prepared to stand. Even as his legs started to push upward he caught the faintest glimmer of light from behind the ones he left behind. He knew what that gleam was: an unsheathed blade.

It streaked toward him and he threw himself back. He felt something strike the edge of the leather saddle, a hard blow that would have killed him, but he was still in a bad position. On his back, and two men leaping over the saddles to kill him.

He rolled to the side and stood, drawing his own blade. They were on him before he was ready. One struck a driving thrust for his stomach, intended to impale him, but the blow was not quite quick enough and Lanrik managed to stumble back. Yet while he was doing that the other man came at him from the side with a wild slash that nicked his shoulder. He grunted in sudden pain.

The soldiers came at him fast, pressing home their attack, but he was better balanced now. Steel met steel in a sudden clash that broke the silence. The horses stomped and snorted.

Lanrik knew that he would have to work quickly. These were his own countrymen, but they had murdered innocent villagers, and he must be prepared to kill them in turn. At least, he thought grimly, that if he could not do so they would still not obtain the shazrahad sword.

A savage blow hissed near his head, the last stroke of that soldier. Lanrik stepped in and smashed the hilt of his sword against the man's head. He slumped to the ground.

Lanrik spun and faced the other man, but he turned, leaped over the saddles, and ran into the fringe of trees.

A moment later a horn sounded, loud and deep in the night. Lanrik cursed. The man was no longer a danger, but he had warned the others. In short order the camp would swarm with soldiers.

He stood a moment in desperate hesitation, but a moment only. Should he flee while he could, or should he take the horses?

His feet moved of their own volition and he was running. Not away from the camp, but to the horses. The ambush must be a good way into the swamp. He was positive the men would have taken the necessary steps to make sure that their intended quarry would not hear horses and receive warning.

He had a few precious moments. The horses were nervous, but still docile, and he ran a loose rope though the bridles of the four closest to him. Quickly, he bunched their reins together and severed the ropes that tethered them to pegs in the ground. Then he paused to listen.

He heard yells, curses and the slamming of boots on the hard-packed earth of the road. The King's Guard would be on him soon, but he had one more task to do.

It would do little good to escape and then let the enemy pursue him. Better that they were on foot, at least for a little while.

He quickly cut the remaining ropes of all the other horses that he could see, and then with a wild shout and slaps to their rumps, he set them into a gallop.

Hooves thundered in the night and there was movement everywhere, whether of man or beast he could no longer tell.

He jumped onto the back of the first horse that he had taken and urged it into a trot. The others followed. The rope was awkward, and so was riding bareback, but it was better than walking. He moved out onto the grass, heard the hiss of some wildly-shot arrows, and looked back as night swallowed the camp. It was nothing now but a memory of a fast fight and lucky escape.

After a little while he slowed and came to a stop. He could still hear a commotion in the distance, but there was no immediate pursuit.

He turned to the left and made for the river. When he found it, he followed it down stream.

Not long after that he came to the others. Arliss saw him first, her face showing relief, and then anger.

"You should have taken me. You nearly got caught, didn't you?"

"Nearly, but I didn't – that's all that matters."

He jumped down from the horse and untied the rope that led the others.

"Quickly," he said. "No one followed me, but they'll be searching. And if they don't find my trail tonight, they'll probably find it tomorrow."

"Assuming any of them can track," Caldring said.

"Probably they can't," he answered, "but it's better not to make assumptions."

In moments they had each mounted their horses and began to walk downriver. It would be another long night.

Arliss shifted her position. "Saddles would have been nice."

Lanrik shrugged. "I suppose so, but I was a little pushed for time." He smiled her. "Anyway, thanks for the blade."

He undid the sword belt and handed her the weapon.

"Did you need it?"

"Yes," he said softly. "I wish that I hadn't."

Arliss studied him carefully. She obviously sensed his distaste at being forced to fight his own countrymen, for she let the matter drop.

Aranloth gave him back the shazrahad blade, which he buckled on promptly. It felt good to have it back.

"How far is it from here to the Angle," he asked the lòhren.

Aranloth thought about it a moment. "A little under two hundred leagues," he said. "A fair way but much closer now that we have horses."

Lanrik sighed. "I guess that we'll be pursued though. How the guard found us in the first place, I don't know. But it won't take much for them to find the trail of four horses. They probably don't even need a tracker for that."

"How long do you think we have?"

"I don't know, Aranloth. But they'll be busy rounding up their own mounts for a while. That should take them the rest of the night. And there'll be trails everywhere from the other horses I set loose. That'll slow them down, too. I'd guess that we might get a day's lead on them. It would've been longer if I wasn't caught."

Aranloth shrugged. "These things happen. The most important thing is that we've got a lead, and we've got horses. Anyway, once we get to the Angle we should be able to shake them."

165

"Why's that?"

The lòhren looked grim "They'll not go where we must. And if they do, they'll not survive."

Lanrik had seen that look before. Aranloth was worried, and he was not about to reveal exactly why. Whatever dangers lay in the tombs of the Letharn must be of concern to him.

Lanrik pondered it. Not for nothing had Erlissa made him swear never to go inside them. He straightened and rode taller. Warning or not, it was what Erlissa needed, and he was determined to do it, whatever it cost him. Still, the memory of her words made him nervous. He promised himself that he would be careful, but the nagging doubt was growing and he could not shake it off. As much as he planned for things, he could not plan for everything. If he could, then the two guards back at the camp would not have taken him by surprise.

They rode through the night. It grew chilly, and he shivered. A mist of light rain started to fall from the darkening sky, and he wondered what was worse: being pursued by enemies for what now seemed all his life, or running headlong toward his own death, a death that had been foretold, and that was, perhaps, unalterable.

16. The Valley of Death

The voices of dead men rode the wind.

Erlissa looked down from a high ridge over the valley of Caladhrist. A dark pit gaped below her; a night-haunted hollow that seethed and roiled with anguish and the haunted cries of the lost.

Late evening cast groping shadows down the ragged valley sides: or the darkness of the pit boiled up to flood Alithoras. Erlissa could not tell which.

She stepped back from the intensity of it. How had she not sensed this the first time that she had come here? The place had left her uneasy, but this, this was something else altogether. She considered it further. Perhaps her growing skills with lòhrengai had opened her senses. That was likely. But even so, it was not enough to explain what was happening.

There was more going on. She felt as though a great wave of evil surged up from the pit and battered against her sanity. The presence of the witch was part of it. So too the cries of the sacrificed and the spilled blood that fed her power.

Ebona was gathering forces here that could destroy Alithoras. And Erlissa knew that she must stop it. Yet she was a pitifully weak challenger, dwarfed by the puissance of her opponent. She was as nothing to Ebona: the witch could swat her like a fly.

167

Erlissa felt a sudden urge to turn and run. She took a step back. Fear rose up within her like a rearing snake and she swayed and shook. Her breath heaved in her chest and she took another pace back.

The lip of the valley began to obscure the pit. A few more steps and it would be out of sight altogether. She would be free!

There was evil down there, and it ran unchecked. Her heart thudded and she felt sick. But she clenched her jaw and stood still. She could turn and leave Caladhrist behind, but as far and as long as she fled, she would never be free of the voices. They would damn her always. The ceaseless crying of a thousand accusers would haunt her dreams. And her own voice would be the loudest.

One step at a time, she forced herself forward. The sense of evil buffeted her, but that at least gave her cause for hope. She was insignificant among the mighty powers that pulsed and throbbed in this valley, but she knew where Ebona was, could track her down and try to stop her, but the witch would be unaware of her presence. At least Erlissa hoped so.

She sensed the struggle that was in play between the witch and Carnona, and she knew that the witch was winning. Not lightly had the Guardian summoned her. Her presence was needed, though exactly what she would do when she found her enemy, she still had not decided.

Slowly and carefully she moved down the rocky slope. It became a little easier as she progressed. Perhaps her decision and determination to fight had cleared her mind. Or maybe her senses, at first overwhelmed by the forces that assaulted her, were growing more accustomed to them.

She walked forward warily, aware that any misstep could be her last. She had shunned the road, it being too visible, and come down through one of the many treacherous ravines.

This area had been mined, though how long ago she could not tell. The ground was broken and tumbled, a mess of loose sand and knife-sharp rocks that formed fragile slopes and ridges. Either could give away at any time, but she stepped lightly until she was deeper in the valley and the slope had become less steep.

Fires burned, red and flickering, far below. The faint and acrid tang of smoke hung in the air. It seemed unlikely to her that any miners were still there, but if not them, she wondered who had lit the fires and for what purpose. But it did not matter. Ebona was not down there. She was somewhere on the slope to the right, probably in one of the many tunnels.

Erlissa turned her steps in that direction. It was hard going, but she kept at it with slow determination. The fires intrigued her, but she had no way, and no intention, of finding out what was going on.

She had only one concern in the valley, and her time was swiftly running out. She concentrated on Ebona and forced herself onward. She was in a race of sorts. The pull of her body in Lòrenta was growing by the hour, and the beasts that hunted her were closing in. Worst of all, the task that she must accomplish remained unfinished, and it would stay that way if either of her other problems caught up with her too soon.

The night grew old around her, and she could now almost understand the plaintive calls that filled the valley. There was meaning in them, over and above pain and anguish that tore directly at her heart.

Erlissa shuddered and walked on. She looked up and saw that the stars were gone. The darkness of the valley was thick like smoke. Shadow had become substance. She wondered anew at Ebona's growing power and what she could do to try to break it.

As she walked along the valley side she knew also that the creatures of the otherworld that hunted her had entered it too. They were coming for her, though she sensed confusion among them. The place was filled with roiling power, and their senses were not as acute as her own. She might be able to avoid them for a while. Long enough, perhaps, to reach Ebona.

She closed her eyes and cast her seeker senses through the valley, reaching out with tendrils of lòhrengai until she knew exactly where the witch was.

She opened her eyes and studied a point of the slope several hundred paces away and half that high again. There, nearly hidden from view, was a deep cleft between two ragged ridges. It was a place where night had gathered, deeper and darker than the rest of the valley, and it was overhung by an outcrop of solid rock. She turned her steps toward it, but moved even more slowly, one pace at a time.

The walnut staff grew warm in her hand, and she used it as a prop, for she suddenly succumbed to dizziness. For a moment she sensed the peace of the fountain at Lòrenta, felt the pull of her true body and the formlessness of her shadow-self here in the valley. She felt like she was falling, and only her grip on the staff kept her upright. She opened her eyes, swayed, and then set her jaw tight. She would not yield. Not yet. Her task remained unfinished.

The slope grew steep, and the rocks larger and sharper edged. It would be a bad place to fall.

Ahead was the opening that she sought. A cave, or tunnel, led into the side of the valley. Ebona was somewhere down there. But there was something else too, unseen but sensed. The creatures of the otherworld that hunted her had beaten her to it.

She paused, trembling in fear and frustration, until she realized something. She frowned as she considered it. The creatures were similar to those that sought to kill her, but not the same. She focused her senses on them. They were dogs, two of them, huge beasts of black as were the ones that Ebona had previously had. Even as she sensed them, she knew that they sensed her. One growled deep in its throat, and the other remained silent.

They were not hunting her but guarding the opening. Nor, did she think, would they abandon their task to pursue her. She sighed and backed away. There would be no entrance for her that way. But she was not put off. Casting her senses deep into the ground she found the network of caves and mine shafts that lay beneath the rock. There were other ways.

She backed away some more, veered a good way to the side, and then climbed higher up the slope until the guarded cleft was below her.

A series of fissures broke the slope. Some were little more than cracks while others, large and gaping, were death traps for the unwary. She chose her path carefully and weaved among them, one more drifting shadow in the valley.

At length, by the use of her seeker senses, she located one that suited her purposes. It was just wide enough for her to fit through, but it ran away up the slope until it was out of sight. She stood above it, alone and unaided, looking down into its blackness while she summoned the strength of will that she needed to enter.

The black chasm, like a malevolent eye, stared back at her. Thus she stood for a long time, until she mastered herself. Waiting would not serve her. Nor would fleeing. The only thing left was to go forward.

She eased herself down the crack and entered the earth. She wondered if it would be her grave and if she was destined to be entombed in two places.

It was dark. The surface of the chasm was rough stone, but it was not a straight drop. It ran at a steep angle into the bedrock of the valley and she slid down it, scraping some of the skin off her arms and legs, until the tunnel flattened out and ran at a smooth but still slightly downward slope.

It was warmer beneath the earth, but darker than midnight, and she sent a gentle flow of lòhrengai through the staff. Its tip began to glow and she walked forward.

The tunnel opened into a wider cave. It was empty of all life and perfectly still. Nothing moved except for her, and yet from somewhere came the unearthly voices of the lost. What had happened in Esgallien since she had left? What control did Ebona have over the realm, and what blood was flowing to sustain her growing power?

The voices assailed her anew. The hair on the back of her neck stood on end and she trembled. She could not distinguish actual words, but she thought that she heard pleas for help over and above the wails of anguish. She moved on, unsure if that were true or just her imagination.

The tunnel ahead of her widened further, and she paused. Reluctantly, she let the light of her staff fade away. But the passageway remained lit. A dim light, flickering and red, came from the far end.

She moved ahead again slowly. Once more she felt dizzy and swayed precariously until she braced herself against the rough wall to her left. A long time she stood there, pulled back toward Lòrenta, but at the same time drawn onward. Ebona was close. She sensed it. And her fate, whatever it was to be, was that way too.

The dizziness passed, and she moved on. The red light flickered, and there was a sense of warmth. She came to a ragged opening at the end of the passageway. The tunnel opened up after that into a cavern of some sort. Shadows writhed in the wavering light. She stared hard, but she could not see with any certainty who, or what, was in there. This much she knew: Ebona was close. And the source of her power, too.

For a while Erlissa trembled in the dark. She was scared to enter, for she still did not know how, or even if, the staff would help her destroy Ebona's cauldron. Yet she must go forward and find out.

She would catch Ebona by surprise. That was an advantage, and she clung to that for hope. She must find a way to use it. She also knew that she was running out of time. The beasts that hunted her were in the valley, maybe even already in the tunnel with her.

Erlissa held the staff up and stepped forward with seeming confidence into the cavern.

The chamber was now visible by the red glow that seethed and roiled from its center. A cauldron, knee high and made of gold, sat there. It was a squat thing, shiny in places, but its rim was blackened, and dark stains groped their way down from its lip. The bottom, set on three short legs, was grimed by charcoal and the smoke of many fires. Embers lay beneath it, half black and half red. Curls of smoke caressed the curved sides and drifted upward.

There was evil in the chamber, a sense of great wrong, but the voices of the dead were unexpectedly stilled.

Ahead of Erlissa stood an elùgroth. Elù-Randùr. She shuddered when she saw him and remembered what it was like to be his captive. The last time they had met, he had taunted her by calling her a sister. Hatred for him rose like hot fire through her brain, but he seemed unaware of her, his head bowed, his blue-veined hands resting loosely against his wych-wood staff.

Erlissa studied the rest of the chamber. She saw no sign of Ebona but still felt her presence. The smoke cleared a little when a sudden breeze disturbed the thick air. It was then that she saw her enemy.

The witch stood on the far side of the cauldron. She was tall, pale haired, more regal than any queen and cloaked with power. Cold eyes, hard as diamonds, looked straight across the chamber.

"Hello, my sweetling. I've been waiting for you."

17. The Wailing Dark

The days were a blur to Lanrik.

One after another he and the others rode. And the riding was hard. They were delayed too, for they had to find good pasture for the horses and allow time for their rest and grazing. More than once Lanrik wished he had taken saddles from the Royal Guard, and some of their grain, too.

It would be futile to complain though. It was a difficult situation, but the only way through it was by endurance. Luck, as always, was two-edged as well. On the positive side of things, the guards had not yet caught up with them.

Lanrik did not doubt the persistence of the guards though. King Murhain would have charged them with retrieving the sword, killing him and anyone else who was with him. It was a task that they would have little choice but to fulfill.

Esgallien's king was not an easy person to work for, and things could only have gotten worse since Lanrik had last been in the city. If the guards returned unsuccessful, they risked punishment. And maybe a hard one at that. For that reason he knew they would be out there somewhere, following. The trail left by the horses was obvious enough, even if it would take soldiers longer than a Raithlin to find it. All it took in the end was a farmer's son used to finding and rounding up cattle, or someone with a little experience of hunting.

The weather grew warmer as the days passed. Summer was well under way. The long grass bent at the touch of hot breezes, and the river, a silver band on their left, provided fresh water and cool camps along tree-lined banks.

As they traveled, the river widened and slowed. Lanrik marveled at the amount of water that ran down its course, eventually to reach the Angle, and beyond that to make its way down to the sea.

He thought of the massive falls at the Angle. They were a spectacular sight. That much he knew, but to think that there were tombs buried deep under river and rock was a strange and disturbing thought. He shivered even in the warm summer sun.

They rode in silence this morning. He was in the lead, looking for tracks or signs of people, but saw nothing. Nor had he seen anything for days and did not expect to until the guards caught up with them. He just hoped they reached the Angle before then.

As they traveled he showed Caldring what it was to be a Raithlin. The excitement of raiding the camp was a one off. It was something they trained for, but most of what they did was less dramatic. Their job, above all else, was to watch and learn without being seen.

Lanrik explained from time to time why he chose one route over another, why he kept to low ground and how he avoided being silhouetted. He taught the youth how to track, and what signs indicated the presence of people. He showed him how to read the land like pages in a book, to listen for the alarm calls of birds, to watch for startled animals that could reveal the presence of someone in hiding or moving through cover. Most of all, he taught him how to avoid an ambush. With everything he said, he imparted a love of the land, for only with that

176

would a Raithlin be attuned to all the signs that they must observe and understand.

Caldring learned quickly and absorbed the many lessons with growing confidence. Lanrik was pleased, but they both knew this was only a beginning. The skills were easy to learn at the start. Progress was swift, but after that, knowledge and skill would be hard won. It was the same with any craft. Yet here there was an urgency, for they were at risk. At any time the guards could find them, or other enemies, and there was the yet unknown dangers of the tombs.

Lanrik would have taught him to fight as well. Sword and knife skills were vital, as well as the last resort of bare-hand fighting, but there was not enough time.

Aranloth remained quiet and watchful during this time. His mind was on other things, whether trying to determine how their enemies so often located them or ensuring the seeking mind of Ebona did not find them, Lanrik was unsure.

Arliss was also quiet. She had withdrawn into herself. She spoke seldom, smiled little and looked as though the weight of the world was on her shoulders. In a way, it was, for danger was behind as well as ahead of them. And yet it was not her way, and that was what worried him. The lightheartedness had gone from her, and her sense of humor.

One afternoon Aranloth approached him as they rode.

"We're nearing the Angle," he said.

"How close?" Lanrik asked.

"We'll not reach it tonight, but probably tomorrow."

Lanrik decided to ask a question about a problem that he had been trying to solve for a while.

"Last time we were there, we came through from the Angle itself. But now, on the southern side of the river, how are we going to reach the tombs?"

Aranloth smiled. "I told you once that I know this land well. I've trod all its paths countless times, even those beset by danger and deep darkness. I discovered its secrets long ago – the lesser, the greater, the concealed and those hidden in plain sight. There is a way. It's in the open, but like all else in this land, the easier something is to find, the greater the peril. Long ago the Letharn built a tunnel at great cost and labor. It runs beneath the river. Where it ends, the tombs begin."

This did not quite make sense to Lanrik.

"I understand the idea of hiding things in plain sight, but everybody must have known where the tombs were. Didn't the Letharn worry that people would find a way in and steal the treasures?"

The lòhren shook his head. "They weren't worried. Many went in seeking the wealth that lies there. None returned. The people soon learned that the tombs were guarded."

"Guarded by what?" Arliss asked.

"By something powerful. I'll say no more until we reach them."

The lòhren was true to his word and made no further mention of it as they traveled, nor did he add to his comments when they camped that night.

The next morning Lanrik could tell for himself that they were close to the Angle. They were walking the horses to rest them for a while, and in the relative quiet he suddenly heard the great falls. They were little more than a distant thrum, but the noise was unmistakable.

He looked at Caldring but saw that the youth was troubled.

178

"What is it?" Lanrik asked.

"I'm not sure. I could be imagining things because of all that you've been teaching me, but I thought I saw movement behind us."

"What do you think it was?"

Caldring did not answer straight away. When he did, his response was hesitant.

"It might have been a horseman. Whatever it was, it was far away, and just as I looked it went under cover. Maybe it was a deer."

Lanrik studied him and could tell that he was not convinced by his own explanation.

"Was that all that you saw?"

"I saw a bird as well. It took flight from the same thicket just moments later."

Lanrik looked, as casually as he could manage, over their backtrail. There were several woods behind them, but he saw nothing out of place. He turned to Arliss.

"Did you see anything?"

She shrugged. "If I had, don't you think I'd have said something?"

Lanrik ignored her tone. She had a right to be upset at the question, but something still nagged at him. Caldring might be inexperienced, but he was not foolish. He had seen something, and while it could have been a deer, Lanrik did not think so.

They continued to ride their horses at a slow walk and Lanrik thought about the situation. He glanced back at Aranloth.

"I think it's wise to assume the guards have caught up with us at last."

"What do you think we should do about it?"

179

"We can keep on going like this, but they'll soon realize that we've caught onto them. When that happens, they'll give chase."

"What do you suggest, then?"

"Let's take the timing of any chase out of their hands. We're close to the Angle as we are, and we have a lead. We can make use of that and race the last mile or two. If we catch them by surprise, we'll reach our destination with some time to spare." Lanrik paused. "But I want to know this first. Is the entrance to the tombs defendable? And is it hidden in such a way that we may be able to disappear from the guards?"

Aranloth thought about it. "The entrance isn't hidden, but it's defendable. If we reach there first, it would be better to just go straight inside, though. The guards might pursue us, but not for long."

Lanrik made up his mind. It was time to race, and if they were pursued, so be it. It troubled him though that the entrance was not hidden. If there really were so many treasures inside, why had the Letharn not concealed it?

"What about the horses when we get there?" Lanrik asked.

"We'll have to leave them behind. The tombs are no place for them. And we won't be coming back this way either. We'll leave by another way."

Lanrik did not like the idea of leaving the horses behind. He had gone to a great deal of trouble to get them.

"Is everyone ready?" he asked

The others nodded.

"Then let's ride!" he yelled. He kicked his mount into a run, and the others followed.

The deep thrum of the falls was overtaken by the thundering of hooves over turf, but not for long. They swiftly approached the falls, and Lanrik could see clouds of water spray in the distance.

He looked back. As he feared, the guards were there. They peeled away from the thicket, one by one, and gave chase.

"They're after us!" he cried. But it was less a warning than an acknowledgement to Caldring of his observation.

The grass beneath them and the tree-lined river on their left blurred. The wind blew from the north and swept water spray toward them.

Within a mile the roar of the falls was loud and the land began to change. Ahead of them was a stone building, ancient and deserted, yet obviously something of grandeur.

They approached it. The structure was made of great granite blocks, each as long and as high as a man, and Lanrik wondered how the ancients had shifted even one of these, let alone the scores that went into the making of the building.

The gray sides were scummed by centuries of water spray, moss and lichen, and yet the building still engendered a sense of awe. It had many strange windows, triangular slits in the stone.

The building itself was shaped as a triangle, and massive entrances, triangular also, stood open at each of its three sides. If there were any doors originally, they were long gone.

Beyond the building was the edge of the escarpment. Lanrik leaped down from his horse and glanced over the precipice. Far below was the Angle, and to either side two bands of silver water. The one on the left a continuation of the Carist Nien, and the one on the right the newly formed Erenian River. He remembered being between the two once before, and then, even as now, guards pursued him.

Regretfully, he took off the bridle and smacked his horse on the rump. It ran, but not far. The others did the same with their horses.

The guards were gaining on them in the distance. They did not let up their ride, but Aranloth gave them a dismissive glance.

The travelers followed the lòhren into the building through one of the triangular entrances. The noise of the fountain grew subdued. It was a quiet place inside: dark, and yet some areas were well lit by light that streamed in from the many openings. The inside was bare of all ornament except for strange carvings on the walls and a four-sided stone monument on the far side.

The carvings were odd, perhaps because the grooves that formed them had once contained some kind of paint or colored clay that had long since disintegrated. Long processions of varied people wound around the walls. Lanrik recognized the aloof style of craftsmanship from the massive carvings in the ravine on the other side of the river. This was much smaller, more refined, and yet eerily similar in the mood of authority and awe that it inspired.

Men, women and children were shown wailing in the procession. Stern warriors surrounded them, heavy swords and halberds in their hands. Long-robed priests, or sorcerers, led them, staffs in one hand and ceremonial daggers in the other.

At the very head of the winding line was a wagon, drawn by two white oxen. It seemed like a funeral procession.

Aranloth paid the carvings no heed. He walked straight to the stone monument on the far side of the room. It was squat and ugly. Tall as a man it stood, though wider than it was high. Each of its four faces was blank, unlike the monument that Lanrik had seen marking the opening of the tombs on the other side of the river.

He soon noticed however that the four sides were not quite blank. There was no writing, yet each face showed a small carving near the top. One a crescent moon, its opposite a radiant sun. The remaining two faces bore the image of a woman. A set of scales held in one hand and a saw-toothed dagger in the other. Her hair was long, and serpent heads sprouted from its ends.

Beyond the stone was a waist-high slab of red granite, pit-marked by age and covered by mold. On its far side was the dark mouth of a tunnel. Stairs led down at a steep angle into the rock, and above the opening was a lintel, inscribed with marks in a series of lines, dots and half circles. Lanrik knew it for the writing of the Letharn, and guessed its meaning.

"What does it say?" Arliss asked.

"There's little time," the lòhren answered, "and yet you should know before you enter."

He did not look at it. But when he continued, his voice was assured, though reverent.

Attend! We who mastered the world are become dust. We possessed the wealth of nations. Gold adorned our hands; priceless jewels our brows; bright were our swords. The world shuddered when we marched! Now, our glory lies unheeded in the dark of the tomb. Servants mutter secret words as they walk the hidden ways. Death and despair take all others!

Arliss snorted. "The ancients didn't have much of a sense of humor," she said.

183

Lanrik frowned. "Don't make light of it, Arliss. I don't think the Letharn made threats lightly. They protected their riches, and that protection still exists."

Arliss shrugged, but did not reply.

"This is the last chance to turn around," the lòhren said. He looked at each of them in turn.

No one moved.

"Then follow me!"

He faced the front again and carefully descended the stairs.

The roar of the waterfall dulled further. The stairs were wide, but the ancient stone was crumbling at the edges. They went deep into the earth before the path suddenly leveled out. It swiftly grew dark, and Aranloth's staff began to glow.

The group kept close together. Aranloth remained in the lead, and Lanrik was happy to walk behind him. His Raithlin skills were of little use here.

They followed the tunnel. It was both wide and straight. Brass brackets were fixed into the stone wall; brackets that once must have held wooden torches for light. Lanrik could picture a long line of people coming through here, and he guessed that the royalty of the Letharn, when laid to rest in the tombs, followed this same path in a funerary procession of pomp and ceremony.

There was room for many to walk abreast and countless mourners to trail behind. He supposed that the carvings in the building above showed exactly that. And yet how did they get the ox-drawn wagon down the stairs? He thought about it as they walked and finally came to the conclusion that the ancients built a temporary ramp for the purpose.

After a while, Aranloth stopped and listened.

"What is it?" Lanrik asked.

"I'm listening for the guards, but I can't hear them. They're probably deciding whether or not to come after us."

"They'll come," Lanrik said.

Aranloth sighed. "I hope not."

He led them on again. Lanrik realized that somewhere above ran an entire river. The weight of the water and the stone above him made him nervous. He wondered if it was safe and feared that it would collapse. Yet that must be unlikely. The tunnel had been here for thousands of years, predating even the exodus of the Halathrin into Alithoras. At one point, he traced a hand along the stone wall, but it, just like the floor, was dry. He put the river out of his mind.

They continued forward until they came to a vast recess. It was triangular, a shape that the Letharn seemed to favor. Stone benches ran along the sides. Here, if not in the building above, were once decorations.

What looked like cushions had rotted to dust on the stone. Around them, the walls were carved with yet more scenes from the funerary procession. The wagon, the white oxen, and the men in long robes featured prominently. The priests now seemed to mutter under their breath as they walked.

Aranloth paid none of it any heed. He walked forward toward an opening on the opposite side of the recess. Lanrik wondered how many times the lòhren had been here. He could read the Letharn's language, he knew at least some of their secrets, and he could find his way through their tunnel system. How had he come by this knowledge?

The lòhren stopped. A portal stood before them. Two naked women were carved into the stone on each

185

side. They were life-size and lifelike. Lanrik repressed a shudder, for the looks on their faces were terrible and cold. They each held high the saw-toothed daggers that he had seen in the building above; a clear threat. The strange writing of the Letharn was inscribed at their feet; the deep grooves filled by black stones. It was short, whatever its meaning.

"What does it say?" Arliss asked.

The lòhren ignored the carvings of the women, but he looked closely at the writing.

"It says, in the tongue of the Letharn, who are no more, *Harak kur likkil, harak ben luluck*. They are words that now no man speaks, and few dared even in the days when the harsh hand of the Letharn ruled these lands. But their speech is dead, was long dead before the Halathrin came. But once those words meant something, and they inspired fright even among the ancients, that race who often knew strife but seldom fear. When they were uttered, the strongest warrior would cringe, kings would bow their head and queens would wail."

"So, what do the words mean?"

"I am death. I will devour you."

No one spoke and Aranloth turned and listened again. Far away there was a dim sound of movement. Thrice the lòhren struck the butt of his staff against the stone floor, and thrice the echoes ran along the length of the corridor. Then he spoke, and by some art of lòhrengai, though he did not shout, his words were loud.

"Turn back, fools! You will die if you follow. I cannot protect you from that which stalks the paths ahead."

There was no answer save for the heavy silence of the dark tunnel.

The lòhren waited several moments, and then gestured to the others.

186

"Come," he said. "Whatever you do, do not touch anything, for the poison on the treasures will kill you. Step only where I step, and listen carefully to what I say. If you follow my instructions, you will live through what comes, though you will gain memories to haunt you all the days of your life."

He stepped through the portal. Straightaway the tunnel changed. It widened again and was no longer so smooth. Here, the caves seemed natural and the Letharn had spared little time carving and shaping them. Even their seeming endless supply of laborers could not do everything.

Lanrik thought of asking what protected the tombs. He wondered why Aranloth had not volunteered the information, but the lòhren was always secretive. Yet in this case there was probably a good reason. It was better to confront some dangers only when necessary, rather than struggle with the fear of them beforehand and thus be weakened.

Alcoves, dark and musty, were set into the walls at irregular intervals. Above each was more lettering in the strange script of the Letharn. The tip of Aranloth's staff did not cast much light in the recesses, but Lanrik saw the remnants of bones and rotted furniture. There were tables, many broken but some intact, and chairs, cups and pottery. The bones were positioned neatly, each laid to rest with the skulls toward the far end of the niche. Other bones littered the floor of the main tunnel, and the travelers stepped carefully around them. Rusted swords and other weapons lay discarded on the ground.

"They are not Letharn," the lòhren said quietly.

Lanrik asked no questions. He understood what they were: grave robbers, killed before they escaped.

A sound of shuffling, of murmuring and whispering, came to his ears. He wondered if it was the river, or the subdued sound of the waterfall, but he knew it was not. Something else walked the tunnels with them.

The stench of ancient death was suddenly strong, and the very dark began to whine; a long and high-pitched moan like the keening of a thousand throats. It filled the shadows, brought them to life, and finally rose to an angry wail.

A chill breeze blew down the tunnel. Aranloth stopped walking. He spoke as before, not loudly, but his voice carried.

Har nere ferork. Skigg gar skee.

The wailing subsided, with seeming reluctance, and the wind stilled. The scent of death remained strong, but whatever was in the tunnel with them dissolved back into the shadows of which it was made and receded.

Lanrik wondered what the Lòhren had done. He had spoken in a language that sounded like the Letharn's own. At least like what had been written on the lintel. He thought about that warning not to enter. It said that servants mutter secret words as they walk the hidden ways. Had Aranloth somehow learned those words? They must be some kind of charm or password that offered protection against whatever guarded the tombs. If so, he understood why the guards would not be protected. They did not know the charm.

Even as he thought of the guards he heard something in the tunnel behind them. The wailing rose again, loud and fierce, but this time it was not directed at them. A little while later there were alarmed shouts, and then fear-driven screams. Then there was silence once more.

Aranloth broke it. "I warned them," he said. "I warned them, but they would not listen." He walked on, his head bowed, and said no more.

Lanrik let out a long breath. Here, in the dark of the tombs, the only thing that stood between them and death was Aranloth and his understanding of the lost lore of the Letharn.

At least they had protection. The soldiers from Esgallien had died. Once more, men lost their lives in service to a corrupt and foolish king. How many had done so because of Murhain's greed for the sword? It was time to do something about it, although he did not know what. Nor was this the time to think about it. The skin of his neck prickled. The wailing pierced the dark again.

18. Wrath of the Wizard-priests

They continued through the tombs. The wailing voice followed them, a constant presence in their wake that muttered, whispered and whined in frustration. At times, it was more than a voice. When Lanrik looked back, he often glimpsed strange shadows that flitted away from the light of Aranloth's staff. He noticed, also, that the somber face of Arliss shone palely in the dim light.

From time to time the lòhren gave voice to the charm that kept them safe: *Har nere ferork. Skigg gar skee.* But as they walked, Lanrik realized that Aranloth spoke it more frequently, and the force that guarded the tombs, whatever it was, did not withdraw so much.

They went forward through the endless dark. The tunnel veered one way and then another, but always it had a slight downward angle.

The niches to either side changed: no more the broken furniture and cheap clay vessels; here rested the wealthy of Letharn society. Carvings decorated the tall walls, intricate and extensive. In places, bright murals gleamed in the fitful light, revealing scenes of hunting, fishing, wine-making and the day-to-day activities of long-ago lives.

On the pointed fingers of the dead glittered jewel-encrusted rings; twisted arm bones ran through bands of beaten gold. About the once-bright necks of women hung necklaces, yet these now shone against a background of grimed flagstones and dark-eyed skulls.

The number of graves was astonishing. Lanrik wondered if all the Letharn dead, through a long and prosperous history, were buried here. For not only was there the main tunnel down which Aranloth led them, but many others that branched continually to either side. Truly, he thought, the rock beneath the river was a catacomb like no other, for here the dead must outnumber the living of all the cities and lands of Alithoras.

The thought depressed him. He began to think that life was futile, that in the end he too would be reduced to nothing but dust. The weight of the stone piled high above, and the mighty river that coursed atop it seemed to press down and crush his spirit. The shadows stirred and groped, and he thought he heard the slap of footfalls in the great dark behind him. Perhaps a quick death at the hands of the force that guarded this place would be best. He would die anyway.

Even as his thoughts darkened, the voice of the lòhren rolled through the caverns once more. *Har nere ferork! Skigg gar skee!* This time he spoke the words with great force. The shadows receded, and the light at the tip of his staff shone hopefully against the night.

"Have courage!" urged the lòhren, and he walked forward with a high head and sure strides.

Lanrik felt a weight lift off his shoulders. Aranloth led them without fear, and he would follow in a like manner. Death would claim him one day, but he need not make it easy. And there was much that he might yet achieve.

The wailing turned to a distant whine, and Lanrik ignored it. He looked instead about him, wondering once more at the size of the place, but no longer intimidated by it.

They did not speak to each other, but they all looked with curiosity as the tunnel began to change again. It narrowed into a passageway. The niches in the wall and the dead that filled them were no more.

On turning a corner, they entered an open chamber. The floor was a grand mosaic of colored stones. Long benches of white marble, where a multitude could sit, ringed the walls. The open center was surrounded by tall walls, carved with massive figures. The whole vast space was overhung by a domed roof, man-made, smooth and painted to show scenes of people and rituals that must have meant much to the Letharn but were lost on Lanrik.

All about the travelers were more signs of a funerary procession. The wagon and oxen appeared again, and the wall carvings were beaded with gold and silver and strange gems that glinted in the first light for tens of centuries.

Aranloth sighed. "It was here that the Letharn rested during funeral ceremonies. After, they moved on to the next level. The rich, the noble, even kings and queens were laid here for an hour while the wizard-priests performed rites and the weary mourners found what ease they could. We should rest, too."

They sat down on one of the benches. It felt strange to Lanrik, for it occurred to him that he now sat in the same place that a race of people, which had not walked the earth for thousands of years, and about whom little was known except for dim rumor, once rested just as he.

He looked at Aranloth and spread his arms wide to indicate everything that surrounded them.

"How do you know all these things?"

The lòhren let out a long breath.

"You know that I am old – that I have lived many lives of men. But I am older even than that. I walked these halls when the Letharn were at their zenith …" He hesitated, and then went on. "I hunted the Angle with the rulers of the land and many realms beyond. I crossed the rivers and explored distant lands – before the Duthenor came, before the Camar, before the Halathrin trod those paths. And I came here also, to the very heart of the Empire that was, and in these shadow-haunted halls watched while the great of an age that is lost were buried."

Lanrik looked at him and did not speak. What reply could he make? There were no words to encompass how he felt, or the awe in which he held the lòhren.

Then, suddenly and unexpectedly, he had another thought. Aranloth had lived through the eons, preserved by some power of lòhrengai or ancient lore of the Letharn, but the world that he knew was gone. It lay about him now, reduced to dust and broken bones. Of everything that he once loved, nothing remained. Now, Lanrik understood better that look of compassion, sadness and regret that often marked the lòhren's face.

The wailing dark seemed to leave them alone in this resting place. Yet they must continue on, and the lòhren eventually stood. Once more he held up his staff, and like a man preparing for some great task, he straightened his shoulders and lifted up his gaze.

"The last stretch lies ahead," he said. "Soon, we'll come to the burial chambers of the wizard-priests where the implements of their trade, and the poison that covers the treasure, as well as its cure, is stored. After that, we will leave as swiftly as we may. This is no place for the living or the light of heart."

He led them to the other side of the chamber. Here, a set of marble stairs wound down into the dark, like a white spiral into a pit of shadow.

Down they went, their steps shuffling along the stone. At length, the staircase ceased. Before them stood a great portal. Three massive slabs of marble formed a doorway. Engraved on either side were the naked women, their saw-toothed daggers held high, their expression wicked and deadly. Gold filled the deep-cut lines of their figures, and it shimmered and sparkled in the light of Aranloth's staff giving them a semblance of life and movement. On the high lintel was more writing in the script of the Letharn.

We serve. We obey. We enforce, intoned the lòhren. "Here are buried the wizard-priests, servants of the emperor, and often members of the royal family," he added.

Aranloth waited no more. He strode forth. The tunnel they now followed was perfectly even, the floor, walls and ceiling clad with white marble. Statues and carvings decorated the long aisle, and to each side were great tombs.

The large alcoves were open, as were the previous niches, but here the rooms were no longer rough chambers hewed out of stone, but like the pleasure-rooms of a great palace. Columns of carved marble formed an entrance to each one, and a single stela of black granite, inscribed with the strange script of the Letharn, stood to the left of each opening.

The stelae, supposed Lanrik, listed the names of those buried within. And within, when the light of Aranloth's staff reached that far, were no collections of rustic furniture and clay pottery, but gold, silver and finely-worked glass.

No room was quite alike, but most had a great table near one of the walls. Over their dusty tops were all manner of bowls, plates and dishes, each filled by the desiccated remains of an ancient and uneaten feast. Chariots, their wheels gold rimmed and their ornate timber carved and inlayed with jewels, stood ready to drive. The skeletons of horses lay before them, age-darkened bits among their white teeth. And beyond that, piled high and deep, were gold coins, silver chains and jewels that sparkled a thousand colors.

Caldring lingered near one chamber of particular luxury.

"Touch nothing," the lòhren reminded him. "It may look tempting, but a fine layer of poison is over all that you see."

They walked on. The tunnel seemed endless, without change or stint in the finery. The wealth of the world was collected here, the treasures of an empire that ruled Alithoras. Lanrik shook his head at the wonder of it, and more so at the fact that this was only the resting place of the wizard-priests. What splendor lay buried with the emperors?

Something else occurred to him. The lòhren now invoked his charm less often, and the shadowy movement that followed them through the dark had retreated. Perhaps some lingering power of the wizard-priests offered protection.

Without warning the tunnel changed. It came to a resting place like the one above. The light of Aranloth's staff flared, revealing a similar dome and new tunnels to left and right.

The lòhren did not enter, though. Instead, he turned to the last tomb on the left. This, they now saw, was larger than the others and resplendent with even greater wealth. There, on a gilded bed, lay a body bedecked in silver, gold and jewels.

Here, there was no skeleton as elsewhere, but an actual body clothed in white robes. A shock of silvery hair sprang from the ancient head. A black beard, stiff and streaked by gray, covered its chin. And there was a face rather than a skull. The skin might have been dry and leathery, the cheeks sunken, the hooked nose a little twisted, but by some art of the ancients, or power of enchantment, the flesh of the long dead remained whole.

"The head-priest of the Letharn," muttered Aranloth. "See the black rod beside him? That marks him as not only a wizard-priest but also of the royal blood. We must enter his tomb, but I warn you again, touch nothing."

He walked through the pillared opening, and the others followed. Straight away they saw another flight of stairs to the left. This led down, and he led them along it, leaving the tomb of the head-priest behind.

"We must yet return this way," the lòhren said. "The rooms we seek lie beneath him. Even in death he guards the accoutrements of power that he held in life. He it was who first learned the uses of the poison that protects the treasures, and he also discovered the cure. His aged steps led the processions for years beyond count. Few priests the Letharn had, and fewer still the number of head-priests, even during the course of the long reign of the empire. But he was the greatest of them all."

Down they followed the lòhren. The stairs soon ceased and a new tunnel began. Rooms lay to each side, but these were not tombs. They appeared to be storage chambers. Ancient timber kegs filled some, tall clay vessels others. The scent came to them strongly of frankincense, myrrh and medicines that Lanrik well remembered from his youth whenever he went to the healer. Some of the smells also reminded him of the dried herbs that were often used in Esgallien cooking to preserve meat or disguise the taste of food that was going bad.

Aranloth stopped before one of the rooms.

"What we seek is in here."

He went inside, his eyes roving the many shelves and tables, but without hesitation he reached out to a smaller clay vessel imprinted with the image of a five-leafed plant.

Dust covered the jar, and for a small container the lid seemed heavy when the lòhren lifted it. Within moments of him doing so, the strong smell of a herb dominated the room. It had a bittersweet scent, and seemed as fresh as herbs just cut from the garden. Lanrik breathed in the smell with wonder, for the dried leaves had been stored here since before a time that was legend.

"This is it," Aranloth said. "I well remember the smell." He pulled a soft leather pouch from his robes and undid the string that held it tight.

He carefully tipped the vessel until its contents, fine stalks and narrow leaves still intact, fell into the pouch. He gathered little more than a few pinches before turning the jar upright again and replacing the heavy lid. Quickly, he drew the string of the pouch tight and placed it back into one of his inner pockets.

"Will that be enough?" Lanrik queried.

The lòhren looked at him with sad eyes. "It's enough. If not, then no amount of the cure will work. Erlissa was well under the influence of the poison before we reached the fountain."

Lanrik did not answer. He always knew there was no guarantee that their quest would be successful, but now that they had the actual cure in their possession, it was hard to hear that there was a chance it would not work.

"We should leave," Aranloth said. "The less time we spend in the tombs the better."

Lanrik did not disagree, and the lòhren led them from the chamber and back up the stairs. They reached, after a hard climb, the tomb of the head-priest once more.

The chamber was not the same. Lanrik paused, trying to think what it was. There was a stronger smell. Incense hung heavy in the air. And resin, too. More subtly, he caught the scent of decay. It was slight, but growing.

He looked at Aranloth, but the lòhren paid him no heed, his eyes fixed on the head-priest. Lanrik followed his gaze.

The priest lay as before, and yet it seemed like there was a thrum of movement beneath his folded arms, as though the long-stilled heart fluttered once more in his dry chest.

The fingers twitched. Dust stirred from the age-darkened sheets, and the air grew cold. With a moan and a creak the body shivered; the arms unfolded and the ancient corpse heaved upright to sit on the side of the bed like an old man waking from sleep. The head turned, the leathery flesh of its neck twisting, and it looked at them.

What gazed at the travelers was like the face of a live man, so great was the preservation skills of the ancients. The eyelids flickered, which had been sealed with fine thread for eons, but did not open.

"Sleep," the lòhren intoned. He reached out a hand, palm down. "Sleep. Rest. Lie in peace."

The dead man shuddered, and then his mouth worked, but it too was sealed by thread.

198

"My sleep is broken. What do you do in my tomb, Harlak?"

"I do nothing, Burik. Lie down. Sleep. Rest in peace."

The dead man shook his head as though casting away a fog that dulled his mind. He spoke again, his lips moving but still sealed, and Lanrik realized that the voice he heard were the thoughts of a dead man conveyed from mind to mind by wizardry.

"Do not try to deceive me. You possess *herenfrak*. This I know, and you intend to take it out, out to the world beyond. But you know better than others that nothing leaves this place, neither the great treasures nor the small ones."

"Sleep. It is not your concern."

The dead man ran his withered hand through his shock of hair. The sleeve of his robe fell down, and the wasted flesh of his arm was laid bare. Corded muscles slid beneath dry skin.

"I am dead, Harlak. Nothing concerns me. And yet, and yet, *all* concerns me. I have seen you in my long sleep, seen how you scurry about helping the lesser races that once we ruled. They roam the lands that we conquered like a plague of mice. They are nothing to us. Why do you waste your time to help them? You, who yet live. You could bring back the old ways. Have you no loyalty to those who raised you up, made you what you are?"

Aranloth straightened. He held his staff firmly, his grip white-fingered.

"The old ways are gone. They will not return, and the world is better for it. Ours was a great people, but they lost their way. I toil now to redeem the many wrongs we did, to make right all our sins. I serve, rather than conquer."

The priest clenched his gnarled hands.

"Thus you dare to treat me? I, who was your master."

"You are no longer my master. Those days are gone."

The dead man shook his head from side to side.

"Gone. Gone! Dust and ashes blown away on the wind of time! Yet hear me now, Harlak." The long-sealed eyes fixed on the lòhren. "You were a good student. The best. You know as well as I that the guardians of the tombs will consume you. You, and all with you. Your spirit will be devoured! No long sleep for you. No rituals. No funerary procession befitting your great station. You cannot defy them, though you utter the charm until the breath is stolen from your chest. Not while you take something that belongs here. Here it shall stay, and your rotting corpse with it."

Aranloth struck the end of his staff against the stone floor.

"Enough!" he cried. "Life is lived by the living. I do what I do, and I take the risks I must. Sleep! Lie down! Rest! We shall leave you."

"Leave me, traitor. That is good. I will sleep the long sleep again, for your babble tires me. But know this!" The head-priest's head turned away from the lòhren and surveyed the others. "The eyes of the dead see all. I know what one of you carries in your false heart – the seed of destruction for the rest. And I know what one of you carries in their strong hand – the seeds of destruction for a nation. Most of all, understand this. You try to save your friend, she who lies in the embrace of ùhrengai, but she is not there. Ebona has her, and that new race of sorcerers that you fight. They shall kill her in the Vale of Gold that once gave us great wealth. Your quest is come to nothing. Go! Go now to your deaths, and I shall dream of your wailing while I rest."

The corpse lay back, and they were dismissed as though an emperor had finished with them. The body rested again on the bed, the long arms crossed themselves. The corpse grew still, and away in the tunnels Lanrik heard the wailing start again. Whatever it was, it stirred once more, and the dead priest's words hung in the air.

"Cranky old bugger," Arliss said.

Lanrik turned to her in amazement. A cold sheen of perspiration clung to his face, and fear made his heart beat wildly in his chest. And yet in the face of all that had just happened, Arliss joked. She was incredible, and he knew that she was a companion to endure the worst with.

"Come," Aranloth said. "The way is long and our hope shorter than it was. My old master has brought the guardians of the tombs to full wakefulness. He was ever spiteful."

"Is there any hope?" Lanrik asked.

"Dead men do not lie," answered Aranloth. "But they do not see all, either. We shall discover now who is mightier. I, or my old master."

19. Queen of the World

It seemed to Erlissa that the world tilted beneath her feet. The witch had been *waiting* for her.

"Foolish, foolish girl," Ebona said. "Yet not so foolish as Carnona. Or maybe desperation drove her to this act of stupidity."

The witch's pale eyes glittered in the dim light.

"Tell me, sweetling, how does my sister fare? Does she fret? Does she worry what will become of her when I triumph? What did she promise you as reward for this act of folly?"

Ebona's gaze was serene, and yet there was a hint of something in her eyes. It might have been the barely-checked power that roiled through her body, for her growing strength was a palpable and wild force in the chamber. Or it might have been madness.

Erlissa made no response. Her thoughts raced, but hope died every second. Yet she would not give up. She did not think Carnona would have sent her had there been no chance of success.

The witch raised her hand and lashed out with sudden and violent force. The slap stung Erlissa's cheek, and she felt the force of it right down to her feet. It made her reel back and sway.

Her face throbbed, but she regained her balance. Anger flared within her, but she made no move to retaliate. Not yet; not until she better understood what was happening.

"Carnona promised me nothing. I came of my own accord. I came … because you must be stopped."

"Stopped? Not even Carnona can stop me now. She may as well have sent a pebble to dam a flooding river."

The witch's words stirred something in Erlissa's memory. Carnona had also called her a pebble. Unexpectedly, Erlissa smiled, for she saw that even with all Ebona's power she did not know everything, and there was still a chance to surprise her, maybe even defeat her.

"You must be stopped, Ebona. How many have died to fuel your strength? Are their lives worth nothing to you? And if you don't stop now, when will you?"

Ebona looked at her sweetly. "I shall never stop. There are realms and races that have not yet heard my name. All the power and people of Alithoras would not serve to glut my greed. And why *should* it be glutted? In this world the strong take, and the weak give."

Erlissa looked at her calmly. "Not always. Sometimes the strong give in order to help the weak. Even if you kill me, others will oppose you."

The witch laughed. "You speak of the lòhrens. Maybe they'll try to stop me. If so, they'll fail. But truly, I hope they try – it'll save me the trouble of hunting them down." Anguish momentarily distorted her face, and she spat on the ground. "Aranloth humiliated me once, but I'll not endure that again. Not ever!"

Ebona swiftly regained her composure, but Erlissa had seen something that further stiffened her resolve: the witch *was* going mad. She had gathered too much power to herself, too quickly. It was a festering corrosion that ate at her mind. And it would only get worse.

The witch gave a shrug. "Anyway, my dear, Aranloth will be my concern. You'll be long gone before he, or anyone else, comes looking for you."

Ebona lifted her arm. She pointed at Erlissa with a long-fingered hand as though admonishing her.

"You should think less of the lòhrens and more of the elùgroth. For with *him* you shall go, and he is not best pleased with you. It may be that living in his service is worse punishment than the slow death I would otherwise have given you. But he wants you, and he shall have you."

Erlissa turned to Elù-Randùr. The elùgroth seemed little more than a black shadow that had not yet spoken. She wondered what his relationship was with the witch. She knew them both, better than she liked, and she believed that neither would give precedence to the other.

Elù-Randùr appeared subservient to Ebona, but he would bide his time and use her even as she used him. In the end, one would prevail over the other, and though the witch ordered things to her will at the moment, it need not stay that way. The elùgroth would have a scheme. Perhaps he understood what Ebona did not: that she was losing her mind, and he intended to take advantage of that.

Erlissa repressed a shudder as Elù-Randùr looked straight at her. The fingers of his blue-veined hand, pallid and sickly, twitched against the black wood of his wych-wood staff.

"Welcome, sister."

"I'm not your sister."

He smiled. "Oh, but you are. More so than any creature that shares my blood, for you and I share the same spirit."

"No, we don't."

204

Elù-Randùr shook his head. It was a slow movement, like the patient crawling of an insect.

"So you say now, but I'll bend you to my will in the end. I'll show you what it is to be an elùgroth, show you powers that Aranloth dare not teach. You'll be mine then. My disciple. My servant. And yes, even my sister."

Erlissa laughed. "You might once have bent me to your will. But not now. I've seen your kind. And I've lived among those who oppose you. I know the difference, and I've made my choice. I'm stronger than I was when you last held me captive." She hesitated, and then added, "Don't you realize that you have no power over me?"

The elùgroth studied her with a long gaze and calculating eyes.

"So confident? Never mind. It'll give me all the more pleasure to break you. And yet your manner intrigues me. I sense that you *have* grown, and that you've realized some of your potential. But there's more yet. So much more. I'll bend you to my will. And if I can't, I'll kill you. I cannot allow the enemy to possess your skills."

Erlissa shrugged. "You talk a lot, but all I see is an impotent sorcerer who serves as a witch's lackey – like a dog that picks up the scraps its master lets fall from the table."

Elù-Randùr drew in a sharp breath, and she knew that her taunting had wrung a chord that disturbed him. And yet he recovered smoothly.

"So quick to judge. You should know that Ebona and I have an agreement. For the moment, our plans overlap, much to our mutual benefit. But it's interesting that you think to try to divide us. Quite devious, in fact. There's hope for you yet, no matter that you deny it."

Erlissa ignored him. She turned back to the witch.

"You understand of course, that he'll betray you in the end."

Ebona smiled. "Yes dear, I know. He thinks of it all the time. But the day he tries to will be his last. He thinks of *that* all the time, too. I know much that happens in these lands. Carnona brought you here, spirited you away from Lòrenta on a river of ùhrengai. I will say this, her skill is great to have done so, but she could hardly have been unaware that I would sense it and divine her purpose. While you're discussing treachery, you should think on that. She abandoned you to this fate, for she knew I would be waiting for you. Just as I know what the elùgroth desires. But in this new world, only my desires matter."

The witch drew herself up. Amid the dark, the pale linen of her dress gleamed. Her eyes flashed, and the power that was in her flared as though an inner light burned her soul.

"I, who once was great, will be great again. Men shall bow before me. Nations shall tremble at my word. I will grind the lòhrens to dust, and even the Halathrin, that proud race of immortals, will serve me. I will rule all! Queen of Alithoras I shall be, and the world will tremble!"

Ebona stood there, a mighty figure, and yet a mere shadow of what she would become if she was not stopped.

Erlissa bowed her head, as though in dismay, but her gaze sought out the cauldron. She could only break Ebona's power if she could destroy the source of it. The witch fed on sacrifice and dark rites, and somehow the cauldron gathered those forces and multiplied them. Break it, and her power would diminish. Carnona could then withstand her.

The witch trembled and regained control of herself. She seemed to shrink, to become more human again.

"Already it starts. Many plans are afoot. Esgallien is in my power. That meddler, Aranloth, will receive a nasty surprise soon, if he has not already. Arliss is in the pay of Musraka, and with her help he will reclaim the shazrahad sword that once belonged to his forefathers, that will one day belong to the Hakalakadan." Ebona smiled at the thought, relishing her words. Then she shrugged. "Or one of my own men will, and he'll give it to Esgallien's king. Either way, it shall unleash bloodshed and ruin in the city. And when that happens, nothing will be able to stop me. Nothing at all."

"Enough," Elù-Randùr said. "You have the cauldron, and I have the girl. It's time to go our separate ways." He looked hard at Erlissa, a flicker of doubt in his eyes. "I sense that there is more going on here than you know. Aranloth is a meddler, but he is not stupid. I have learned not to underestimate him. Carnona you know, and I do not, but she sent the girl here with some sort of hope. We have her now, and it's time to move on to the next step. She'll come with me to the south. There, she'll serve that which I serve, or she'll die."

Erlissa looked at him with more calmness than she felt. That Arliss was a traitor was a surprise, a surprise that in truth she did not believe, for she thought she had read the girl's feelings for Lanrik like a book.

Another wave of dizziness crashed through her, but she ignored the incessant pull of her true body in Lòrenta. It was a fact that both the elùgroth and the witch, for all their boasting, had not understood.

She raised her arms, and the walnut staff throbbed with power in her hand.

"Truly, I shall come with you, brother."

Elù-Randùr looked at her in surprise. That moment would not last, and the moment, the one moment that Erlissa had waited for, the one moment she had in which to act, was upon her.

20. On Wings of Darkness

The light of Aranloth's staff flared and bobbed as he strode ahead. He led them from the aisle of buried wizard-priests into the domed chamber at its end. The rasp of their boots filled the eons-old silence that haunted its vast space.

Lanrik saw two tunnels. One ran to the left and the other veered right. They probably housed the crypts of the royal families. Yet Aranloth headed for neither.

The lòhren moved to the nearest marble bench. He put his weight against it and pushed. Nothing happened for a moment, and then Lanrik heard the loud groan of stone sliding over stone.

He could not pinpoint where the noise came from. He turned around, his eyes searching, and suddenly he saw a vertical line split the wall to his right. A second ago it had been tall and intricately decorated; now a great door stood open, black and forbidding.

"Quickly," Aranloth said.

They moved into the dark, and Aranloth followed them.

"Give me a hand," the lòhren said to Lanrik.

Together they braced themselves against the stone wall and slid the door back in place. It thudded shut, and a deep boom reverberated through the many-tunneled tombs.

Lanrik listened for some moments, and when the last echo died he realized a complete silence lay over everything. The wailing in the dark had ceased as swiftly as it had earlier begun, but he had a feeling the peace would not last long.

Around them was a rough-hewn tunnel. He studied it carefully as they began to walk. It had none of the luxury of the previous passages. Nor were there niches for the dead.

Aranloth glanced at him and must have noticed his puzzlement.

"This place is vast, and none but the wizard-priests ever learned all its secrets. There are areas even they dared not go. But wherever they went, they wanted to get there quickly. The stately and winding tunnels were for the conduct of rites and the passage of large processions. Lone servants on minor errands used narrow ways such as this that lead directly to where they wanted to go."

He led them on, and soon other tunnels intersected with the main one that he followed. After a while, he started to take some of these. Many that they saw led down, but he always chose those that led upward.

The wailing began again. Lanrik could not tell if it came from behind them, or ahead, it seemed to be all around. And it was loud.

"It's getting closer," Arliss said.

"Too close," Caldring added. "How far do we still have to go?"

Aranloth's long strides did not slow while he answered over his shoulder.

"Still a while yet. Have faith, you'll see the daylight soon enough. In the meantime, try not to listen to the wailing. It's meant to unnerve you. Ignore it."

Lanrik thought that was good advice, but it was advice that he could not follow. The wailing had a way of

210

getting inside his head, of swirling through his every thought like a snake slithering through tall grass.

At times the wailing seemed more than simple noise. He heard words, and the more he thought about it, the more certain he became. He realized that whoever, or whatever, guarded the tombs was only playing with them. It could reach them swiftly if it wanted to. It had wasted no time in dealing with the royal guard.

He thought of Aranloth. That was the difference between the fate of the soldiers and this group. Aranloth had powers, great powers, and even the guardian of the tombs was respectful of him. It bided its time, or gathered its strength in preparation for an attack. But however strong the lòhren was, if the head-priest was to be believed, there was no escape while they carried the herenfrak.

Whether or not the head-priest was to be believed was a good question. He had claimed that Ebona and Elù-Randùr had taken Erlissa. That seemed impossible, for she was entrapped in the ùhrengai of the fountain. And yet he could not dismiss it either. Aranloth had said that dead men do not lie. Perhaps they could be mistaken, though. Either way, his first concern was to escape the tombs. He could not do Erlissa any good if he died here.

They raced ahead. From time to time they climbed stairs, narrow and twisting. Lanrik's thighs ached, and his breathing was labored, but he noticed a change. The air was fresher, maybe even more humid, and if his ears played no tricks on him, he heard the faint thrum of water carried through a maze of tunnels from the great falls. Or perhaps from the river itself.

Suddenly the lòhren chanted the charm. *Har nere ferork! Skigg gar skee!* As he spoke, the light of his staff

211

flared and lòhrengai sparked at its tip. What danger he was responding to, Lanrik could not tell, but his lòhren senses, or his ancient knowledge of their foe, must have given some warning.

A moment later, Lanrik saw what Aranloth had sensed. They turned a corner, and there ahead of them were three creatures: the living embodiment of the naked women on the carvings. Their faces were contorted in rage or pain at the lòhrens words, and they gave ground, but only a little. In their long-fingered hands they carried the saw-toothed knives, and they held them forth as though eager to rend flesh.

Har nere ferork! Skigg gar skee! The lòhren yelled, but just as the head-priest had foretold, the charm now seemed to have little effect.

The women hissed, long tongues curling in their red-lipped mouths, their eyes flashing hatred.

One stepped ahead of the others. She pointed her knife at Aranloth, singling him out.

The lòhren stood his ground.

"I must have it," he said, referring to the herenfrak.

The woman shook her head. Her hair swung, black and lush, but as she moved snake heads darted among the long ends. A piercing cry that might shatter stone burst from her throat. Lanrik put his hands to his ears. Caldring and Arliss reeled at his side.

Aranloth took a single step forward. He raised his staff high and lòhren-fire flickered at its tip.

"I *must* have it," he said.

The woman hissed louder, and the other two joined in, stepping forward to meet him while they unleashed their own screeching cries.

Lòhren-fire erupted and sizzled through the air with a blinding flash. The sound of thunder rolled through the hollow halls and the floor shuddered.

Lanrik raised his arm to shield his eyes, and when he lowered it the women were gone.

"Are they dead?"

The lòhren shook his head. "No. They are the *harakgar*. They do not die."

"What are they?" Caldring asked.

"The lore of the Letharn delved into many secrets. Some that it would have been better to leave alone. They created the harakgar to serve as guards for the tombs."

"If they were created, then surely they can be killed?" Lanrik asked.

"Not by blade or shaft. Not even by magic, for they are creatures of ùhrengai, of the very power that shapes and substances the world. It runs strong here, deep in the stone that forms the bones of the earth. The Letharn woke it, transformed it and used it. The harakgar are the result, but even if I could kill them, I would not." He paused, leaning on his staff while he rested. "Too many secrets, too many powers and artifacts lie buried here besides the bodies of a long-dead nation. It is better that they never see the light of day again, and the three sisters ensure that."

"Then how can we get out?"

"Have courage!" Aranloth said. "Now, walk fast, but keep your eyes open! They are far from done yet. So far, they are only testing me."

The lòhren led them forward again. His stride was sure, his staff high, but Lanrik, who knew him well, recognized that worry vied with his confidence. But the lòhren did not have to fight alone. If the creatures were of magic, the shazrahad sword would be of use. He

213

reached down, drew it, and felt the warmth of its hilt seep into his hand.

He heard a soft rasp as Arliss drew her own behind him. He glanced back at her. She walked with seeming confidence, as she always did. Of what she really felt or thought though, he saw nothing. It was as if she had drawn a veil over her face. Caldring paced nervously at his side, a knife in his hand, but he was white with fear. This was a hard learning experience for him. He was too young for this kind of danger, and yet regardless of his fear, it did not hold him back. If he lived, he would make a good Raithlin.

Aranloth led them through another door and once more they were in the tombs. Here seemed to be buried warriors of some renown, for weapons, strange and cumbersome to Lanrik's eye, were piled high in the niches beside the bones of those who once held them.

No sooner had they entered this new tunnel than the wailing began again. This time it rose to a maddening shriek of laughter.

A green mist flowed low over the floor just ahead of them. They stopped and watched. The vapor swelled and rose. Swiftly it coalesced into a great serpent, tongue flicking, tasting the air. Its scales glittered as it undulated and rose up, head held back, poised to strike.

The creature was as thick as a man and its trailing body disappeared back into the vague gloom. Eyes, like black diamonds, stared at them malevolently.

Aranloth moved forward, the end of his staff pointed at the serpent. It arched its head higher, and then suddenly struck. The great head shot forth, fangs bared.

Lòhren-fire flared to meet it. A flash of white light and the roar of thunder filled the tunnel. When the light blinked out, the serpent was gone.

"Quickly," Aranloth said. "They won't relent and my strength diminishes."

They strode through the tunnel of buried warriors. Soon new tunnels branched out everywhere, but the lòhren chose his path unerringly. They came to another of the domed recesses. Now, the lòhren slowed and then stopped.

"What is it," Lanrik asked.

"I don't know. Keep your eyes open."

Lanrik looked about him. He saw nothing, but then heard Arliss gasp.

"The walls!" she said

Lanrik spun around looking at them. As with many of the others, they were carved. Tall figures, six feet high, ringed the domed chamber. There seemed to be all manner of Letharn. Men and women. Nobles, peasants, warriors and dancers.

It was the dancers who caught his eye. They were girls, lithe but muscular, the taut flesh of their curved figures barely concealed by thin veils. They lifted their arms high over their heads, entwining their fingers while their hips swayed to music gone silent for long eons.

As Lanrik watched the stone shimmered. Like oiled muscles the stone undulated and rippled. He let out his breath as the figures stepped off the wall. Stone had become flesh. Dark-eyed girls now danced over the dusty floor. Veils wove to and fro, parted red lips smiled and perspiration glistened over silken skin.

Unexpectedly, one of the girls began to sing. Her voice was rich and pure. Lanrik drank it in like chilled water on a hot day. He yearned for it, and it lulled him. It made him feel that all was right in the world.

The song dropped into a deeper tone, low and husky. And then it rose to a high sound, sweeter than the air he breathed. Lanrik could not understand the words, but he longed to learn their meaning.

The singer looked at him, her red lips parted, her dark eyes smiled, teasing him, inviting him to come to her.

The other dancers moved in growing frenzy, their bare limbs gleaming in the light, the perfect blend of muscle and impossible grace.

The singer wrung ever-sweeter sounds from the air, and her long fingers ran through her shadowy hair, but her dark eyes, deep like pooled night, gazed at Lanrik.

He took a step forward, enchanted.

Arliss moved behind him. One moment her hand was on his shoulder, holding him back, and the next she was in front of him. As quick as the eye could see, she lifted her hand and flung something.

Cold steel glinted, and one of her knives flashed through the air.

The singer ducked, unnaturally fast, and the knife clattered into the wall. But the dark-eyed singer was gone. In her place stood one of the harakgar. Tall, statuesque, naked. She was as beautiful as the singer, but her hair writhed in a fury and her hand, holding a saw-toothed dagger, trembled in rage.

Har nere ferork! Skigg gar skee! shouted the lòhren.

He reinforced his words with a flicking motion of his staff. This time, there was no lòhren-fire. The room darkened and the air became thick like muddied water. A wave of shadows crashed through the chamber and rolled over the harakgar. She made no noise, nor did she struggle.

The wave of shadows dissolved, and when the light returned, faint and fluttering at the tip of Aranloth's staff, the harakgar was gone. Of her two sisters, there was no sign.

216

The lòhren wasted no time on words. He strode ahead, turning left at a tunnel that opened up on the other side of the domed room.

They moved swiftly, dark shadows flickering through the tunnel like bats. Shadows flitted across the looming walls, for here there were no burials. The ground ran at an upward slope, quite pronounced for the first time, and it was uneven, as though a natural cave had been hewn roughly into the semblance of a man-made tunnel.

Their path curved one way and then another, but it always led upward. Their breathing was loud in the closed space, but the air seemed fresher than before.

Abruptly, the tunnel ended. Now Lanrik knew they really were in a cave. Sand and loose stones covered the floor. The walls, or at least what he could see of them, were natural and uneven. The vault of the ceiling was lost somewhere in an echoing space above.

"Be careful," warned Aranloth. "The outside is close, and the harakgar will try to stop us in earnest."

"You mean they've been playing so far?" Arliss asked.

Aranloth peered about him, measuring the great cave for signs of ambush.

"That's exactly what I mean. They're creatures of immense power. So far, they've just tested me. They know who I am, but they have not measured my strength. They show caution, learning what they can. Now, near the exit, they'll use that knowledge in a concerted attack."

"What happens if we break free of them?" Lanrik asked. "Will they follow us outside?"

"No. They're linked to the tombs. They can't go anywhere else. That was the way the Letharn created them. But this is their world, and here they are all-powerful. Only the charm protects us, and even that is close to useless now."

"Then how do we escape?" Caldring asked.

"A good question," Aranloth answered. "They might be all-powerful, but I have delved deep into the lore from which they are made. They can be defied, but only with great power, and only briefly. When they attack, I'll repel them. In those few moments you must flee to freedom. I'll hold them back as long as I can. Use the time wisely."

They moved ahead. Aranloth led them slowly now, careful of every step, and casting light into every nook and cranny ahead of them. Arliss walked behind, quiet and watchful.

Lanrik held the shazrahad blade ahead of him. The hilt remained warm, and he felt the powers inside it rise and surge in response to the harakgar.

To the right a chasm opened up. It was a gash in the earth, deep and dark. Aranloth stayed away from it.

A drop of water struck Lanrik's forehead. He looked up, but saw nothing. Another one hit his arm and he realized they were very near the surface. Deep in the tombs it was dry as dust, but here, the river was close.

The cave veered to the left, and Aranloth led them around a great boulder. On the other side were more chasms and the sound of running water. It was a place of small but swift-flowing streams. Aranloth worked his way through a maze of fissures.

The ground was almost flat now. It was pure sand, deep and soft beneath their feet. Ahead was a glimmer of light that was not from Aranloth's staff. Fresh air moved among the travelers and ruffled their clothes. Freedom and escape were close. Yet as they walked, Lanrik's sudden hopes sunk.

Ahead was a span of stone. It arched over a great chasm between them and the light. The rush of water came loud from its hidden depths, but on the span stood the three sisters.

The harakgar made no sound. They stood, tall and regal as queens, cruel as mad women, beautiful but evil.

Lanrik felt his heart beat wildly in his chest.

"We *will* pass," Aranloth said. His voice was quiet, but it filled the cave. The harakgar hissed in response. As one, they walked forward, their saw-toothed knives raised, red tongues licking the blades and a deathly smile on their lips.

They came to the end of the narrow bridge and stopped.

Far away Lanrik thought he could hear the calls of birds, and he saw the movement of something in the light at the end of the tunnel, as though trees leaned and leaves rustled at the touch of a breeze.

They were close, but this, he knew, would be Aranloth's greatest test. The lòhren had defied Elù-Randùr when Lòrenta was besieged by sorcerers, but this was a trial of a different order. Here were creatures of ùhrengai, created with only one purpose, and they were in their home. Aranloth was the outsider here. He did not belong, for he was alive, and there were three harakgar, but only one of him.

Lanrik stepped forward to stand by the lòhren. The three figures watched him, their eyes glinting.

Without warning, the harakgar stretched forth their arms and green fire streamed from their fingers.

Aranloth raised his staff. Lanrik lifted high his sword, but before any flame reached them a wind blew. It smelled of the tombs below: dry and stale. It rushed forward, sweeping the green flame aside and smashing

219

into the harakgar. They staggered back. The flame died. The wind ceased.

In the momentary silence the harakgar began to laugh.

Truly, thought Lanrik, they were creatures of power. There was something immutable about them, as though they were forces of nature. Not by any ordinary means had the treasures of an empire remained inviolate for eons.

Aranloth stood calmly, poised but unmoving. If he felt fear or doubt, he did not show it. The harakgar ceased their laughing and watched him through narrowed eyes, sensing that he was doing something.

Breathless moments passed. The combatants remained motionless despite the forces at their command. Then suddenly Aranloth raised his staff.

The harakgar crouched, their eyes staring hard at the lòhren, seeking the source of his attack. They did not see it. But Lanrik did. The chasm that the bridge spanned must have been filled with a deep river. Lanrik watched as a swell of water rose up high, white crested, towering, silent behind the three sisters. A shadow fell over them, and they swung around.

Too late they saw their danger. The wave crested, rolled forward, and swept them off the bridge with a roar that drowned their screams.

The water smashed back into the chasm, though some of it spilled onto the sand in front of the travelers, and the spray of heavy droplets whipped against their faces like pelting rain

"Run!" Aranloth commanded.

The travelers scrambled across the wet sand. Of the harakgar, there was no sign. Whether the wave had drowned or destroyed them, Lanrik did not know.

The stone of the bridge was smooth and wet. As swiftly as they could they crossed it. Below was a dark gulf, filled with the crash and rush of seething water. It was not far below, but darkness hid it.

They came to the other side, and the light at the end of the tunnel was close. But their ordeal was not yet ended. The harakgar remained undefeated.

The three sisters did not seem to be bound to any form. They could be a mist, a noise, or even stone. Now, they rose up from the chasm on wings of darkness, their long-fingered hands, that once carried saw-toothed daggers, had transformed into talons that gripped and squeezed the air while shadowy wings beat above.

"Flee!" shouted Aranloth.

The travelers ran.

Aranloth and Lanrik were in the lead, Arliss came last. Ahead, a fresh breeze blew and a pool of late afternoon sunlight dropped like a fountain of water into the darkness. They made for it, sprinting for freedom and escape.

They were nearly there when Arliss fell. Lanrik heard a muffled cry and turned back. She lay sprawled on the ground, a misstep on the loose sand having sent her sprawling. Over her, the harakgar hovered.

Lanrik did not think. He turned back and stood between Arliss and the harakgar while she scrambled to her feet. He had already lost one Raithlin; he did not intend to lose another. They had pledged their loyalty to him as Raithlindrath, but that loyalty went both ways.

The shazrahad sword was hot in his hand. A blue shimmer of flame ran along its length, the lòhrengai inside it coming to full wakefulness. But the shadows above him darkened and the harakgar screamed with glee. Their wings folded and they dived.

221

Suddenly, Aranloth was there. His white robes billowed wildly, and he extended his staff in a stiff arm.

"Flee!" he yelled. "I'll hold them off!"

Lanrik lifted Arliss. Blood trickled down her forehead. He held her, his sword still in his hand, and carried her to the mouth of the tunnel.

Warm sunlight streamed on his face and he looked back into the darkness of the cave. The harakgar had surrounded Aranloth. They fluttered above him, dark wings beating and talons stretching forth. They dropped from the air and reached for him.

21. The Light Within

The harakgar screamed. Their beating wings flung a whirlwind of sand and dust into the air. For a moment they hovered above the lòhren, and then they plunged, talons outstretched.

Once more Aranloth called out the charm. His voice boomed through the hollow cavern, and white fire burst from his staff. Dust and sand sizzled in the swirling air, and the lòhren shone with the power of lòhrengai that was within him.

The three sisters screeched. Their pain-maddened cries tore the air. One fell to the side, her form twisting while she plummeted, her dark wings aflame. The others wavered, but then dropped and reached for the lòhren.

Lanrik leaped into the chamber. The shazrahad sword, hot in his hand, caught the lòhren-light and silver-white flame ran along its length.

He charged into the fight, sword swinging, and its bright edge struck one of the harakgar a glancing blow. She screamed and spat, her dark hair streaming while the snake heads hissed.

Aranloth sent a bolt of lòhren-fire into the other. It blew her to the side, and she tumbled from the air.

They turned toward the remaining harakgar. She plunged once more at the lòhren. At the same time, fire darted from his staff and Lanrik stabbed with his sword.

The creature writhed in sudden fury, and her shadowy wings arched high. She lifted herself beyond the reach of the sword. Yet, just when Lanrik expected Aranloth to finish her off, the flame died.

The lòhren swayed, nearly spent. At that moment, the first harakgar pulled herself off the ground. What injuries she had suffered Lanrik did not know, but her power seemed endless, for she appeared whole and unharmed again. Her wings were gone, but her long legs, sleek and rippling with muscle, propelled her across the ground.

She leaped like a striking serpent, and her body smashed into the lòhren and sent him sprawling. His staff flew from his hand and landed in the sand. She perched atop him, clawed hands tearing, and her mouth sinking into his shoulder.

Red blood spurted over his white robes. He yelled, his voice made harsh by pain and anger. Fire burst from his fingers and stabbed into the harakgar. She screamed, but the noise was muffled, for she would not unclench her jaw. Instead, she worked her teeth deeper into the lòhren's flesh.

Lanrik staggered toward them. He had never seen Aranloth so beset before. He might at last have met his match, but the hot blade of the shazrahad sword slid through the harakgar's body before she could drive home her advantage.

She arched her back and lifted her head. Blood frothed at her lips as she screamed, and the lòhren threw her off him and reached for his staff.

Lanrik heard the beat of wings above. He started to turn, knowing that he would be too late. He began to lift the sword, but though his mind raced with swift thoughts, his body was too heavy and sluggish to match them.

224

The harakgar would be on him before he could bring any weapon to bear. He would die in the tombs of the Letharn, and Erlissa's warning not to come here ran through his mind. She had seen this. He would miss her, and his heart ached at the thought.

He felt the thrum of lòhrengai in the blade, felt the exultation of that other power that was in it, that force of will or prophecy that was pulling on the strings of fate, drawing him into the net of his enemies.

And then suddenly Caldring was running and leaping. He held his knife high in one hand and a rock as big as his fist in the other. The harakgar saw him and shied away, though little harm could come to her from such weapons. Yet that momentary pause altered Lanrik's fate, and the destiny that Erlissa had long ago seen was averted.

A thin streak of lòhren-fire smashed into the harakgar. Her dark wings blazed and she unleashed a mad cry.

The lòhren stumbled to his feet. "Run!" he yelled.

And they ran. It was a short stretch to where Arliss lay in a daze outside the mouth of the cave. But the beat of wings was loud behind them as well as the sand-dulled thud of running feet.

Darkness loomed behind. Light lay ahead. Lanrik sprinted, the sword heavy in his hand. Caldring reached the opening and dived outside. Lanrik and Aranloth were a moment behind him. They sprawled to the ground, rose and turned, ready to fight, but the harakgar remained inside in a fume of shadow and swirling sand.

The three sisters were not visible, but they could be heard. Their wail rent the very air. And then abruptly their torturous cries ended.

The travelers lay on the ground, panting for air. At length, Lanrik roused himself and looked to clean his sword, expecting to see blood, but there was nothing there. The steel glimmered at him coldly.

He went to Arliss. She had used the palm of her hand to stem the bleeding from her forehead, and she waved him away.

"Look to the lòhren."

Lanrik did so. Dark blood flowed from the wound on his shoulder and his face was white, his teeth clenched in agony.

Carefully, Lanrik pulled aside the cloth of the lòhren's robe to expose the harakgar's bite. The wound looked angry, and it had already begun to fester. It was red where teeth had rent deep into the flesh, but along the jagged edges its hew was a sickly green.

"The bite of the harakgar is a grave injury," Aranloth said softly. "But magic can heal what other magic harmed." He looked up, the skin around his eyes drawn tight, and his face deathly pale. "But this will use the last dregs of my strength. For the next few days I'll be little more than a burden. I'm sorry. I know there's far yet to go, and other dangers ahead."

Lanrik placed a hand on the lòhren's other shoulder.

"You've already done so much to help Erlissa. Between the rest of us, we'll manage from here. Do what you must to heal yourself."

Aranloth nodded but did not answer. He placed a hand over his wound and groaned as he pressed hard.

For a moment nothing happened, and then white light stuttered to life. It flickered tenuously around his palm before it suddenly flared. There was a hiss, as though one of the harakgar was still present, and then a green mist uncoiled from the wound like a sluggish

226

snake. It rose and hovered in the air, swaying one way and then another, before it shuddered and then shot like a cast stone into the cave. It disappeared from view, swallowed by the black mouth of the tombs.

When Lanrik looked back to the lòhren, he saw that his friend lay unconscious on the ground. Of the wound, there was now little sign, though the stain of congealed blood on white robes gave mute evidence of what once was there.

Aranloth slept, and as there seemed no further danger from the harakgar, Lanrik decided to stay where they were and rest. They had traveled all during the day and seen and heard things in the tombs that drained them. He was exhausted, and he doubted the others felt better.

Caldring seemed uninjured, and Lanrik marveled at his daring. If not for him, he would have died. Perhaps Aranloth too. He was a youth no more, for he had shown the bravery of a man. And not only that, but a man with a sure future as a Raithlin. All the skills of tracking and concealment could be taught, but courage was the one thing that must come from within. It was the force that bound the others together.

The sun began to set. The sky, a pale pink blushed by the last rays of light, grew darker as he approached Arliss. The cut on her forehead seemed minor, but Lanrik checked on her anyway.

She looked up at him as he walked over, but did not speak until he sat down beside her.

"You came back into the tombs for me. Why did you do that?"

Lanrik did not know how to answer. "Why wouldn't I? You're one of us, and you'd have done the same for me."

227

Arliss shook her head. "I've never known loyalty like that before."

Lanrik reached out and put an arm around her shoulder. "Get used to it. You're one of the Raithlin now, and we look after each other."

He stood up after a little while.

"I'll collect some timber while there's still light. We could do with a fire tonight."

He moved out of the camp. The ground was rocky, and he took his time. Firewood was not the only thing on his mind. He also wanted to get the lay of the land. They must be somewhere on the north side of the river, but he wanted to know exactly where.

He found an ancient trail. It ascended a little further, but most of it ran down hill. After a moment he recognized the features, and though it was too dark to see properly, he knew this was the same path that he had climbed once before. Somewhere down below was the recess where Aranloth had brought down stone and rubble to block their pursuers. Further below that were the great falls and the beginning of the Angle.

He made his way back to the camp, collecting fallen branches that were dry enough to burn. He soon had an armful. On the way he noticed a stone, just like the others that carried the writing of the Letharn. A mass of grass and twisted vines covered it, which explained why he had not seen it earlier. There were many ways into the tombs, but leaving them alive was hard.

He made a fire when he reached the camp and Arliss and Caldring gathered around it. They did not speak much, and the lòhren still slept, his face pale.

One by one they settled down and slept. There was little chance of setting a watch tonight, for they were simply too exhausted. Lanrik's mind was working though, and as much as he needed sleep, it eluded him for a while.

He thought of Erlissa, and he longed to talk to her. He did not think the head-priest was right. Ebona could not do her any harm. She was in Lòrenta, secure in the ùhrengai of the fountain, and the witch was far to the south. And yet the thought disturbed him. Ebona would pay if she had done anything. Too long she had influenced Esgallien, too long a weak king had put the city and its people in danger. It was time to do something about it, but he was not sure what.

Once more he had the strange sense that he was reliving events that had already occurred. What the prophecy of the sword was doing, what power it had to shape the days ahead, he did not know. But he thought that it was time to resolve that issue too.

He eventually fell asleep, troubled by the past and worried for the future. When he woke it was bright morning. Arliss had gathered more timber and a smokeless fire burned hotly.

They ate a warm breakfast, all save the lòhren who still slept. Lanrik chose not to try to wake him. He was not sure if that was wise or even if he could.

When they were done, he stood up.

"We can't go anywhere with Aranloth the way he is. But I better have a proper scout around and see if there's anybody nearby. I looked last night, but I didn't go far."

Caldring and Arliss both stood up, ready to go with him.

"Stay here," he said. "I won't be going too far. Last time I traveled this way there was nobody about, and I don't expect that's changed. But I better make sure. Anyway, we could use some more water."

He took their near-empty water flasks, strapped them around his shoulder, and moved off.

He quickly found his way back to the main trail. Now, he could see the recess far below and the tumbled rock below it. He turned west, the direction they must go, and followed the path upward. After some long minutes of hard walking he reached a crest that overlooked the river.

He moved slowly, his natural caution always making him proceed with care, and lay down to look out over the ridge. It was for this reason that he spied Musraka's men before they noticed him. He slunk down as low as he could, not so quick as to attract their eyes, but as quickly as possible.

On his belly, he lifted his head just enough to peer over the top of the crest.

Down below, the river swept toward the falls. Its banks were shallow, for the river was wide and trees and lush grass grew along its verge. Deep within a straggly copse were horses. And with them were Azan. He saw no sign of the shazrahad, and wondered what that might mean, but he watched for some time to tell what they were doing.

They seemed to be waiting, for had they only been watering the horses they would have long since moved on. And though they were waiting for him, their presence offered hope as well as worry.

It was curious that they did not make a better attempt to hide, but he guessed that they felt sure of themselves, outnumbering those they pursued.

He eased himself back down the trail until he could stand and walk once more. He wanted water, but there was still some left in the flasks, at least enough to last for the rest of the night.

He returned to the camp, careful to leave little sign of his trail, though experience had taught him that the Azan, at least these ones, were no better at tracking than they were at hiding.

He got back and gave the near-empty water flasks to the others.

"We've got a problem," he said. "But for every problem there's a solution."

Arliss gazed at him, and her face suddenly broke into a grin, the first he had seen her give in what seemed a long time.

"I know *that* look," she said. "Keep your eyes open Caldring – you're about to see the Raithlin skills at work again."

22. Wet Feet and Cool Heads

The travelers waited through the day. There was no way around the Azan, at least not while the sun rode high. At night, it was a different matter. Yet it was not Lanrik's plan to try to slip past them.

Evening groped over the land, sending dark shadows ahead that gathered in deep pools beneath the trees. A pink blush once more painted the sky. High clouds, thin and stretched, trailed from west to east. True darkness, when it came, fell swiftly and stars sparked to sudden life.

Halathgar gleamed and twinkled. Lanrik knew the constellation better than most, for few men had lived as he, sleeping so often under the open sky with the dome of the heavens his ceiling and the earth his bed.

When the time came, he pulled his Raithlin cloak tightly about him and led the others from the rocky hollow.

He was not sad to leave the place. The harakgar were creatures he would not forget, nor did he doubt that they would haunt his sleep for the rest of his life. But he had escaped them, and the death that Erlissa had foreseen, because of Aranloth and Caldring.

The youngest member of their party now helped the oldest. Aranloth, his arm around Caldring's shoulders, trudged along at a slow pace. They stopped frequently to rest, but Lanrik did not mind. He was just glad that the lòhren had woken during the course of the day, though it disturbed him to see how weak he remained.

They had plenty of time to reach their destination, for he hoped to find the Azan camp late at night while they slept.

The ancient path over the ridge was a pale line in the starlight. They followed it, the hill too steep for Aranloth, who at times stood still, leaning on his staff and catching his wheezy breath while Caldring supported him.

At length they came to the crest. Lanrik signed for the others to sit down and rest, but for Arliss to come forward.

Together they used the Raithlin crawl to get right to the top, and then they lay motionless on their bellies, listening for any sound out of place. It was far too dark, and the camp of the enemy too distant, to see anything.

A long time they waited, but they heard nothing. So far, so good, Lanrik thought.

There was no guarantee that the Azan had remained at the same camp, but he took a guess that they would. There was water there, and concealment, even if they did not use it to best effect.

After a while he led the group forward. They passed over the crest, moving even more slowly now and sure to walk quietly, for sound traveled far at night, although the muted roar of the falls covered all but loud noises.

To the left lay a tract of rutted ground, thick with a confusion of shattered stones and ankle-deep hollows. Lanrik thought that once a building had stood there, perhaps something constructed by the Letharn. If so, it was not one of their important structures, for it had not lasted through the long years as had the others.

As soon as possible, he moved off the ancient road. The disturbed ground soon gave way to a gentle slope that led toward the river, and this is where he wanted to go.

The grass was lush, and though they treaded softly their passing made some noise. But as they neared the river, trees grew more thickly, the grass thinned, and sand and loose soil thrown up into drifts by floods softened their footfalls.

The gurgle and plop of the river as it ran to the falls was a gentle and calming sound. It too would help mask their presence, yet as they approached Lanrik felt the flush of nerves and the churning fear in his stomach that always accompanied a dangerous task. He was more familiar with it than he wanted to be, but he had learned to accept the reactions of his body, and in accepting them, to diminish their influence.

Once again he must steal horses. It seemed as though that was all he ever did: take the horses of the enemy and evade pursuit. This time, however, he had a different plan. He hoped it would prove safer than the last.

They reached the river and sat down beneath the canopy of an old willow. Its ancient trunk, fissured and flaking, was pale in the darkness. The enemy camp was several hundred paces upstream, but Lanrik was in no hurry. They rested quietly, waiting for the night to grow old.

Far away an owl hooted and a fox yelped. The river noises filled the night and the chirp of crickets and frogs rose and fell in some rhythm known only to them.

Aranloth rested, his back against the tree, his staff held loosely in one hand. Lanrik nodded to him, and the lòhren nodded back. He was awake, and he would wait for their return.

"Time to go," Lanrik said to the others.

They began to put in place the plan he had devised during the day. First, they took off their packs and left them near the lòhren, and then moved to the edge of the river.

"It's time for wet feet and cool heads," he said.

Lanrik took the first steps into the water. It was cold, and they could not stay in it too long, so now they would have to work not only more quickly but also with greater silence.

They waded out some twenty feet until the water pushed hard at them. Leaning forward into the current, so that little of their body could be seen, they began to walk upstream.

It was hard work against the strong flow, and their trousers and tunics clung to them uncomfortably, but it was safer than approaching the enemy by dry land. The Azan would have a guard, or more than one. Lanrik doubted that they expected trouble from the river, though. They would be watching the road, ready to spring their ambush.

He kept a close eye on the riverbank as they pushed forward. He could not be sure exactly where the camp was, but yesterday he had marked a clump of trees, thick and tall, and he thought he saw its outline coming up now.

With his left hand he signaled the others. With his right, he drew his sword, and Arliss did the same. Caldring only had a knife, but their weapons were drawn as a precaution rather than in anticipation of a fight. If it came to combat, his plan had failed.

They moved close, and then Lanrik paused. A long time they stood in the river, the chill water rushing past them, the stars glittering coldly above. At length, he saw what he had waited for. A horse moved, and he noticed the dim outline of its flicking tail and twitching ears. He had located the camp; now it was time to start the second part of his plan.

He gestured to the others, and they moved toward the bank. Caldring came last, for he had no real training in the Raithlin skills, but he was a good hunter, and he had some talent for moving quietly.

Lanrik reached the shore first. He studied the bank carefully, seeking out the quietest and most sheltered route as best as the dark allowed.

He moved up onto dry ground, stepping along a drift of sand that would dull the noise of their steps more than the rocks and gravel that formed much of the bank. When they were all clear of the water, he stood still and waited again.

His eyes were well adjusted to the night, but he could see little. The shadows at the base of the trees were thick, but he made out the shapes of more horses to the right. He could only see a few. The others, probably just better hidden, would be close by.

Now was a time to make a guess, and he hoped it proved right. The horses were to the right, and the breeze was coming from the left, as it had done since they escaped the tombs. Most likely the Azan had established their camp to the left too, for that way the smell of horse manure and urine would be taken away from them; a factor at any time, but increasingly important the longer the Azan stayed in the one place.

Lanrik made his decision and signaled to the others. It was time to get on with things.

He set the example, moving with soundless steps, first feeling the ground with the toe of his boot to determine if anything lay there that might make a noise. Only when satisfied did he place the rest of his foot down and transfer his weight to it.

There was movement among the dimly seen horses, and he froze, but it turned out to be another one that stepped into view. He eased his way forward again. Of Arliss, he heard nothing. She was a gifted student and had learned his lessons well. Caldring made more noise, but it was nothing against the background sounds of the river, and Lanrik was pleased with him.

A clearing came into view. It was the heart of the copse, and the long dark line of a fallen tree ran across its length. Above, where the tree had once grown tall, was open sky.

Beneath the shadow of the remaining trees Lanrik made out the shapes of sleeping men. At least he thought they were sleeping; he would not assume it as a fact. They did not move, and the night was now old, but that did not prove the point.

He got down onto his hands and knees and began to inch forward on his belly. It was the Raithlin crawl, a tactic that scouts all over Alithoras must use, but it was one that Caldring was not versed in.

This was the greatest moment of danger, for not only were they close to the Azan, but Caldring was now at risk of making more noise than before. Yet to stay on their feet was to increase the chance of being seen, even in the dim light.

Lanrik led the way, finding a route beneath the trees that kept them in the deepest shadow. Once more he worried, for although it would be harder for the Azan to see them that way, there was conversely more chance of noise from fallen debris.

Just as he thought that, there was a rustle of dry leaves from behind him. He froze. The sound stopped straightaway, and he waited. One of the Azan rolled over in his blanket, but he did not get up. It might have had nothing to do with the noise. Perhaps the man had just turned in his sleep. Yet Lanrik was grateful to be in the deep shadows. The sleeper was visible in the open, but the three intruders, motionless and low, would not be.

He waited a long time before he moved again. There was no hurry, for his plan was not to steal four horses, but *all* of them. If they achieved that, there could not be a pursuit, and that was his main priority. Too many times the Azan had tracked them down. Now, he intended to ensure that even if they knew where their quarry was, or where they were going to, they would not be able to do anything about it.

One thing concerned him though: he had caught no glimpse of the shazrahad yesterday. Nor could he see more than five Azan now. It was possible that another ambush was set up further along the ancient road, but doubtful. It would be better tactics for the Azan to keep together and force a fight where their numbers must win.

Alternatively, the shazrahad was hedging his bets. He might have sent this group to intercept them as they left the Angle, but he could not know for sure which side of the river they would emerge on until it was too late. Even Lanrik did not know exactly where they were as they traveled through the tombs. That being the case, Musraka might have divided his forces. The one place that he knew they would eventually return to was Lòrenta.

Lanrik thought about it. It made sense, but if so, it was a problem for another day.

They neared the horses. The clearing could not be seen anymore, and he stood up slowly so as not to disturb the animals. He counted them. There were six,

238

and yet he had seen five men in the camp. That made sense, for there would be a watch. But where would that man station himself?

Lanrik took a step closer to the horses, and he sensed Arliss and Caldring behind him, now also on their feet. He made no move to touch the animals yet. He wanted to ensure that they saw him first, knew that there were people about them, and had a chance to grow used to them. Sometimes little more than a strange smell could disturb a horse, and he wanted to make sure they did nothing to alert the Azan.

The animals cocked their ears and snorted once or twice, but they showed no sign of agitation. Slowly, Lanrik walked among them. He ran his hand along their flanks, patted their high withers and ran his hand over their rumps.

Arliss and Caldring moved among them too. They were all careful to keep at least one horse between them and the sleeping Azan, for if their enemies happened to wake there was less chance of being seen, and if attacked, there was cover.

Yet the Azan did not wake. Nor was there any sign of the sentry. Lanrik thought of taking saddles, but he dismissed the idea quickly. They were now used to riding bareback, and while it was true that they could not ride quite as fast that way, it was no great problem. More harm would come from being discovered, and the chances of that increased every moment they lingered.

He began to untie the ropes that secured the horses, and the others, seeing what he was doing, did the same. Soon, the mounts were ready. They each held the reins for two animals, and steadily began to walk them from the camp.

239

Lanrik felt a fresh shiver of fear. The movement of horses would be visible, and they were making some noise. Leaves rustled, hooves clicked and the odd twig snapped.

He was ready at any time to give a yell for them to mount and ride, yet he saw no sign of the enemy. It was better to slip away unseen if they could manage it, for riding at night was dangerous, especially with horses that were unused to new riders.

He angled back toward the river, away from where he believed the sentry was stationed. The gurgle and plop of the water grew strong in his ears and he let out a sigh.

They had done it. His choice this time had proved right, for although taking the others was a risk, especially the untrained Caldring, they had managed to steal all the horses. That would make a big difference.

They should have a free run from here back to Lòrenta, and although he was sure that Musraka was not here, he knew that they would meet once more. Near the fortress of the lòhrens would be as good a place as any. And so long as Aranloth could take the herenfrak to Erlissa, it would be time to settle things with the shazrahad, once and for all.

They were now out of the trees and onto grass. Above, there was a faint graying of the starry sky.

"Let's ride," Lanrik whispered.

The other two smiled, the release of tension on their pale faces obvious, and they mounted.

At first, it was awkward. Although they had only nudged the horses into a quiet walk, leading the remaining three by hand was difficult. They were not so well trained as the horses of the Royal Guard. Yet Lanrik was pleased. They were still fine animals, and though they had been given little in the way of grain, they seemed at first glance strong and healthy.

The gait of the horses was smooth and they appeared fit and eager for work. And work was what they would get, for it was a long way back to Erlissa. The additional mounts would help. By rotating them, all the horses would be better rested and travel faster.

"I feel sorry for the sentry," Lanrik said.

Caldring gave him a puzzled look.

"Why's that?"

"Because the others will blame him when they find that their horses are gone. They might even mete out some sort of punishment."

"Then he should have done a better job."

Lanrik shrugged. "Just as well for us that he didn't. Still, it's no easy task being a sentry, and people like to find someone to blame when things go wrong. Really, their leader was at fault – he should have arranged for two sentries, but some leaders have a way of reprimanding others for their own mistakes."

Arliss rolled her eyes, and the whites gleamed in the dim light.

"How could he know that you've got a fondness for stealing alar horses?"

Lanrik grinned, but did not answer.

They soon reached the old willow where they had left the lòhren. He was still there, his back resting against the weathered trunk and his staff held loosely in his hand. At first he looked asleep, but a closer glance assured Lanrik that regardless of how tired he looked, Aranloth's eyes were alert and watching them closely.

"You didn't have any problems?"

"None," Lanrik answered.

He studied the lòhren some more.

241

"We'll camp here for a few more hours and rest. You look like you could use it."

Aranloth looked at him kindly.

"That would be nice, but you and I know it's best to take advantage of the tail end of the night. It won't be dark for much longer."

"Are you sure you're up to it?"

The lòhren grunted and stood.

"My strength is returning, even if slowly. I can't do much, but I can manage to ride."

The travelers gathered their equipment. The sky was going gray in the east when they rode off.

They headed for the ancient road, and then crossed it, moving somewhat to its far side. Beyond was a long belt of trees, and Lanrik chose not to get too close. He did not believe there was a second group of Azan, but there was no point in being foolhardy. The trees provided a good place for an ambush, and Lanrik was not prepared to take that chance. Better to accept the known risk of the Azan camp to their left.

When they neared it, he gave a signal and they broke into a gallop. The thud of hooves was loud, and in moments they saw a dim figure run at them. It cried out, a strident yell in the Azan tongue, and other cries quickly answered from the dark behind it. But in moments the dim figure was lost to sight and the cries went silent.

Now, thought Lanrik, they were on the last leg of their trip. Nothing stood between them and Lòrenta, although Musraka would if he could.

A nagging doubt gnawed away at Lanrik. What if the head-priest was right? What if Ebona really had captured Erlissa?

He gritted his teeth and rode on. The river streamed by to his left, and the green grass flowed beneath the long gait of the horses.

The old road of the Letharn soon dwindled to nothing but grass, as he remembered it would. He was not sad to leave the land of that ancient race, and their works, behind. But he was glad of the herenfrak. Now, it was time for Lòrenta and Erlissa.

23. The Earth Groans

Erlissa sprang toward the cauldron. Her hair billowed behind her, and the walnut staff was hot in the tight grip of her hand.

She was only a step from the blackened vessel when Elù-Randùr struck. His own staff, the dark wych-wood implement of the elùgroths, whipped through the air. It struck her ankle like a barbed lash. She reeled, regained her balance, and prepared to thrust her staff into the cauldron's murky interior.

Ebona cried out, and flame coursed from the tips of her fingers. Red fire sizzled through the air and Erlissa flung up a wall of blue light. The witchery struck it, knocked it down, but it sputtered to life again and repelled the attack.

The elùgroth moved like the black shadow of a hawk. His robes flew and fluttered, and he crashed into Erlissa. She sprawled to the ground and hit her head hard against the stone.

The room swirled with power, and a tremor ran deep in the earth until the whole valley of Caladhrist shook. Lòhrengai, elùgai and ùhrengai charged the air – too much for the confined space of the chamber. Dust and grit rained down from the ceiling and the cauldron tottered.

With a heave and a reckless burst of lòhren-fire, Erlissa flung the elùgroth from her. She came to her feet, blood dripping down the side of her face, and stumbled toward the cauldron.

Once more the witch flung fire at her, but she ducked and rolled, closing her eyes to the brightness as the flame roared over her head and thundered into the wall.

The many-tunneled rock of Caladhrist groaned, and a noise came from somewhere in the stony deeps as though mountains tumbled into the sea.

Erlissa plunged her walnut staff into the cauldron. Its tip sunk deep and smashed into the bottom. The wood thrummed with power, and a shock traveled along its length as the dark forces of witchcraft and sacrificed blood reacted to the intrusion.

Fire dripped like water from Ebona's fingers, and she raised her hands to strike.

"Wait!" the elùgroth shouted.

There was fear and desperate urgency in his voice.

The witch paused a moment, her hands uplifted, and a snarl contorting her once-beautiful face. Her glaring eyes shifted from Erlissa and bored into the elùgroth.

Erlissa fought a new wave of dizziness, and only the staff in her hand kept her upright. Or was she lying down in a block of ùhrengai in Lòrenta? Her two worlds now seemed as one.

The elùgroth spoke quickly, but his voice was calm.

"There's too much power here," he said. "One more move from any of us might bring the whole cave down over our heads."

Ebona stood still a moment, her arms extended, the madness inside her raging across her face. Erlissa thought it had control of her, but after a few moments she lowered her hands and the flame at her fingertips snuffed out.

"You are correct, elùgroth."

Her gaze turned once more to Erlissa.

"You do not have the power to destroy the cauldron. It is a relic of an older age, and far beyond your understanding."

The witch paused, and a mysterious smile played across her red lips, but her high-cheeked face was void of humor.

"But know this. Should you assault it with lòhrengai its own powers will stir to life. And they are vast, far stronger than the paltry forces so far unleashed. It will destroy you."

Erlissa felt sudden doubt, but she kept it from her voice.

"Perhaps. But if it destroys me, it'll destroy us all. And what does it matter if the caves collapse upon us? At least there'll be an end to this abomination."

Ebona laughed. Once more there was a hint of madness about her.

"Fool! It will destroy you. It will destroy the elùgroth. It will *not* destroy me. Did you not know? I am as old as the earth, and I shall endure so long as the world spins through the void."

Erlissa wavered. What the witch claimed might be true. If she tried to destroy the cauldron, its powers might rise up against her, and her skill at lòhrengai was not equal to the forces of ùhrengai bound within it.

Her lòhren senses probed the cauldron. She felt the latent forces within it. They seethed and roiled, their tendrils reaching out and infusing themselves into earth and air alike. She was no match for those powers. Nor was she any match for the witch.

It was one thing to face a task beyond her strength. It was another to try to achieve the impossible. For the first time she felt as though the Guardian had sent her on a hopeless quest, and the strength of her will, which had kept her going while she journeyed to Caladhrist, faltered.

She swayed. Doubt and despair made her weak, and the pull of her body in Lòrenta grew by the second. She could not resist for much longer.

Ebona smiled again.

"Yes. I see that you realize the truth, now. Don't you, sweetling? My sister betrayed you. She sent you here as a sacrifice of her own, a strategy to buy herself a little more time, for time is precious even to immortals. You never had any hope of success, and she had no power to give you anything that would help."

Erlissa dropped her head. Her gaze fell upon the cauldron, and she looked deep within it. It was dark and murky, filled with sliding shadows and churning blood. She felt the antiquity of it. It was as old as the staff in her hand, or the tree from which it had come.

Something stirred in her mind at that thought. Carnona was not like her sister. She was aloof. She was primal; she was less human than Ebona. A long time the witch had dwelled among humankind, trying to dominate them, using them to feed her power. She had grown to be like them. Carnona, on the other hand, lived a remote life, rarely seeing people at all. She did not show anger or anxiety, as did Ebona. Still less did she show fear.

The more Erlissa considered it, the more her faith returned that the Guardian would not have sent her here as a strategy to gain only a few extra days. She had summoned her, taken her to the ancient walnut tree and sent her to Caladhrist for a reason. She herself had hope, even if it was slight.

Erlissa had a moment of sudden understanding. It was true that she was no match for the witch. It was also

247

true that her lòhrengai was not strong enough to break the cauldron. But Carnona had never sent her to do either of these things. Her role was to bring the staff, an implement of ùhrengai, a force of nature as old, or older, than the cauldron. The staff might do what she could not. All that was now required was that she waken its powers.

Erlissa ran her hands along the dark timber. She sent her mind into it, and found its core.

"Grow," she whispered, and led the thought deep inside the staff.

She took her hands from it, letting it rest within the cauldron, and stood unaided. The room spun and she swayed.

Ebona smiled, and Elù-Randùr approached.

"There is no escape," he said.

The pallid hand of the elùgroth, spider-veined and cold, gripped her arm. It sent a chill into her bones. She remembered his touch, remembered what it was like to be his captive, devoid of hope and facing torment. But she also remembered Lanrik, and saw his face once again just as it was in the dark tent of the shazrahad. He was hope unexpected, and she would never forget that feeling.

The elùgroth started to move, to drag her away, but at that moment the staff in the cauldron began to glow. They all paused and looked at it.

The dark grain of the walnut glimmered with waves of light. The cauldron and cavern, until now engulfed in shadow, were suddenly clear and visible.

A soft radiance, like the dappled light of the forest, white and yellow and green, flickered and pulsed. For a moment it shimmered, and then sudden light blossomed

248

as though the sun had burst through a tree canopy onto a dark forest floor.

Shadows fled from the chamber. The dark-cloaked elùgroth was revealed, his pale face and hard eyes, the hooked nose and high forehead. For a moment he reminded Erlissa of Aranloth, and then his eyes shifted. They were black pits of malice, though uncertainty glinted in them now. All semblance to the lòhren dropped away.

Elù-Randùr looked to the witch. She returned his gaze, her blonde hair shimmering in the bright light, and a flush of doubt was on her face also.

She lifted a long arm and pointed at Erlissa.

"What have you done?"

Erlissa shrugged. "I haven't done anything."

Ebona shook her head. "Don't play games with me. Where did the staff come from? What is its nature?"

"It's from a walnut tree."

For the first time Ebona dismissed her entirely. Erlissa felt the witch's attention shift and focus on the staff.

"It's from Enorìen."

Her eyes flashed with fire, and she turned to the elùgroth.

"Remove it from the cauldron."

Elù-Randùr looked at the staff. He hesitated, and even as he watched its light intensified and a quiver ran along its length.

"Remove it!"

The elùgroth let Erlissa go, and it was a relief to be released from his clammy grip. What happened now was beyond her control. Still, she doubted that Elù-Randùr would find removing the staff as simple a task as it seemed. His hesitation told her that he knew that as well.

His pallid hands settled over the timber. The staff thrummed and writhed at his touch; the wood, like a living sapling, began to bend.

He pulled, but nothing further happened.

"Remove it!" the witch screamed.

Elù-Randùr looked at her. His dark eyes glinted.

"I cannot. It is stuck … almost as though it has grown roots."

Erlissa felt heady with excitement. Ebona's face twisted in fury, but whatever she was about to say was stilled in her throat.

The wood quivered once more. It was no longer a staff, but a growing tree. Smooth bark filmed it, twigs and leaves sprouted from it. High it shot, branches and leaves unfurling until it reached the domed ceiling of the cavern.

A harsh groan tore the air. The metal of the cauldron rippled. There was a high-pitched shriek that pierced ears like a knife, and then the bloodstained sides buckled and broke. Shards flew everywhere.

Ebona screamed. Elù-Randùr wheeled away. The earth trembled and dust and rocks fell from above.

The elùgroth fled. Swift he ran, a dark shadow that flitted past both Erlissa and the witch, and he was gone. He sought to escape the destruction that was coming, for surely now the cavern would collapse. Little did he know that the creatures of the otherworld that hunted her were near, and Erlissa smiled. Even if he escaped, he might yet be attacked when he least expected it.

The two left in the cavern ignored him, and made no attempt to flee.

Ebona's eyes raged with hatred and the need for vengeance. Erlissa stepped back, and the witch followed.

The ground heaved beneath their feet. Erlissa felt sick. There were only seconds left before the cavern collapsed, before they were both buried beneath the rubble.

She reached out and gripped the walnut tree. It was warm to her touch, just as the staff had been. She felt its power ranging into earth and air, felt the souls of the damned sigh and sink. Ebona's victims had freedom, and with a final sigh they faded from the world.

Ebona screamed again. Fire dripped from her fingers as she raised her hands for a final attack. The cavern shook, and the rock of the far wall slid like a wave of water and collapsed.

Erlissa gave in to the pull of her true body. She leaned against the tree, and began to fall. Her vision spun. Flame erupted around her. A boom thundered in her ears, and blackness took her.

24. As it Began, so it Ends

Lanrik sat astride his alar mount. Ahead, a silvery veil of mist lay over the land. He saw little, and heard less. If Musraka and his men were nearby, their presence was impossible to detect.

He shifted his weight, trying to relieve the deep aches that had penetrated flesh and bone. It was futile. No momentary shift in position could relieve him from the accumulated soreness of many days of hard riding. He felt tired and filthy as well, but nothing would ease any of his discomforts until he was inside the fortress of Lòrenta.

Yet he knew, with a certainty born of instinct more than logic, that Musraka was somewhere ahead. What had started in a dark tent hundreds of leagues away was not finished. The shazrahad wanted his sword back. He had sworn an oath to reclaim it, and nothing except success, or death, would turn him aside.

Lanrik, in his own way, without oath or wild words, was just as determined that Musraka would not have it. He clenched his jaw and nudged the horse forward.

The others followed. They looked worse than he, for he was better used to the demands of long days and short nights in the wild.

Aranloth, however, had regained much of his strength. Each day brought him renewed vigor, and the color was creeping back into his face. He still looked weak, like a man who had suffered a life-threatening

252

illness, yet the worst was over. He would need to be in good health, for Lanrik doubted releasing the enchantment that protected Erlissa would be easier than its establishment had been. It was another worry. There was a long list of them, but only one course of action: return to the fortress and save Erlissa.

Aranloth now rode beside him, for they were in the Hills of Lòrenta, a place that the lòhren knew far better than he. The old man chose the paths, and Lanrik studied them for signs of ambush.

"We're getting close," Aranloth said.

Lanrik relaxed his scrutiny of the trail long enough to glance at the lòhren.

"How can you tell? Everything looks the same in this mist."

Aranloth shrugged. "I could find my way to the fortress through a nighttime blizzard – with my eyes closed."

"Well, we'll soon put that to the test. Maybe not with snow, but with rain. There's some on the way, and it might be heavy."

The lòhren glanced at the sky. There was nothing to see except mist, but he nodded.

"I sense it too. It rains here a lot. If it's not raining, a gale blows or a fog covers the land more thickly than a forest. The clear days of summer are few and short, and yet when they arrive, there are no fairer places in all Alithoras."

Arliss pulled her hood up and shivered. "I can think of fairer places right now. A hot bath is one. And a warm hearth another. I'm sick of all this riding. Most of all, I'm sick of the dirt. I'm not sure if I'll ever feel clean again."

Lanrik did not answer. She had been short with him lately, though what he had done to upset her he did not know. But they were all on edge, even Caldring who never complained, though he had more reason than any of them.

"Which entrance are you heading for?" Lanrik asked the lòhren.

"I haven't quite decided yet. We're coming at the fortress from the south-east, so perhaps the front gate is as good a place as any."

Lanrik thought about it. He supposed that if Musraka were waiting, he would have all the entrances watched, even if he had to divide his men to keep lookouts all around the castle.

"Do you think we can use the birch wood for cover, and then make a dash for it?"

"That's what I'd suggest, but it's more your field than mine."

Lanrik turned the idea over in his mind.

"It'd have the advantage of surprise," he said. "The woods offer better concealment than anywhere else close to the fortress. I think it'll be the best way."

He glanced back at Arliss. "What do you think?"

"I think Musraka will be waiting for us. We left six of his men behind at the Angle. That leaves about fourteen. He'll have the castle watched at every side, and he, or some of his men, will try to stop us no matter where we come from or what entrance we use."

Her comment was probably true, but it was unlike her to be so resigned to the situation. Still, her assessment was correct, and there was little point dwelling on it. The woods would provide the best cover, and if Aranloth was right, they were close.

Lanrik thought about it some more. He was not going to wait until nightfall to try to get inside. He did not know what was happening with Erlissa. Was the head-priest's claim believable? There was no way to know for sure, and he had no intention of waiting any longer than necessary to find out. The sooner she was given the herenfrak, the better he would like it.

"The front gate it is," he said to the lòhren.

They rode on, and the mist faded under the influence of a chill breeze that blew from the northern mountains. Yet even as it dissipated, the flow of cold air drove clouds, ominous and low, before it. A drizzle started, faint at first, but it grew steadily stronger. The travelers pulled up their hoods. It was a mark of defiance rather than a practical solution, for the cloth offered little protection against the weather.

When they reached the birch woods the drizzle turned to rain. The leaves above them constantly dripped, and it was as dark as dusk beneath the trees.

At least the timber offered shelter from the breeze, and it felt warmer. Lanrik thought once more about waiting until nightfall, but dismissed the idea again. It was too long to wait, and they would be wet and miserable all the while. Moreover, he knew the Azan would feel the conditions more keenly, for they were a desert people and unused to this climate. It would hinder their watch, and the rain would subdue noise and reduce visibility, especially if it grew heavier. And it showed signs of doing so.

They passed quietly through the wood. There was no need for Lanrik to ask them to be alert. They all knew the risks and that the Azan might be near.

The rain increased. The forest trail ran with water. In places, swift runnels formed and cut through the leafy mulch beneath the trees. The silver-white trunks glistened with moisture and shimmered as though an

255

army of phantoms marched over the land. The travelers, like gray ghosts themselves, continued silently.

Lanrik slowed their pace. He knew exactly where they were now. If not for the rain, and the last fringe of trees, the fortress would have come into view. Instead, all he saw was dripping leaves and scudding cloud. He veered to the left. If the Azan were watching, they would likely do so from a position straight out from the gate, rather than to one side. That way they would have less distance to travel in order to intercept anyone.

He signaled the others to stop. "I'll go forward and have a look."

Handing Aranloth the reins to his horse, he dismounted. Carefully, he walked ahead. He saw nothing unusual. Nor was there any sound, except for the pitter-plop of rain on leaves and earth.

When he neared the edge, he lowered his body to the ground and used the Raithlin crawl to bring him to a point where he could see the stronghold. Even more important was the green sward that lay between forest and fortress.

The earth, usually soft with leaf mulch, had turned to mud. He disregarded that – his Raithlin cloak and other clothes were already filthy. In fact, the new stains would help him to blend with his current surroundings. What he did not like was the clamminess that permeated his leather boots and all his clothes. He felt cold and uncomfortable, and that was the kind of nuisance that made people impatient. Impatience, in its turn, led to poor decisions.

He drew up beside a tree. He did not get too close, for the pale trunk would cause his darker clothes to stand out. It was better to merge with the background color of the forest floor.

He studied the situation carefully. Nothing moved on the sward. There were no enemies there. Nor had they gathered at the gate. That was too close to a possible attack from the ramparts. He doubted that there had been any fighting between his men and Musraka's, but that did not mean that the Azan would place themselves in a vulnerable position. But there *were* horsemen.

To the right, about a hundred paces away, was a group of five men. They were not mounted, but their horses stood saddled and ready nearby. Musraka was among them.

Of the other Azan there was no sign. No doubt they were spread out around the fortress, perhaps even patrolling it. They would be ready to bring word to the shazrahad if they spied the travelers.

Lanrik had no intention of trying to find another way in though. All ways were guarded. All ways were dangerous. Here, at least, the numbers were fairly even. Of one thing he was confident: he and Arliss could hold the Azan off long enough for Aranloth to take the herenfrak inside the fortress. That was what mattered. And Caldring could go with him. The young man had courage, of that there was no doubt, but he did not possess fighting skills to match Azan warriors.

He watched them for a while, studying their habits. They were established in that spot, and showed no sign of riding off on a patrol. They also remained alert. There was one at all times who eyed the fringe of trees and another who observed the fortress.

Lanrik smiled. He had instructed his men not to engage in fighting, but the Azan did not know that. Nor did it mean that the Raithlin had not harassed any warriors who ventured near the walls. By the Azan's wary appearance, he judged that they were frightened of arrow shot, perhaps even of a sally from the gate.

He started to consider the best way ahead. There were Raithlin on the walls, and they would see the travelers when they crossed the sward. If he could somehow signal them sooner, they might be ready to provide help when the travelers made a dash. But was there any way to send a message?

Nothing was changing, no matter how much he thought about it, so it was time to go back to the others and let them know how things stood.

He eased back into the cover of the timber. When he was deep enough in the wood, he stood and went back to the others.

"Best to dismount and talk," he said quietly when he reached them. "But do it quietly. They're near."

The group settled down beneath a tree. It gave them shelter from the rain, but they did not remove their hoods.

He was not worried about the horses. There was no wind to carry scent, and the rain stirred up many smells from the forest floor. It was possible that they would detect others of their kind and whinny, but he thought it unlikely. Nevertheless, he kept a careful eye on them. They seemed disinterested in the world, though. They stood still, their heads down, and appeared just as miserable as their riders.

He explained the situation to the others. They listened to his description carefully.

"So, what do you think?" Aranloth asked.

"There's no point trying to get in elsewhere," Lanrik said. "We've got as much chance here as anywhere else. Besides, the more we roam around the more likely we'll run into Musraka's men by accident. At least here, we know about them, and they don't know about us."

"Should we just make a dash for it?" Caldring asked.

Lanrik hesitated. "Probably. I think we can get through that way. One or two of us at least." He glanced at Aranloth. "Everything we've done is futile if you don't reach Erlissa with the herenfrak. That's our most important job."

The lòhren returned his gaze, and after a moment gave a slight nod. Lanrik looked at Caldring, and then back at the lòhren. Aranloth gave another nod. He would do what he could to protect him.

"The only question," Lanrik said, "is whether it's possible to alert the Raithlin on the ramparts without letting the Azan know we're here. If we can do that, it'll give us an advantage."

Arliss looked up at the sky. "A fire is out of the question. The Raithlin on the battlements would see smoke before the Azan and know that something was happening, but we couldn't get one going in this wet."

Lanrik frowned. "We might, but it would take forever to search out enough dry material. Even as wet as it is, there'd still be tinder beneath logs and fallen branches. But we don't have the time for it."

He turned to the lòhren. "Is there anything you can do?"

Aranloth pursed his lips. "Perhaps. I could use lòhrengai to make fire or cast light, but the Azan would likely see that at the same time as our own men. There are other things that I could do, but they take more power. Even though I'm regaining strength, it might tire me enough that I'd have to wait several days before I could release the enchantment around Erlissa."

Lanrik shook his head. "That's a no, then. The sooner she gets the herenfrak the better I'll like it."

"Then we'd better just make a dash for it and see how it plays out," Arliss said.

Lanrik took a deep breath and let out a sigh. "It's not the greatest of plans, but it's all we've got. Anyway, sometimes the simplest approach is best."

He looked at them all. "Remember. Our first goal is to get Aranloth through the gate. Only he can wake Erlissa." He turned to Caldring. "After that, you'll go in. Arliss and I will hold the Azan off until the Raithlin inside the fortress come to our aid."

Arliss nodded decisively. "Count on it."

They mounted and drew their weapons. Lanrik deliberately moved to the right flank, closer to the Azan, and Arliss joined him. Their sword arms would be free, while the Azan would have to slash across their horses. Also, Aranloth and Caldring would be better protected. Lanrik knew what Erlissa would say about all his planning, and the thought of her, and of being so close to achieving the quest, brought a lump to his throat. He would not let her down.

The lòhren said nothing, but glanced at him and then at Arliss who was busy stretching her arm and freeing her muscles. Lanrik took his meaning. Aranloth still mistrusted her.

He acknowledged the warning with a slight nod. Aranloth was not right about her, but now, if ever, her loyalty would be tested. He straightened, and nudged his mount forward. Whatever else happened, he would ensure Aranloth and Caldring got through the gate.

They neared the fringe of trees. Rain battered them. It fell in a thick curtain between them and the fortress, obscuring it completely. That was good, for the Azan

260

would be less watchful, but also bad, for it would likewise influence the Raithlin on the battlements.

He looked at everyone, making sure that they were ready, and lifted his sword arm.

"Ride," he said, and slashed the blade downward. Drops of rain sprayed from the metal and flashed through the air.

His alar mount responded to a quick nudge of his boots. It shot forward, clearing the trees and gathering speed as it raced across the wet grass.

The others galloped with him over the open sward. From their right came a series of cries, and in moments the Azan mounted and raced to intercept them.

Lanrik's heart pounded, and the hooves of the horses thundered. Clods sprayed behind them. The ground was even wetter than he thought, and the riding was dangerous. He felt the mount beneath him scramble, but it regained its footing.

They were ahead of the Azan, but Musraka's men had the shorter distance to traverse. They might cut them off.

Lanrik bent forward, keeping his head down and urging his horse faster. Out of the corner of his eye he saw one of the alar mounts slip and fall. It crashed into the ground and tore a long rent in the grass. The rider, thrown over its head, landed hard.

Lanrik looked ahead again. Rain drove into his face, and he could barely see the ramparts. He assumed his men had noticed what was going on, and that someone was getting ready to open the gate, but he could not be sure.

He glanced to the side again, and even as he did so his own horse slipped. This time it did not regain its balance but skidded and toppled. He leaped off, glad for the lack of stirrups. Had his foot been caught the horse might have crushed him.

He landed heavily, but somehow managed to keep a grip on his sword. Rolling several times, he came to his feet and cursed. Pain shot up his arm, but nothing was broken. He looked for his horse. It was up again, mud smeared all over its flank, but it was some way off. He would not reach it before the Azan surrounded him.

Aranloth rode ahead, his white robes billowing. Sudden light flashed from his staff. The fortress must be alerted now, but it would take the Raithlin time to get out here.

Arliss must have noticed his fall, for she pulled up her mount. It too nearly went down, but somehow kept its footing. She galloped back, but the Azan reached him first.

He cleared his thoughts, paying no attention to the wild yells and shrieks of Musraka's men. He could not ignore the shazrahad's face though; he resembled a hawk about to pounce on a rabbit.

Lanrik took deep breaths, willing himself to relax. He got ready to fight for his life, or to sell it dearly. Arliss approached and dropped off her mount to stand next to him.

Musraka hawked and spat. "The sword!" he yelled. "Give it to me!"

"Come and get it," Lanrik said quietly.

"Fool! Don't you know when you've lost?"

"I haven't lost yet."

Musraka bared his teeth in a feral grin. "It'll take at least a minute for help to arrive from the fortress. You'll be dead before then. Give it to me, or I'll kill you where you stand."

Lanrik did not answer straightaway. Every second of delay was a chance at life, and he knew Musraka did not want to fight. It would be quicker to be given the sword. Also, if he killed him, he knew the Raithlin in the fortress would be more likely to pursue him. With them on his trail, it would be near impossible to reach the southlands.

"The odds could be worse than two against four," he said. "It'll take you a while to kill us both, and while you're trying, help will arrive."

Musraka smirked. "Fool," he said. "The odds are worse than you think. The girl works for me. Give me the sword. Give it to me now, and you shall live. Delay any longer, and you'll die. Choose!"

Lanrik glanced at Arliss. She did not look at him. Her gaze was fixed on Musraka. She looked cold, devoid of emotion, but ready for anything.

The shazrahad pulled a silver medallion from his tunic.

"See this? It's a gift from Ebona. You'll have seen that Arliss also wears one. Ebona's witchery has allowed us to talk to each other. How else do you think we found you all the time? Now, the sword!"

Lanrik felt empty inside, but he showed nothing.

"Like I said – if you want it, come and get it."

For a moment, all was still. None of the Azan moved. Arliss remained motionless, but he knew she was poised to act. He was ready to pivot away from her, and yet to do so would propel him straight at one of the riders.

All at once, everything erupted in a blur of motion.

Musraka stretched out his left arm. The glint of metal shone dully as a knife dropped from his sleeve and into his hand. At the same moment the gate of the fortress opened. Aranloth was through, and men raced over the wet grass on foot toward them.

The shazrahad hurled his knife. It was likely filmed by poison, the same substance that he had used on Erlissa.

Lanrik began to move, to try to fend the blade away with his sword, for to dodge right was to be impaled by the waiting rider. Arliss moved also. He thought for a moment that she was thrusting at him, but her body came across in front of him instead. She held her blade up, slashing it through rain and air.

Lanrik cried out. He saw what she had tried to do. But her strike missed the knife, although her body continued to move and the dagger blade, unhindered by her attempted block, drove into her shoulder. It struck bone and bounced up, its hilt smashing into her head.

She made no noise but stumbled and fell. Lanrik leaped over her body at Musraka. The shazrahad's horse shied away. Musraka pulled the reins hard, forcing the horse to shift position, but Lanrik was quicker. He need not fight; he had only to delay long enough for the Raithlin running toward them to intervene.

The other Azan wheeled around him, but he ducked and weaved. Throwing his arms up and shouting, he scared their horses. They did not lay a blade on him, but as they tried he led them away from Arliss so that she would not be trampled. He saw that she was struggling to her feet, but she would play no further part in the battle. Blood drenched her shoulder, and she swayed dangerously.

Either the Azan killed him swiftly now, or they must flee. Musraka leaned forward over his saddle and struck a vicious blow. Lanrik narrowly avoided it, but as he darted back, another horse shouldered him and knocked him down. Hooves churned the wet earth near him, but he avoided them. Rolling beneath a horse that pranced and kicked, he came to his feet on the other side.

All the horsemen wheeled on him again, but only Musraka attacked. The others paused, and then backed away. They yelled urgently at their leader in their own tongue, and though Lanrik did not understand what they said, he guessed the import of the words. The Raithlin were nearly here, and though they were on foot, they outnumbered them.

Musraka hesitated, his face contorted by anger and frustration, and Lanrik saw his lust for the sword. He needed it as other men needed air. It was his birthright, it made him who he was, and with it he wanted to conquer the north.

Lanrik knew he would always seek it, and no one in Lòrenta would be safe until the matter was resolved. He lowered the blade and looked straight at Musraka.

"Parley!" he called.

The shazrahad stared at him. He knew what those words meant: the Raithlin would not harm him.

"Can I trust the word of a thief?"

"You've already done so. Otherwise, you'd have fled."

Lanrik drew a deep breath while the Raithlin gathered around him.

"It's time to sort this out once and for all." He held up his hand and spoke to his men. "Parley has been called. Let every man here sheath their swords. Musraka and I will settle this by ourselves."

The shazrahad dismounted. He handed his reins to one of his men and stood before Lanrik.

"How do you propose we settle this? The sword is mine. You know it, and I want it back."

Lanrik spoke quietly, without anger or haste.

"You brought war into our lands and held an innocent Esgallien girl prisoner. You've forfeited your rights to ownership."

Musraka was about to respond, but Lanrik held up his hand to forestall him.

"We could argue all day. It won't resolve anything. What I propose is this: we shall fight, just the two of us, and to the death. I know you won't ever give up the sword, not in life. And I can never give it to you."

Musraka, his eyes hard and dark, studied him for a long time.

"If I win, I shall have it?"

"Yes."

"Do I have your word, and the word of your men, that they'll let me go?"

"Yes."

Musraka smiled. "Then you will die. For I am a great swordsman in my land."

Lanrik shrugged. He had seen Musraka wield a blade. The same blade that he carried now, an elug scimitar. He was not worried. There was risk to what he did, but the benefit outweighed it. At least to his way of thinking. Musraka would never give up the chase, and how many others would die by a hidden blade or poison? They must settle the issue now.

"Perhaps," he responded. "But I don't think so. It's more likely that I'll kill you, and swiftly." He paused, and looked earnestly at Musraka. "I don't tell you this as a boast. I say it so that you know what's going to happen."

"Enough words," Musraka said. "Time to fight!"

The Raithlin backed away at a sign from Lanrik. The remaining Azan also kept their distance.

The shazrahad was tall and well built. He moved with speed and agility, but he was a man born into a position of power. He had never struggled to prove himself, never competed with other men to gain his rank. Lanrik thought he had his measure. Still, doubt nagged at his mind. He was taking an immense risk. He knew Aranloth and Erlissa would advise him against it. But the truth was that things could not go on as they had.

The two men stepped forward and circled each other. Lanrik was tired after many days of hard riding, yet danger made him feel fresh once more. He put the Raithlin and the Azan warriors from his mind. His only thoughts were of his slow drawing of breath, the feel of the wet grass beneath his boots and the balance of the sword in his hand. He felt strong and nimble.

Without warning, Musraka slashed. The curved elug blade sliced through the air. Lanrik leaned back, feeling his weight shift onto his rear leg. The point of the scimitar tugged at his cloak, but it did not touch his skin. Even as Musraka's swing continued, and he started to divert the blade into a return stroke, Lanrik lunged. He thrust the point of his own sword forward, propelling the weight from his rear leg to the front one.

Swift he struck, and like an arrow the sword-point drove through the air. It pierced the shazrahad's belly, slowing little as he pushed it forward and up.

Musraka staggered back. He dropped his blade, his eyes wide with stunned disbelief. Rain sheened his pale face.

Lanrik withdrew the sword. Blood coated it, yet only a trickle ran from the wound. Red froth foamed at the shazrahad's lips as he tried to speak, but no words came. He dropped to his knees, gazing at Lanrik in astonishment. The pain of his injury washed over him, and he shuddered. For several long moments he convulsed, and then he died.

The corpse toppled to the ground. There was silence except for the heavy patter of rain on the grass.

Lanrik stepped away and sighed. So much had changed since that night in the tent long ago. And yet so much was the same. He had intended to kill Musraka then, although he did not want to, and he had killed him now, although he wished not to have needed to. It ended as it began.

He turned to the Azan. "Does anybody else wish to claim the blade?"

One of them took a step closer. He was scrawny, but Lanrik read self-assurance in his every move.

"I'm Nurhaq, and I now lead these men. The blade isn't worth anything to the rest of us. We weren't born to it, and the pursuit of it has led us to disaster." He turned dark eyes on Lanrik. "For myself, I care nothing for conquering these lands. I'd just as soon never be cold and wet again."

"Then go in peace. But do not return."

Nurhaq tilted his head. "Know this, though. A man's fate is rarely his own. I go where I'm commanded, and so too for my nation. Whether it is me, or my brothers, you will undoubtedly see Azan again. Those whom we must obey, have decreed it."

"So be it," Lanrik said.

Nurhaq spoke no more. A moment, he and the other Azan looked at the body of the shazrahad, he who once had led them, and though the expression on their faces was unreadable, Lanrik did not think he saw love there. Together, they trotted off. Lanrik watched them go, and then he walked to Arliss.

She did not look at him. Her eyes were downcast, as though something on the ground was of vital interest. She had torn a square of cloth from her tunic and pressed it over the wound in her shoulder. Blood seeped through it. The wound did not seem to be overly

268

dangerous. More worrying was the poison that Musraka had used. She would need the herenfrak as well. He just hoped there was enough of it.

It surprised him that she had been working for Musraka. He had misread that, and Aranloth had been right. Yet it did not surprise him that in the end she had sided with the Raithlin. He had never doubted her loyalty.

"You took a knife for me," he said. "Why did you do that?"

She glanced at him for the first time. There was a new look to her face that he had never seen before. Gone was her bravado, worldliness and humor. She seemed unexpectedly young, and he saw only vulnerability. It was something that she had never shown before.

"You would have done the same for me," she whispered.

Lanrik thought about it a moment. He *had* done something similar when they escaped the tombs of the Letharn. And she had just now echoed his own words at the time.

He nodded slowly. "That's what it means to be a Raithlin," he said.

He noticed something else. She had pulled her tunic a little to the side so that she could press the cloth to the wound on the shoulder. He could not see the medallion.

She read his look. "It's gone. I threw it away. If Ebona wants it back, she'll have to take on the three harakgar."

Lanrik realized that he had not seen the medallion for a long time.

"I don't think anyone's going to wear it any time soon," he said. He searched a moment for the right words to his next question. It was something he needed to know.

"When did you meet Musraka?"

She closed her eyes. "He was in Cardoroth. Somehow the witch knew you would go there to recruit Raithlin. She also knew that you would seek me out. I suppose it's true what Musraka told me, that she has the sight. Anyway, he offered me money to spy for him." She paused, seemingly unwilling to go on, but then continued in a rush. "I'm sorry. I didn't know you then. And money was hard to come by. You have no idea how poor my family is. I supported them by knife fights. Men bet on me to win. And I rarely lost. It was the only real skill I had. My only way to earn money. It was all I was good at, until I came here."

A tear rolled down her rain-wetted check. It was another look on her face that he had never seen before.

"You're a natural at all our skills," he said.

The other Raithlin were nearby, but not close enough to hear the conversation. They were busy catching the horses.

"As things went on," she continued, "I loved that I belonged somewhere. I loved that I no longer had to risk my life for nothing but money. There was a reason for things here. To help Alithoras. I felt a sense of belonging that I've never felt before." She looked at him, and wiped the tear away. "I'll never forget that. I'll miss it."

Lanrik winked at her. "You won't miss it – you'll still be here. Once a Raithlin, always a Raithlin. There's a place here for you as long as you want it."

She gazed at him with disbelief in her eyes.

"You'll keep me on after what I did? How can you trust me?"

270

"How can I not? You just risked your life for me. I trust you more than ever."

She would have said more, but he waved her comments off.

"First things first," he said. "We need to get to the fountain."

He helped her onto her mount when one of the men brought it over, and then took the reins of his own. They rode to the fortress in silence.

The gate was open, and there were more men there. Lanrik passed through swiftly, only pausing to acknowledge greetings with a quick wave. After that, he helped Arliss dismount, and as she was still unsteady on her feet, he picked her up and carried her through Lòrenta's passageways.

Rain splattered his face once more when he entered the courtyard. The square of sky high above the enclosure was dark gray. The grass, trees and flowers seemed drab and motionless, except for the glistening water drops that gathered on every surface.

The great spray of water from the fountain was just as peaceful as ever, though no sunlight played over it today. Aranloth stood nearby, leaning on his staff. The lòhren looked down at the block of ùhrengai that encased Erlissa, and seemed oblivious to all else, but he glanced at Lanrik.

His gaze took in Arliss. Concern crossed his face that she was being carried, and then surprise when he saw the blood on her shoulder.

He was about to speak, but Arliss spoke first.

"I chose the right side, at last."

Aranloth stared hard at her, and then he nodded. "So you have."

271

Lanrik laid her down on the grass, and then looked back at Aranloth.

"We'll need herenfrak for her, too. Musraka was fond of poison."

Aranloth raised an eyebrow, but did not ask any questions. He probably realized by Lanrik's choice of words that the shazrahad was dead.

"There is enough to spare. But no matter how much we have, it may be of no avail for Erlissa. The head-priest was right. Ebona had her."

Lanrik stepped close enough to see. His breath caught in his throat. Erlissa lay there, but not as she was when they last saw her.

Blood marked her face from a long cut that ran above her eye. Soot and dirt covered clothes and skin alike. Her long black hair was burnt at the tips. Worst of all, there was still fire about her. It gave off light, yet did not leap and twine. It was caught, just as she, in a moment of time. Strangest of all was the black staff in her hand. It had not been there before.

Lanrik shuddered. It looked like the wych-wood staves that elùgroths carried. Yet as he studied it he realized that it was not. It was walnut, a timber that he knew and liked. And there was something about it that seemed at the same time both strange and familiar.

He looked at Aranloth, and tried to keep his voice steady.

"How is this possible?"

Aranloth shook his head. "It was done by some art or power beyond my own. I sense Ebona at work. The fire is certainly hers, but the staff is something else. It belongs to Enorien, and I think Carnona has been involved. The head-priest did not lie, but he did not tell all the truth."

Lanrik forced himself to ask the single question that burned in his mind.

"Is she alive?"

Aranloth straightened. "She's alive, although it's clear that when I release the spell that binds her, the blast of witchery will strike. I cannot say if she will survive that. She may wake for a single breath only."

"Is there anything we can do?"

Aranloth looked at him, his age-old eyes deep wells of sympathy. He shook his head.

Lanrik gritted his teeth. "Then the sooner we find out the better. Do what you need to do."

Aranloth took a firm grip on his staff. "Stand back," he ordered.

Lanrik moved away to where Arliss sat on the ground. Together, they watched as the lòhren stilled himself. He seemed a statue that mirrored the one in the fountain. The only motion was the slight rise and fall of his chest as he breathed.

When he had focused his mind, he lifted the staff high. Water ran along its length, dripping from its end onto the green grass. Suddenly, lòhren-fire flared. The water sizzled and turned to mist, and a tongue of silver light leaped like lightning into the earth.

The fire flicked back and forth between ground and staff. With a heave, the lòhren thrust the tip higher. Lòhren-fire shot upward, arcing into the air and driving deep inside dark clouds.

Aranloth relaxed, lowering the staff, but the lòhren-fire thrummed steadily. Once more he drove the tip high, and the silver light shone with a blinding flash. There was a clap of thunder, and the gray clouds flickered with inner light.

Once more he relaxed. This time he swayed a little, but he did not allow the staff to touch the ground.

He steadied himself, and Lanrik and Arliss put their hands over their ears. A third time he drove the staff up. Blinding light flared. The air hissed and crackled, and a vast boom rolled over Lòrenta. The earth shook with it. The fortress shuddered. Far away birds cried in the woods and took flight, wheeling in confusion across the sky.

The boom receded. The land grew still. There was an answering rumble, distant and subdued, like an echo of the first. The ùhrengai that encased Erlissa turned to water and sank swiftly into the earth. It left her resting on the marble bench.

Erlissa gasped for breath, and even as she did so the witch-fire burst all around her. She screamed, and her hand twitched on the walnut staff. The fire engulfed her, bathing everything in red.

The others staggered back. Even as they did so, a white light, tinged by forest-green, flared to life inside the red.

Lanrik fell to his knees. A voice bellowed from the very earth.

"Die!" it screamed.

Lanrik knew it. It was Ebona.

As swiftly as they had burst forth, fire and voice dispersed. There was only Erlissa, partly shielded by the forest-green light. She reefed herself into a sitting position, wisps of flame curling over her clothes and through her hair.

Lanrik raced over to her. He tore off his Raithlin cloak and tried to smother the flame. After a moment, he picked her up, and then stepped into the basin of the

274

fountain. Water sprayed over him, and ran up to his knees.

He laid Erlissa down, soaking her and putting out whatever flame was left. He held her head above water and splashed her face.

She called out, but he could not understand her words until she reached up with her free arm, the staff still in her other, and pulled the Raithlin cloak away.

"Enough," she said.

Lanrik looked at her. She was injured, but perhaps not so badly. Her hair was shriveled in places, but the fire had not reached her skin.

He rested his head against hers for a moment. But then he forced himself to pick her up and move out of the fountain. There was more yet to do.

His legs ached as he carried her over to Aranloth. The lòhren lay on the ground, groggy but unhurt.

"The herenfrak!" Lanrik said.

Aranloth stirred. He reached into his robes and pulled out the bag that Lanrik had last seen in the tombs of the Letharn.

The lòhren moved close to Erlissa, and then stopped.

"You do it," he said to Lanrik. "My hands are too shaky."

Lanrik took the bag.

"Just a small pinch," Aranloth said.

Lanrik opened the bag and reached in. There was little of the herb there. It was powdery to the touch, and so light that it felt almost as though nothing was there. He pinched a little between his fingers.

Aranloth looked at Erlissa. "Eat it," he said.

Lanrik placed the dried herb in her mouth. There was a pungent odor, and for a moment he was reminded of the tombs. And then the smell was gone.

Erlissa lay down as she chewed and swallowed.

Lanrik leaned over her. "Are you all right?"

She nodded, but took some time to speak. "I think so. I feel the cure begin to work. I'm already stronger, but I could still sleep for a week."

"She's had enough," Aranloth said. "Now for Arliss."

Lanrik stood up and walked to her. The few paces that separated them tired him like a ten-mile walk. He nearly collapsed, but sat down and gave her the cure.

She looked to Aranloth. "I don't feel anything," she said. "Neither better nor worse."

"You would not. Erlissa did because she is adept at lòhrengai and felt the cure run through her body. Trust me, you'll be well."

The lòhren retrieved the bag and looked inside.

"There's still some left," he said. "I'll store this properly." He drew the strings of the pouch tight. "It's hard to get."

Lanrik would have laughed if he had enough strength for it. *Hard to get* was an understatement.

He signaled the Raithlin, who had kept a distance while powers beyond their understanding moved around the fountain, and gestured to Erlissa and Arliss.

"Take them to their beds. See that they get rest."

Erlissa and Arliss did not resist as the strong hands of the Raithlin picked them up and carried them into the fortress.

Lanrik and Aranloth were left alone. Above them, the clouds parted and sunlight filtered down into the courtyard. He felt the peace of the fountain, and all seemed well with the world.

"Have we just achieved the near impossible?" he asked Aranloth

The lòhren ran a hand through his hair.

"Yes, but that's only a beginning."

Lanrik knew what he meant. Musraka was dead. But other enemies were not: both their own and those who wanted to conquer Alithoras.

"We've got a lot to think about."

Aranloth nodded. "And a lot to decide when all counsels are considered."

Lanrik stood. His thoughts went to the shazrahad blade, and his hand dropped to it. It felt comfortable by his side, yet he knew that its pull on destiny was getting stronger. That would be their first task, to figure out what to do with it.

He extended a hand to Aranloth and winked at him.

"Come along, old friend. The girls aren't the only ones who need some rest. You're not as young as you used to be."

Aranloth raised an eyebrow. "That's true. But you'd better hold onto that sense of humor. You'll need it."

Epilogue

The following weeks were quiet and restful. And rest was needed, for Lanrik had never felt so exhausted. Yet, the more the discomfits of his body eased, the greater his disquiet grew. He became anxious to learn of events in Esgallien.

He visited Erlissa and Arliss regularly. They were recovering well, though Erlissa was slower to return to health. The poison had brought her to the very brink of death, and the confrontation with Ebona had nearly pushed her over.

She had explained Carnona's use of ùhrengai, and of the task the Guardian had set her. It amazed him then, just as it amazed him every time he thought about it since, that she possessed such courage as to challenge the witch in her own stronghold. There seemed no limit to her nerve, and he wondered how many lòhrens, even those with greater experience, would have attempted it.

It was clear that Erlissa's efforts had broken the witch's attack on Enorien. It was not clear what influence she retained in Esgallien.

Arliss regained her humor, but there was often an introspective cast to her eyes when he came upon her unexpectedly. She avoided him, and he knew why. But he found no words to say to her. Only time would remedy what ailed her.

The Raithlin honed their talents. He taught them, taking them on expeditions all over the hills, and they learned with diligence and determination. They did not forget that one of their companions had been killed, and they understood better than ever the dangers of their profession and the necessity to become adept at a multitude of skills.

The new order of Raithlin were now a band of people who shared a common desire to help Alithoras. They had the skills of their namesake in Esgallien, though it would take many years of real-life experience to match the level of expertise the old Raithlin possessed.

Lanrik often wondered how his former companions fared, particularly the Lindrath. His old leader was no friend to the king, nor would Ebona sway him. Those things, and his fondness for direct speech, might cause him problems.

When Erlissa was strong enough she sent word across the land for healers to come to Lòrenta. Lòhrens took her messages, and traders who brought food and other supplies. In the meantime, she translated the book of healing that they had retrieved from the tower of Narvil, into the Camar tongue. In time, she intended to have it translated into all the other languages of Alithoras, even Azan. The work was slow and arduous, but she seemed to enjoy it.

He found her one day, vexed by a difficult passage, and she seemed ready for a break.

"It looks like hard work," he said.

She put down her quill.

"It's harder than I thought it would be. The translation itself is difficult, and Aranloth has to help me when I get stuck. But copying the plant drawings so accurately that they can't be confused with anything else

279

is the worst. They have to be perfect. Too much rests on getting the right herb."

He looked over at her work, awed by the detailed drawings in the Halathrin book, but surprised at how accurately she rendered them in her own.

"They're works of art," he said. "I can barely draw a straight line."

She smiled. "Maybe. But your Raithlin skills are their own kind of art."

He nodded. "At least that's one thing that I'm good at."

She narrowed her eyes. "Yes. One thing you're *not* good at, though, is keeping promises."

Lanrik knew what she meant, but he was not going to admit it so easily.

"What do you mean?"

Her eyes narrowed further, and he realized he had made a mistake.

"I mean that you promised me the last time we were in the Angle that you would never enter the tombs. It was a promise, and you broke it." She shuddered. "I never told you exactly what I saw in my vision, but you had to know I made you promise for a reason. You must have guessed that I saw your death."

Lanrik held up his hands. "What was I to do? I couldn't let you die. You needed the herenfrak. So I helped get it. And just as well. Had Aranloth attempted it on his own, he might have died."

Erlissa clenched her hands into fists, but she spoke calmly.

"I saw *his* death too, although that was less clear in my vision. I can't make him promise me anything. But you, at least, I thought *you,* would do as I asked."

280

He had no answer for that. He would keep any promise that he made to her, except one that would see him safe and let her die. But she knew that, and there was no point getting into an argument over it.

"And what of Caldring?" he asked.

"Him, I did not see. It proves that visions need not come true." She gave him a cool look. "But it came close enough."

Lanrik changed the subject.

"Caldring is quite a find. He excels at the Raithlin skills. He's better than I was at his age."

Erlissa narrowed her eyes further and added a frown. He knew that she understood that this was an attempt to change the subject, and she let it go after a long sigh.

Some days later on a morning when the wind blew cold and chill, and the inhabitants of the castle sought refuge in the kitchen and in the common rooms where fires burned red in the hearths, Aranloth saw him in a hallway.

"A moment," the lòhren said. "I need to talk to you."

Lanrik fell in beside him and Aranloth led him out to the courtyard. The wind did not blow here, but it was icy cold despite the bright sunlight. Autumn was approaching, and the long days of winter would follow fast.

They sat down on a bench, the very same on which Erlissa had been encased in ùhrengai.

Aranloth absently ran his hand along his oaken staff. It was clear that much was on his mind, and Lanrik was happy to wait for him to order his thoughts.

"It's peaceful here," the lòhren said unexpectedly.

Lanrik glanced at the fountain. "It's always peaceful here."

"It's not like that in other places."

That got Lanrik's attention. "Have you heard word of Ebona or Esgallien?"

"Yes. A wandering lòhren returned this morning. He passed through Esgallien on his way here."

"What's happening there?"

"The power of the witch is reduced. But lòhrens are not welcome. Not in Esgallien, or its surrounds. There's great unrest. Murhain still rules, and Ebona now openly advises him. The people mutter that she rules their land now. They don't like it, but those who voice their anger have a way of disappearing."

"Was there any word of the Lindrath?"

"Of him the lòhren specifically asked. No one knew where he was. Some supposed that he had left the city."

Lanrik thought about it.

"I don't think so," he said. "Esgallien is his home. He would do all he could to protect it, and that means staying there."

"I hope he hasn't done too much," Aranloth said.

"So do I. Ebona and Murhain would deal with him harshly. But he's cunning. I don't think he'd be caught unguarded."

"No," Aranloth said. "But I think we'll soon have to find out exactly what's going on there. Or you and Erlissa will, at least."

"What about you?"

"I have other tasks. First among them to travel to the Graèglin Dennath. You're fulfilling your promise to Carnona every day that you teach the Raithlin to love the land. And Erlissa has kept her own promise, though it nearly killed her. It's time for me to plant the seeds the Guardian gave me."

"Will that be safe?"

Aranloth shrugged. "Nowhere is safe these days. But I'll be as safe as you and Erlissa in Esgallien. I can help you with a disguise of sorts, but you must not get caught."

Something that Aranloth said disturbed him. It took him a moment to realize what it was, and then he had it. The lòhren had tasks, but he only named one of them. There was something else going on.

As for him, he knew that Esgallien was a place that he could not take the shazrahad sword. He would be vulnerable without it. He must hide from his enemies and not fight them, at least not for the moment. But the thought of going there without Aranloth was a worry. He had grown accustomed to the lòhren. Together, they had achieved much. By himself, without the sword, he felt at greater risk.

The lack of news about the Lindrath was the thing that disturbed him most, though. His old mentor was in danger, that much was obvious, but he was sure that he had not fled the city.

Thus ends *Lore of the Letharn*. The Raithlindrath series continues in book three, *Courage of the Conquered*. Once again, Lanrik and Erlissa are caught up in events destined to shape the future of the land.

Sign up below and be the first to hear about new book releases, see previews and learn of upcoming discounts. http://eepurl.com/Rswv1

Visit my website at www.homeofhighfantasy.com

Encyclopedic Glossary

Many races dwell in Alithoras. All have their own language, and though sometimes related to one another, the changes sparked by migration, isolation and various influences often render these tongues unintelligible to each other.

The ascendancy of Halathrin culture, combined with their widespread efforts to secure and maintain allies against elug incursions, has made their language the primary means of communication between diverse peoples.

For instance, a soldier of Esgallien addressing a ship's captain from Camarelon would speak Halathrin, or a simplified version of it, even though their native speeches stem from the same ancestral language.

This glossary contains a range of names and terms. Many are of Halathrin origin, and their meaning is provided. The remainder derive from native tongues and are obscure, so meanings are only given intermittently.

Some variation exists within the Halathrin language, chiefly between the regions of Halathar and Alonin. The most obvious example is the latter's preference for a "dh" spelling instead of "th".

Often, Camar names and Halathrin elements are combined. This is especially so for the aristocracy. No other tribes had such long-term friendship with the Halathrin, and though in this relationship they lost some of their natural culture, they gained nobility and knowledge in return.

List of abbreviations:

Azn. Azan

Cam. Camar

Chg. Cheng

Comb. Combined

Cor. Corrupted form

Duth. Duthenor

Esg. Esgallien

Hal. Halathrin

Leth. Letharn

Prn. Pronounced

Alar: *Azn.* A strain of horses raised in the southern deserts of Alithoras. Bred for endurance, but capable of bursts of speed. Most valued possession of the Azan people, who measure wealth and status by their number.

In their culture, where a person on foot is likely to die between water sources, horse-theft is punished by torture and death.

Alithoras: *Hal.* "Silver land." The Halathrin name for the continent they settled after the exodus. Refers to the extensive river and lake systems they found and their appreciation of the beauty of the land.

Alonthùril: *Hal.* "White wolf." See Arliss.

Anast Dennath: *Hal.* "Stone mountains." Mountain range in northern Alithoras. Contiguous with Auren Dennath and location of the Dweorhrealm.

Angle: The land hemmed in by the Carist Nien and Erenian rivers, especially the area in proximity to their divergence. Once the homeland of the Letharn people. Their empire is gone, but the tombs of their dead remain.

Aranloth: *Hal.* "Noble might." A lòhren.

Arliss: A young woman from Cardoroth City. Recruited into Lanrik's new band of Raithlin. Called Alonthùril in the knife-fighting competitions that she entered.

Arn: See Letharn.

Assurah: *Azn.* A renowned sword-smith of ancient Azanbulzibar, capital city of the Azan people. He was also adept at elùgai, and his work was sought by the rich and powerful of many nations.

Auren Dennath: *Comb. Duth.* and *Hal. Prn.* Our-ren dennath. "Blue mountains." Mountain range in northern Alithoras. Contiguous with Anast Dennath. Home of the Duthenor, a tribe of people related to the Camar.

Azan: *Azn.* Desert dwelling people. Their nobility often serve as leaders of elug armies. They are a prideful race, often haughty and domineering, but they also adhere to a strict code of honor.

Brinhain: *Comb. Esg & Hal.* First element unknown, second "hero." A captain in Esgallien's Royal Guard.

Burik: Head-priest of the Letharn.

Caladhrist: *Hal. Prn.* Kal-ath-rist. "Gold gorge." A valley north of Esgallien. Rich in gold and the source of much of the city's wealth subsequent to the depletion of closer alluvial deposits. Many others mined the valley through the history of Alithoras, including the Letharn. A dangerous place and believed by many to be haunted.

Caldring: A youth who lives by the shore of the Carist Nien. The people of his village, and the other villages scattered along the bank of the river, are descendants of the Letharn race. They have long since lost any memory of their origin. It was Aranloth who saved their ancestors when their empire fell into ruin, and he is a friend to them still.

Camar: *Cam. Prn.* Kay-mar. A race of interrelated tribes that migrated in two main stages. The first brought them to the vicinity of Halathar; in the second, they separated

288

and established cities along a broad sweep of eastern Alithoras.

Camarelon: *Cam. Prn.* Kam-arelon. A port city and capital of a Camar tribe. It was founded after Esgallien as the waves of migrating people settled the more southerly lands first. Each new migration tended northward. It is perhaps the most representative of a traditional Camar realm, while Esgallien is the most influenced by Halathrin culture.

Cardoroth: *Cor. Hal. Comb. Cam.* A Camar city, often called Red Cardoroth. Some say this alludes to the red granite commonly used in the construction of its buildings, others that it refers to a prophecy of destruction.

Carethgar: *Hal.* "Great man-beast." A shortening of carethlingar. These are creatures of swamps and thick timber. They are shy of men and rarely seen, though tracks and fleeting glimpses keep their legend alive.

Careth Nien: *Hal. Prn.* Kareth nyen. "Great River." Largest river in Alithoras. Has its source in the mountains of Anast Dennath and runs southeast across the land before emptying into the sea. It was over this river (which sometimes freezes along its northern length) that the Camar, Duthenor and other tribes migrated into the eastern lands.

Careth Tar: *Cor. Hal.* "Careth Tar(an) – Great Father." Title of respect for the leader of the lòhrens.

Carist Nien: *Hal.* "Ice River." A river of northern Alithoras that has its source in the Hills of Lòrenta.

Carnona: *Cam.* The Guardian of Enorìen. A creature of ùhrengai who has remained in her birthing lands.

Conrik: *Esg.* A former Raithlin and uncle of Lanrik.

Crimson Hand: An inn in Red Cardoroth. Famous in the city for the cheapest ale, the most fights and as a meeting place of criminals.

Durnlath: A citizen of Cardoroth. Recruited by Lanrik into the new order of Raithlin.

Ebona: *Cam.* A witch. A being of ùhrengai who has long since left her birthing lands.

Eleth nar duril: *Hal.* "Lie in peace." A phrase from Halathrin funerary rites.

Elùgai: *Hal. Prn.* Eloo-guy. "Shadowed force." The sorcery of an elùgroth.

Elùgroth: *Hal. Prn.* Eloo-groth. "Shadowed horror." A sorcerer.

Elugs: *Hal.* "That which creeps in shadows." A cruel and superstitious race that inhabits the southern lands, especially the Graèglin Dennath.

Elù-Randùr: *Hal.* "Blade of the Shadow." An elùgroth leader. Formerly a lòhren.

Enorìen: *Cam.* The Eastern Hills. A land where ùhrengai runs strong. Protected by the Guardian Carnona.

Erenian River: A river in northern Alithoras. Some say its name derives from a corruption of the Halathrin word "nien," meaning river. Others dispute this and postulate the word derives from a pre-exodus name adopted by the Camar tribes after they settled the east of Alithoras.

Erlissa: *Esg.* A young woman of Esgallien. Also known as the Seeker. Now being trained as a lòhren.

Esgallien: *Hal. Prn.* Ez-gally-en. A city established by King Conhain. Named after the nearby ford.

Esgallien Ford: *Hal.* "Es – rushing water, gal(en) – green, lien – to cross: place of the crossing onto the green plains." A ford of the Careth Nien.

Exodus: The arrival of the Halathrin into Alithoras from an outside land. They came by ship and beached north of Anast Dennath.

Feldring: A citizen of Cardoroth. Originally a trader plying goods to the villagers along the Careth Nien. Subsequently, he established a thriving business in Cardoroth where Lanrik met, and recruited him, into the new order of Raithlin.

Foresight: Premonition of the future. Can occur at random as a single image or as a longer sequence of events. Can also be deliberately sought by entering the realm between life and death where the spirit is released from the body to travel through space and time. To achieve this, the body must be brought to the very threshold of death. The first method is uncontrollable and rare. The second exceedingly rare but controllable for those with the skill and willingness to endure the danger.

Founding: The arrival of Conhain and his people near Esgallien Ford. This was nine hundred and fifty three years ago at the time of Lanrik's meeting with Erlissa and Aranloth.

Free cities: A group of cooperative city states that pool military resources to defend themselves against attack. Founded prior to Esgallien. Initially ruled by kings and queens, now by a senate.

Galenthern: *Hal.* "Green flat." Southern plains bounded by the Careth Nien and the Graèglin Dennath mountain range.

Graèglin Dennath: *Hal. Prn.* Greg-lin dennath. "Mountains of ash." Chain of mountains in southern Alithoras. The landscape is one of jagged stone and boulder, relieved only by gaping fissures from which plumes of ashen smoke ascend, thus leading to its name. Believed to be impassable because of the danger of poisonous air flowing from cracks, and the ground unexpectedly giving way, swallowing any who dare to tread its forbidden paths. In other places swathes of molten stone run in rivers down its slopes.

Great North Road: An ancient construction of the Halathrin. Built at a time when they had settlements in the northern reaches of Alithoras. Warriors traveled swiftly from north to south in order to aid the main population who dwelt in Halathar when they faced attack from the south.

Guardian: A creature of sentient ùhrengai that preserves its birthing land.

Gwalchmur: *Esg.* A former Raithlin of Esgallien.

Hakalakadan: *Azn.* A revered title among the Azan peoples.

Halathar: *Hal.* "Dwelling place of the people of Halath." The forest realm of the Halathrin.

Halathgar: *Hal.* "Bright Star." Actually a constellation. Also known as the Lost Huntress.

Halathrin: *Hal.* "People of Halath." A race named after a mighty lord who led an exodus of his people to the continent of Alithoras in pursuit of justice, having sworn to redress a great evil. They are human, though of fairer form, greater skill and higher culture. They possess an inherent unity of body, mind and spirit enabling insight and endurance beyond other races of Alithoras. Reported to be immortal, but killed in great numbers during their conflicts with the evil they seek to destroy.

Halls of Lore: Library of records maintained by lòhrens of the history, knowledge and wisdom of the nations of Alithoras. Accumulated over millennia and one of the treasures of Lòrenta.

Harakgar: *Leth.* The three sisters. Creatures of ùhrengai brought into being by the lore of the Letharn. Their purpose is to protect the tombs of their creators from robbery.

Hargil: A young man from Cardoroth City. Recruited into Lanrik's new band of Raithlin.

Harlak: *Leth.* An ancient name of Aranloth.

Headdress: A turban. Worn by the Azan people as protection from desert heat. Can be lowered in a sandstorm to protect the eyes and breath. Its color, and the manner in which it's worn signify military rank or social status.

Herenfrak: *Leth.* An ancient and potent herb. A cure for many poisons.

Lake Alithorin: *Hal.* "Silver lake." A lake of northern Alithoras.

Lanrik: *Esg.* A Raithlin. Also called the Raithlindrath.

Letharn: *Hal.* "Stone Raisers. Builders." A race of people that in antiquity ruled much of Alithoras. Only traces of their civilization remain.

Lindrath: *Hal.* "People lord." A shortening of Raithlindrath. Commander of the Raithlin organization.

Lòhren: *Hal. Prn.* Ler-ren. "Knowledge giver – a counselor." Other terms used by various nations include wizard, druid and sage.

Lòhren-fire: A defensive manifestation of lòhrengai. The color of the flame varies according to the skill and temperament of the lòhren.

Lòhrengai: *Hal. Prn.* Ler-ren-guy. "Lòhren force." Enchantment, spell or use of arcane power. A manipulation and transformation ùhrengai, the natural energy inherent in all things. Each use takes something from the user. Likewise, some part of the transformed energy infuses them. Lòhrens use it sparingly.

Lonfar: *Hal.* "Way of peace." The librarian of the Halls of Lore. Formerly known as Conrik, and once a Raithlin of Esgallien. Also, Lanrik's uncle, and a sword-master of renown.

Lòrenta: *Hal. Prn.* Ler-rent-a. "Hills of knowledge." Uplands in northern Alithoras in which the stronghold of the lòhrens is established.

Marsh hen: A member of the rail family. The variety that live by the shores of Lake Alithorin are found nowhere else in Alithoras. Their alarm call is eerily similar to a human scream.

Mecklar: *Esg.* Was once a senior member of King Murhain's retinue. A traitor slain by Lanrik in single combat.

Merlon: The vertical stonework on a battlement between crenels. The merlon offers protection, the crenel a gap through which missiles are fired.

Murhain: *Esg.* The current king of Esgallien. He was a younger son of the previous king and assumed the throne unexpectedly. Earlier in his life, he had attempted to train as a Raithlin but failed their vigorous standards.

Musraka: *Azn.* A shazrahad.

Narvil: *Hal.* "Pinnacle of knowledge." A tower built by the Halathrin near the shores of Lake Alithorin. Ransacked by Shurilgar the Sorcerer and a band of elugs.

Nurhaq: *Azn.* Cousin to Musraka.

Otherworld: Esgallien term for a mingling of half-remembered history, myth and the spirit world.

Pattern-welded: A blade forged and reforged from bundles of iron rods that are twisted and beaten. This creates a flexible core to which a hard edge is added. The process produces superior, distinctive and sought-after weapons.

Raithlin: *Hal.* "Range and report people." A scouting and saboteur organization. They derive from ancient contact with, and the teachings of, the Halathrin. Disbanded by the king of Esgallien, but founded anew by Lanrik and dedicated to the service of all Alithoras.

Raithlin motif: A trotting fox looking back over its shoulder. A half moon rides above the animal. Symbolizes cunning, stealth and boldness.

Raithlin crawl: A famous technique of stealth. It requires that the palms rest on the earth and the elbows remain tucked in to the body for support and silhouette reduction. The bodyweight is borne on the forearms and only one leg. The other is carefully brought forward in order to avoid making noise while moving.

Raithlin creed: "Our duty is to serve and protect. Our honor is to fight but not hate. Our love is for all that is good in the world."

Raithlin principles of concealment: The Raithlin believe the eye recognizes movement first, silhouette second and color last. Using this principle enables them to best determine how to remain unseen in varying circumstances.

Raithlindrath: *Hal.* "Lord of range and report people."

Rhamon: *Azn.* A servant of Musraka.

Ruthark: A young man from Cardoroth City. Recruited into Lanrik's new band of Raithlin.

Seeker: A person with a rare talent of finding lost things. It stems from a latent use of lòhrengai.

Shazrahad: *Azn.* The Azan who commands an elug army.

Shuffa: *Leth.* A type of boat. Small, fast and ideal for travel by river. Favored by the villagers who dwell along the Careth Nien, and based on a design carried down from ancient times when the Letharn fished the two rivers of the Angle.

Shurilgar: *Hal.* "Midnight Star." An elùgroth. Also called the betrayer of nations.

Sorcerer: See elùgroth.

Tombs of the Letharn: The ancient burial place of the Letharn people. All members of the population, throughout the course of their long civilization, were laid to rest here. It was believed that to be interred elsewhere was to condemn the spirit to a true death, rather than an afterlife. The dead were preserved, and returned even from the far reaches of the empire. This was withheld from perpetrators of treason and heinous crimes. These were buried in special cemeteries near the river. Petty criminals were afforded an opportunity to redeem their place in the tombs on payment of a fine determined by the head-priest.

Ùhrengai: *Hal. Prn.* Er-ren-guy. "Original force." The primordial force that existed before substance or time, light or dark, life or death, good or evil.

Witchery: A type of elùgai. Distinct from the common spell-craft and potion making carried out by some village healers.

Witch-fire: A potent attack of elùgai.

Wych-wood: A general description for a range of supple and springy timbers. Some hardy varieties are prevalent on the poisonous slopes of the Graèglin Dennath mountain range and are favored by elùgroths as instruments of sorcery.

From the author

I'm a man born in the wrong era. My heart yearns for faraway places and even further afield times. Tolkien had me at the beginning of *The Hobbit* when he said, ". . . one morning long ago in the quiet of the world . . ."

Sometimes I imagine myself in a Viking mead-hall. The long winter night presses in, but the shimmering embers of a log in the hearth hold back both cold and dark. The chieftain calls for a story, and I take a sip from my drinking horn and stand up . . .

Or maybe the desert stars shine bright and clear, obscured occasionally by wisps of smoke from burning camel dung. A dry gust of wind marches sand grains across our lonely campsite, and the wayfarers about me stir restlessly. I sip cool water and begin to speak.

I'm a storyteller. A man to paint a picture by the slow music of words. I like to bring faraway places and times to life, to make hearts yearn for something they can never have, unless for a passing moment.